PICKERING PLACE

Pickering Place

H.M. JONES

HMJ Books

CONTENTS

Copyright Page

Introduction by the Author

Dedication

Table of Contents
8

~ one ~
Becoming a Heroine
11

~ two ~
Morgenstern and Milestones
22

~ three ~
First Time Flier
25

~ four ~
Shopping Montage!
32

~ five ~
Tech Ballers
39

~ six ~
Two Baths are Better Than One
53

~ seven ~
Only Colin Firth Would Make That Lagoon More Romantic
65

~ eight ~
Getting to Know You
76

~ nine ~
Huevos Rancheros With a Side of Discomfort To-Go, Please!
85

~ ten ~
Fifty Shades of Xaiden
94

~ eleven ~
Some Baths are Dirty
106

~ twelve ~
Thornes in Chloe's Side
120

~ thirteen ~
A Girl Can Buy Her Own Damn Popcorn!
128

~ fourteen ~
A Pocket Full of Condoms and a Head Full of Dreams
141

~ fifteen ~
Bath Time at 5:20 Sharp and Not a Minute Later!
150

~ sixteen ~
It's Black and White
161

~ seventeen ~
The Mysterious Staircase Behind a Bookshelf
170

~ eighteen ~
Dead Man's Toe, Dead Man's Toe!
183

~ nineteen ~
Salem Sights
194

~ twenty ~
Bewitching Mr. Bath
198

~ twenty-one ~
Chloe Totally Kills Her Chances
211

~ twenty-two ~
Dr. Drama Queen Ruins Everything While Sally Saves the Day
216

~ twenty-three ~
That's Why They Call it Growing Pains
226

~ twenty-four ~
Pirate Island is for Lovers
234

~ twenty-five ~
If You Plant Love in Fall, It Will Bloom in Winter
242

About the Author
244

Other Books By H.M. Jones

Footnotes to Introduction
249

Copyright Page

This is a work of fiction. Unless otherwise indicated, all the names, characters, businesses, places, events and incidents in this book are either the product of the author's imagination or used in a fictitious manner. Any resemblance to actual persons, living or dead, or actual events is purely coincidental. It is loosely based on the public domain novel, *Northanger Abbey*, by Jane Austen.

Copyright © 2023 H.M. Jones [Hannah Jones]

All rights reserved. No part of this book may be reproduced or used in any manner without the prior written permission of the copyright owner, except for use in brief quotations in a book review.

To request permissions, email hmjoneswrites@gmail.com

Paperback ISBN: 979-8-218-38182-0

First paperback edition December 2023.

Edited by Hazel Walshaw

Cover Design and Layout by H.M. Jones [via Canva]

Book Formatted by H.M. Jones

Print version Ingram Sparks in the USA

HMJ Books

www.hmjoneswrites.com

Introduction by the Author

"Northanger Abbey and Pickering Place: Satirizing and Simultaneously Applauding the Novelette Mind"

H.M. Jones here. I thought I'd include a little author forward to the book as a nod to my source material, *Northanger Abbey*. *Northanger* is my favorite Austen novel and was Austen's first completed novel (though posthumously published). *Northanger* is not one of Austen's most popular novels. As a matter of fact, many Austen fans will sometimes give me a blank stare when I say it's my favorite. It's likely that some of these stares come from not having read the book, as it's not one of her better-known novels. It might also suffer from not having the wonderful reputation of an adaptation in which Colin Firth emerges, dripping wet from a pond, in a 90s baptismal-style sexual awakening for almost every viewer who watched it.[1] Either way, as a huge fan of satire, I argue that *Northanger Abbey* is an ideal satire. In it, Austen managed not to vilify the novels she satirized, nor the readers who enjoyed the tropes she toyed with.

Instead, Austen made use of the popular cliches of Gothic romance to engage readers, while also allowing her heroine, Catherine Morland, to learn that life is not as romantic, sexy, or over-the-top as her novels led her to believe. Austen played with the line of romance and realism perfectly in this and many of her novels, which is why they still stand the test of time.

The "novelette mind"[2] was used, in Austen's time, to belittle women for how they spent their free time in a period where men spent much of their free time belittling women and shooting things (sound familiar?). Religious leaders railed against the dangers novels presented to young women's virtue. Novelette minds were those interested in entertainment, not enlightenment. For example, fiction novels about women who had the power to choose men/sex vs. nonfiction manuals about how to be an upright woman and wife.[3]

Austen showed Henry Tilney taking part in the world of feminine entertainment without embarrassment, thus elevating it. This move was undeniably sexy. Henry unabashedly read *Udolpho* and other novels, he "had an understanding of muslins" (i.e. fashion), and even made reference to journal writing. Was he a little tongue in cheek about some of these pursuits? Yes. Did he simultaneously see the value in them? Also, yes.

Austen gave Tilney the strongest case for novels as entertainment when he said, "It is only a novel [...] or, in short, only some work in which the greatest powers of the mind are displayed, in which the most thorough knowledge of human nature, the happiest delineation of its varieties, the liveliest effusions of wit and humour, are conveyed to the world in the best-chosen language" (Austen, *Northanger Abbey*). Henry Tilney allows Catherine to have her amusements, *and* he shares enjoyment in them. The only time he denigrates her obsession is when it goes too far, and her imagination is hurtful to him. This, without question, makes Henry Tilney the most shaggable clergyman in any Austen work.

The novelette mind is still being used to vilify women's interests and how they spend their free time today. Women are not allowed to enjoy *Twilight, 10 Things I Hate About You, Pride and Prejudice, Fifty Shades of Grey,* or even *Hocus Pocus* without being teased. It's strange how little a few hundred years has changed the opinion of society's view on feminine forms of entertainment.

I hope *Pickering Place* can do even a tenth of what *Northanger Abbey* did for justifying female made and feminine driven entertainment for our day and age. I want readers to root for Chloe's fantastic imaginings, while also laughing a little at how ridiculous they are. Let's face it, romance entertainment in its many forms has kept women sane. It has kept us hopeful. It has allowed us to dream of partners who uplift the things we love rather than lecturing us about the frivolity of such things. If male entertainment can have their obnoxious war games, why can't female entertainment be proudly idealistic about empathetic, good looking, charismatic partners who like the same things we like?

P.S.A to Straight men: you should be happy many of us flock to these forms of entertainment. It is, after all, why we can brag to our friends that we married a real-life Mr. Darcy, instead of being honest and saying our partner is a stand-offish dick who at least has the good sense to be rich.

Dedication

I dedicate this book to my many sunny-minded friends who've asked me to write something less depressing. This one's for you, you romantic fools. I hope this book puts a smile on your beautiful faces.

TABLE OF CONTENTS

Chapter One: Becoming a Heroine
Chapter Two: Morgenstern and Milestones
Chapter Three: First Time Flier
Chapter Four: Shopping Montage!
Chapter Five: Tech Ballers
Chapter Six: Two Baths are Better Than One
Chapter Seven: Only Colin Firth Would Make That Lagoon More Romantic
Chapter Eight: Getting to Know You
Chapter Nine: Huevos Rancheros With a Side of Discomfort To-Go, Please!
Chapter Ten: Fifty Shades of Xaiden
Chapter Eleven: Some Baths are Dirty
Chapter Twelve: Thornes in Chloe's Side
Chapter Thirteen: A Girl Can Buy Her Own Damn Popcorn!
Chapter Fourteen: A Pocket Full of Condoms and a Head Full of Dreams
Chapter Fifteen: Bath Time at 5:20 Sharp and Not a Minute Later!
Chapter Sixteen: It's Black and White
Chapter Seventeen: The Mysterious Staircase Behind a Bookshelf
Chapter Eighteen: Dead Man's Toe, Dead Man's Toe!
Chapter Nineteen: Salem Sights
Chapter Twenty: Bewitching Mr. Bath
Chapter Twenty-One: Chloe Totally Kills Her Chances
Chapter Twenty-Two: Dr. Drama Queen Ruins Everything While Sally Saves the Day
Chapter Twenty-Three: That's Why They Call it Growing Pains
Chapter Twenty-Four: Pirate Island is for Lovers 307
Chapter Twenty-Five: If You Plant Love in Fall, It Will Bloom in Winter
About the Author
Other Books By H.M. Jones

~ One ~

BECOMING A HEROINE

No one who'd met Chloe Mora in her childhood would have imagined her to be heroine material. Her tomboy manners, her plain looks, and her poor situation in life were all against her. Chloe was an awkward, elbowy child with a habit of preferring the company of rough and tumble boys from a young age. At ten, she was more likely to be found building forts in the copses near the crick with Tommy Tookers rather than burping baby dolls with her two younger sisters and Amy Bayers. Jumping puddles, scabbing her knees, and pretending pirate attacks from "the Tetanus Fort"–as it was dubbed by her mother–were her reasons for living. It seemed fated that she would remain unremarkable forever.

Her parents didn't despair of it. They loved each of their six children as much as they loved each other. And if any indication of love was procreation, they loved each other, perhaps, a little too much to be sensible.

Indeed, it was the opinion of the coffee sipping, porch gossiping blue-haireds of Williamston, IA that Mr. and Mrs. Mora had not made *many* sensible decisions in their life choices. Mrs. Mora, then Anne Jones, was from a respectable farming household. Her mother had been a third-grade teacher, her father an owner of the majority of the farmland surrounding Williamston. Mr. Mora was the son of one of Mr. Jones' underpaid farm laborers, Luis. The same age,

Mateo and Anne attended school together during the day. In the evening, Anne worked with Mateo on his English, and Mateo taught Anne how to say rude phrases in Spanish to the girls who gossiped about her in class.

Nowadays, Mateo Mora was a field manager for a wealthy farmer in the next town over. He made just enough money to make payments on their quaint but well-appointed mobile home, pay the bills, put food on the table, and keep up maintenance on his early 2000s Ford Truck and the family's second-hand mini-van. His marriage to Anne Jones, a local preschool teacher at the time of their notorious marriage, did not improve his fortune, even if it did improve his happiness.

Most heroines' characters were sewn in bitter, acrid fields–their mother died a tragic death, they were somehow disgraced, or they were beaten down by the grueling persecutions of life. Not so for Chloe. No bitter beginnings birthed her into romantic tragedy. Her mother *did* become pregnant with her at a young age, but she finished high school without distinction or much trouble. "Missing out" on her wild twenties to manage her growing family didn't turn her into an angry, embittered, tired-beyond-her years hag. Instead, Chloe was raised by steady, loving parents who allowed her space to explore, but set appropriate boundaries to keep her safe.

Mrs. Mora found joy in her role as a homeschool teacher and mother to her six children, leaving her job at the local preschool with no regrets after her second child was born. They had very little money, but this was never a point of contention or stress for either of them. Their expenses were simple, and their days largely contented. Mrs. Mora was a doting mother and an adept seamstress who could rework the children's clothing to last several years past their expiration date. She earned a little money selling honey, jarred preserves, and handmade clothing at the weekend farmer's market, which offered the family the opportunity for little treats like Sunday Sundaes–their weekly banana sundae and movie rental ritual.

Chloe was their oldest child and, at age 13, became a second teacher and parent to her two younger sisters and three younger brothers. Where before her teen years, she'd been flighty and distracted in her studies, having the responsibility of her younger siblings helped her to become more structured. She taught her siblings how to manage the family's small but healthy gardens, care for their few farm animals, and hem jeans. She helped her mother with the more difficult chores and assisted her siblings in learning how to collect chicken eggs and milk their docile Nubian goats, Bessy and Clementine.

At about age fourteen, some truly heroine-like changes overcame Chloe. She became more well-read, if reading B+ paranormal thrillers like *Twilight*, *Frankenstein* and *Dracula* and writing impressive online fanfiction could be considered well-read. She also followed fashion trends and presented herself in a more sophisticated way. Gone were her holey jeans and overlarge t-shirts. She began watching sewing videos on their shared family laptop, and making herself mid-length skirts with fabric she picked out from what Mrs. Mora called the "Halloween Clearance" section at the Joanne's in Des Moines. She'd pair her dark skirts with brightly colored, patchwork jackets she'd made of her mom's fabric scraps.

Tommy Tookers stopped coming over to ask if Chloe wanted to find smashed pennies on the railroad tracks. Amy Bayers started bringing over magazines with brightly colored titles and boy bands looking pouty and dreamy on the covers. They would giggle over articles and quizzes about how to "Get the Guy" and "Kiss Like a Boss *itch," even though neither of them were ready to take either of those steps anytime soon. It was enough to prepare and to dream.

At age fifteen, Mrs. Mora was impressed by Chloe's inventive, outlandish, creative imagination, thinking to herself that her daughter was, while perhaps a little silly and naive, a very talented writer, and much cleverer than her early years promised she'd be. She'd also become aware of the fact that Chloe had grown into her gangly arms and knobby knees. She'd started to take after some of the females on her father's side of the family and was gaining curves her waifish mother never had. Her dark, thick hair and light brown skin were also a trait of her husband's that combined to make her a much prettier fifteen than her mother's had been. She had her mother's narrow nose, well-proportioned face, wavy but not curly hair, and her father's proud chin and intelligent eyes. Mrs. Mora could claim the beautiful gray coloring of her daughter's eyes as her own most fetching trait, and was happy to see it carried on in her daughter.

Today, seventeen-year-old Chloe made flower chains from some of the tall wildflowers Mrs. Mora filled their small patch of land with. "Land is for the birds and bees," she'd told Mr. Mora, frowning at his lawn mower, which she only allowed him to use to make paths through the gardens and wildflowers she'd planted around the house. He'd winked and told her he loved birds and bees as much as she did and would not dare do anything to disturb them.

Issa and Bella, Chloe's little sisters, giggled as Chloe placed crowns of black-eyed Susan's and daisies on their foreheads, and talked animatedly about the dress she was going to wear to her community college graduation on Friday. She'd graduated with an online associate of the arts degree and a 4.0 gpa, making her mama and papa the proudest parents in Williamston. Next week she'd be turning 18, and would be ready to lead a life increasingly separate from her parents.

Her papa's eyes filled with this very thought. "Chloe is a young lady, now. She begins to be almost as beautiful as you," Mr. Mora sighed.

"I'd argue that your family's good genes made her much more beautiful than me, but she *is* a pretty thing these days," Mrs. Mora squeezed her husband's hand. "And a good girl. She helped me make Issa and Bella matching dresses for the church play. Not to mention smart. What can she do with brains like that in a town like this? If only she'd use those brains and that talent for less silly things. She can't just write fanfiction all her life. It won't put food on her table." Her mother smiled at her father. "We can worry about that later, I suppose. We did good, Mr. Mora."

"We did very good, Señora Mora. Many young ones are silly and romantic. She'll grow out of some of that. I hope not all. Your romantic nature is one of my favorite things about you."

Mr. Mora kissed his wife's hand and stared into her gray eyes. The kiss on the hand turned into a rather passionate kissing session that made the boys, Sam and Christopher and Collin, groan and run away, made Issa and Bella giggle, and made Chloe, who watched her parents with only a little embarrassment, sigh.

Chloe plucked petals off the flower crown on her lap, wishing she had a name and face to think of when plucking petals, like other girls her age. "He loves me..." smile! "He loves me not..." frown. Amy Bayers went through this ritual over Tommy Tookers, but that made Chloe a little queasy. Tommy ate too many worms on a dare to make Chloe think him kiss worthy.

Being homeschooled her entire childhood and taking free college courses online since she was fifteen had not exposed her enough to other young people, specifically young men, apart from her brothers and the too young, too annoying boys who attended Williamston church. Besides, her melanin was not an asset to her in a town where beauty was blonde and anemic.

She smoothed her purple and black skull paisley, calf-length skirt and sighed again. Her eyes drifted to their happy, bright yellow home. As well-kept and recently painted as it was, it felt more stifling and smaller than ever these days. She longed for the type of excitement that befell small-town girls in the books she loved.

There had been no new-to-town bad boys, no paranormal love triangle with an Edward or a Jacob, no morose, sullen poets like Patrick in *10 Things I Hate About You*. What's more, she never expected such men would present themselves in Williamston. Where was her Four, shaking her out of her simple, selfless life into a life of tattoos, excitement, and danger? What about her Mr. Darcy, pushing into her rural humdrum with his intelligence, good looks and fortune and sweeping her, slowly and steadily, off her feet? Did a heroine have to be powder sugar white and thin to be a heroine?

Chloe was of a sunny disposition, however, and she didn't allow herself to wallow too long in loneliness. She had a creative imagination that could, at any moment, sweep her into the warm embrace of a stunning werewolf or the cold kiss of a moody and misunderstood vampire. She stared at the dirt road running parallel to her house and let her mind drift.

The rumble of a motorcycle broke into her reverie. She felt the dangerous vibration of the machine in her stomach before she saw it or its rider. The motorcycle rounded the corner by the old oak a quarter mile from her house. Her heart pounded in her chest. Just before her house, the rumbling of the motorcycle hacked and sputtered to a stop. A tall, lean man with shoulders that would not quit languidly removed his helmet and kicked the stand in place. The wind swept back a riot of long, black hair from a sculpted, brown face and keen, passionate dark eyes.

The dark stranger, in painted-on jeans and an open leather jacket that showcased his toned brown chest and abs, was walking directly toward her house. Chloe stood, dropping the wilted flower chain in her hand, and smoothing her skull paisley skirt. The stranger caught sight of her, threw his thick black hair over his shoulder and grinned. She melted where she stood.

The stranger's dark, alluring lips parted in a smile. "Chloe?"

"Yes?" Chloe answered, wondering how this handsome stranger knew her name.

"Chloe?!" Chloe shook herself out of the dream and turned to papa's voice.

"Hija, I've been calling you. Your Tía Miranda is here. Come. I've been calling your name over and over. ¿Dónde está tu cabeza?" Her father stood on their back porch, waving her inside their small, white trailer.

Chloe blushed. "Sorry, papa. I'm coming." She brushed the flower chain off her skirt and put a pin in her very promising daydream.

Tía Miranda was a short, big hipped, stylish woman in her mid-thirties. She was known for her ability to talk so quickly people wondered if she was attempting to set a record. It didn't signify, since much of what she talked about had gone over the heads of her peers for ages. With fingers as quick at coding as her mouth was speaking, she'd been somewhat of a prodigy in her youth. Williamston was still not sure what to think about her, and she quit the town so quickly it gave the porch folk whiplash and left them with no time to form an opinion. She met Chloe on the back porch and swept her niece into a very bosomy embrace. A cloud of strong citrus perfume enveloped her.

Tía had always sought Chloe out as her young confidante and protégé. Not having any children of her own, yet, Tía had adopted Chloe's company when her niece's enthusiam for fashion, novels and social media surpassed even her own. Tía had a youthfulness she'd not grown out of, an intelligent if somewhat flighty mind, and a pocketbook that allowed her the flexibility to do pretty much what she wanted exactly when she wanted to.

As it turned out, an ability to travel did not necessarily make a person more well-rounded. For, though Tía Miranda was always bustling here and there looking to experience the fullness of life, she never came back much altered. Her conversation was always about the same three things–fashion trends, celebrity and political gossip and her next excursion. However hard it would be to guess from her very wholesome and frivolous way of conversing, Tía was a graduate of the illustrious MIT, Course 6.

At MIT, Tía created a social media app focused on fashion trends, politics, and celebrity as a final project. Her advanced algorithm app had taken off thanks to some wealthy sponsors, and had set her up for life, financially speaking. It had become one of the most used social media platforms of its time–ITfactor. Having become so successful early in life, she surrounded herself with financial advisors who could worry about her money for her and an artist partner who was well known in her own right, and who was often busy in France or Italy or New York showcasing her somewhat disturbing modern mud art paintings for obscene amounts of money.

"Oh, Chloe! You're so grown! So beautiful. I came, of course, for your graduation, but your parents and I also have a little surprise for you!" Tía's dark eyes, so like her father's, lit up.

"Well, less a surprise and more an offer," Chloe's mother corrected, smiling at Tía. "A very generous offer. You don't have to do it, but you have our blessing if you choose to."

Her father half hugged his sister. "Sí, but we think you cannot say no to your Tía's very kind offer."

Tía, rather used to getting her way and certain of succeeding with Chloe, waved the careful objection of her sister-in-law away. She was certain Chloe was growing as tired of this stifling town as she had when she was Chloe's age. The short, curvaceous thirty-something winked at her brother, who'd already given his full approbation of her plot for his daughter. She wove her arm through her niece's, making her way inside to her family's soft, well-used floral sofa and sitting next to her niece.

"Oh, Chloe! I hope you will make your Tía happy and tell me you will come with me in one week to Boston. I have an alumni association reunion, my fifteenth if you can believe it, and I need your help. I am going to have surgery on my foot in two days. Tía Pheobe will not be able to come, so I was hoping mi dulce sobrina would come with me and help me get to all the parties and events for a week. Of course, I'd make up for you having to hang out with your old Tía by taking you shopping and spoiling you as much as possible, as a graduation and birthday present."

For a young woman of seventeen to become a true heroine, she needed more than good looks and a moderate amount of sense. She needed adventure, newness, and a test of her character. This, it seemed, was Chloe's chance to thrust herself into the sort of teenage romance novel drama she'd only dreamed of.

Chloe was so overwhelmed by her luck, she was speechless for a full minute. Leave Williamston? Leave Iowa for the first time in her life? Go to a fashionable, huge, college city and hang out with her fashion-forward, rich Tía and go shopping in trendy shops? Maybe she would even run into Chris Evans! He'd made the list of best-looking celebrities living in Boston in her favorite magazine *In or Out*, after all. Perhaps they would lock eyes in a ritzy Boston shop...

Bumped from behind, Chloe dropped the blouses she'd hung over her arm, and they fell to the floor. She immediately dropped to her knees to retrieve them. At $90 a pop, these four blouses were worth more than her entire wardrobe.

"Oh, excuse me, Miss. Let me help you with that..."

A shockingly handsome man with eyes the color of bluebells knelt to help her with her blouses.

"I'm so sorry about that. I was in a rush. Looking for a present for..." the man began to explain.

"Your girlfriend?" Chloe ventured, already knowing someone this beautiful had to be shopping at Exposé with the sole purpose of wooing an equally beautiful woman.

The man grinned, his full lips parting to reveal even teeth under perfectly manicured facial hair.

"No, no. I don't have a girlfriend." His eyes met hers and he smiled meaningfully. "I'm shopping for my sister," he replied, dropping his crystalline eyes shyly.

"Oh...well, did you need help?" Chloe ventured, her heart in her throat. Why did she say that?! Of course this god wouldn't need help from the likes of her.

"Really?! Oh, wow! That would be perfect!" His eyes were even bluer when he was excited. "My name is Chris. Chris Evans."

"That sounds familiar," Chloe replied, trying to place this beautiful man in front of her, but too caught up in those perfect azure orbs to manage it.

"Oh, well..." he waved a hand, helping her to collect the rest of her blouses and stand. He offered her his hand, which she took. He held onto it a little longer than proper, and she blushed and looked away.

"Captain America ring a bell?" he asked, his face hopeful.

"Oh! Yes, now I remember," Chloe answered, calm and cool and absolutely unwilling to fawn and make a fool of herself like every other woman this man had probably met. "I haven't seen the movies, but that must be it."

"Well, maybe after you help me find a fitting present, we can change that?" Chris asked her, his eyes hopeful.

Chloe bit her lip. "I'd like that very much..."

"It's a date then..."

Chloe realized he was waiting for her name. "Oh! Sorry. Chloe. Chloe Mora."

"Chloe? I like that. Chloe. Chloe." He savored her name on his tongue.

"Chloe! Earth to Chloe! What do you think, sobrina? Would it be too boring to tag along with your decrepit Tía? You could tour some of the colleges. I know you aren't that interested in sciences, but Boston has a lot of colleges to pick from. MIT is the best, of course..."

Chloe blushed over her daydream, squealed happily, and hugged her Tía. "Yes! Gracias, Tía. I'd love to help you. You are the coolest Tía a girl could have!"

"Lo sé!" Tía replied, accepting the hug with vigor. "We leave Saturday, after your graduation party, and will return in a week and a half. Pack lite. I'm buying you a big bolsa. We are going shopping!"

Chloe and Tía squealed together in like-joy. The younger girls, Issa and Bella, mumbled their discontent with their age and situation. And the youngest boys, Julio and Brian, covered their ears to block out the sound of joy. A peaceable girl at heart, Chloe promised each of her siblings a very special present each from her tutoring savings, which worked to soothe their hurt feelings and made her parents smile proudly. Tía, shocked, would not hear of her niece spending her hard-earned money on anything apart from college, but promised that each child would be getting a very nice present upon their sister's return, with her financial backing.

The Moras looked around their tiny home. It was clean, bright, full of love and well cared for, but it was also second-hand, cramped, and out of the way. They were proud that they had such a godsend in Tía Miranda to help provide such experiences, here and there, for their beloved children, especially Chloe, who was, above all of them, the most selfless and responsible.

~ Two ~

MORGENSTERN AND MILESTONES

Chloe's graduation day went off without a hitch. Tía Miranda headed back to Nantucket to prepare for her surgery and the upcoming trip. Mr. and Mrs. Mora got Chloe her very first phone for her birthday and graduation present. Despite it being the best value Smart Chat phone plan and most basic phone the store had, Chloe could not believe her luck. For her entire seventeen years, she'd made do using her friend's phones or the old folk's landlines if she was away from home, which had been very seldom.

Chloe, like many coming of age heroines, was beginning to understand the real cost of life. Her running start degree was paid for by the state, but she'd taken a job online as a tutor for the community college's writing center. Now that she had her AA degree, she also had to move on from the community college tutoring job that helped pay for books and supplies and pocket money for discount fabric.

Her college advisor and supervisor at the tutoring center, who she'd never met in person, sent her a card with a coffee gift card and a letter of recommendation for any college she chose to pursue next. Chloe, though grateful, seriously doubted she could afford a B.A. degree even from the most affordable public schools, but appreciated the kind gift and words of affirmation all the same. The card was so dear to her, in fact, that she read it several times with feeling tears in her eyes.

Dear Ms. Mora,

Your online work at the tutoring center this year was unparalleled. There are few young people your age who are as responsible and caring as yourself, and there are even fewer who are as creative and inventive. I do hope you'll accept the enclosed letter of recommendation for the college of your choice. I am willing to edit it to reflect your preference of schools. I beg you to set your sights on continuing your higher education, to further the growth you've shown the last two years. Please stay in touch and let me know how I can help see your goals to fruition, as you have done for the students who sought your help at our tutoring center. I've post-scripted my email and office number if you need an updated letter for your applications. You've graduated on an off semester, due to your advanced pace as a homeschooling student, but many colleges will accept winter applications, too. I hope you will seriously consider applying broadly.

Kind Regards and Well Wishes,

Professor Phineas Ballamy

She smiled over the card and put it in her special memories box under her bed before reaching for her copy of *The Starless Sea*. Chloe's creative writing teacher, impressed with her skill in storytelling but rather worried by the unvaried books she was accustomed to reading, gave the gift of Morgenstern's prose as a hopeful bit of inspiration to fuel a more refined passion in her hungry, romantic mind.

Graduation was the first time Chloe met any of her teachers or fellow students in person, though she'd seen some of their faces online. Creative writing was her favorite class, and Dr. Lark her favorite professor by far. Dr. Lark looked just like she did online—petite with short cropped springy caramel curls and deep, almost black eyes. She wore fashionable green glasses and was one of the teachers who shook Chloe's hand when she walked across the stage.

It was a hot outdoors ceremony and was a bit shorter and much less momentous than she'd anticipated, but it had been nice to meet Dr. Lark and get such a thoughtful gift.

She sunk into Morgenstern's marvelous, strange, and uncanny worlds and drifted off to sleep dreaming of painted doors, keys, bees and thrilling and forbidden sounding drinks and dreams. She had little to concern her thoughts now, except the coming trip with Tía Miranda in a week's time.

~ Three ~

FIRST TIME FLIER

Mr. and Mrs. Mora watched with tense, sad smiles as their oldest child wheeled her new, neon purple bag, a graduation gift from Tía Phoebe, up to the security checkpoint. Both being fairly rational beings, however, they were happy to finally see their daughter venture off into her own story. Her father even went so far as to give her fifty dollars for travel expenses, a sum not large by most standards, but not insignificant to the Moras. Passers-by in the Des Moines International airport were not disturbed by loud sobs, overt displays of affection or demands from Chloe's sisters that she call and tell them EVERYTHING that happened. No, the Mora family were quietly touched and wistful. Mr. and Mrs. Mora even waited to shed tears until their younger children led them away from the checkpoint line hoping their parents would splurge on a fast-food dinner on the way home.

As for Chloe, her apprehension about being surrounded by bustling, tired, and stressed looking people was tempered by happier feelings. Today was just the type of day to prove that she had made it to full "heroine goes on a romantic journey to find herself and find love" status. Her spirits were such that no number of grumbling travelers could quiet her excitement. She stared, wonderingly, at the airport security gates, grumpy TSA agents, and would-be passengers incomprehensibly removing their shoes. She removed her own shoes, almost rapturously, even though she would not have been able to tell you why it was necessary.

Her smiling was so excessive that the blonde, forty-something TSA agent looked at her suspiciously and made her walk through the scanning machine *and* waved the strange black wand over her torso for good measure before letting her into the terminal. Chloe smiled in polite acquiescence the entire time, putting the grumpy agent even more off his guard. The agent was only dissuaded from being more of a nuisance by the appearance of his coworker, Carl. Tía Miranda had paid the unaccompanied minor fee to have Carl escort Chloe to her gate and help her settle in the plane.

Chloe put on a show of acting put out over having an escort at age eighteen. Though, in reality, she was happy for the gruff older man's presence. Being a heroine out on your own was all well and good, but the airport was an intimidating place even for well-traveled people, and Chloe was a *never* traveled person. The airport was much bigger than she expected, and she had no idea how to read the digital screens scrolling with different city names, gates, and times. Not to mention the crowds of pushy people shoving past her with bags that clipped her heels. Carl also reminded Chloe a little of her abuelo Mora, which put her further at ease.

Carl made quick work of finding Chloe's gate, expertly weaving around bags and irritated people staring at screens. He even stopped at a cafe on the way to grab her a hot chocolate, courtesy of the probably outrageous service fee Tía had paid to see she was comfortable and safe. Once at the gate, which smelled faintly of socks and sported the most uncomfortably thin cushioned plastic seats she'd ever sat in, Carl sat next to her working on a sudoku book. Once in a while, he showed her a tricky block of numbers and asked for the use of her "young eyes", nodding when she saw the pattern he missed. Otherwise, he sipped his coffee and said little while she nervously drank her hot chocolate and imagined which of the good looking twenty something college boys scattered around the terminal would be her seatmate. The wait, thankfully, was not a long one. The hard plastic chair was hurting her backside and her excitement left her unable to focus on her book.

She was in the first group to board, embarrassingly referred to as the "unaccompanied minors" boarding. Carl helped her find her seat–FIRST CLASS like a proper heroine thanks to Tía–and stowed her bag over her head. She thanked Carl with a five-dollar bill, calculating that she now had only $45 pocket money left from her parents. He smiled at her and patted her hand, calling her a good sort of girl. Carl motioned towards her as he left, drawing the attention of a pretty black-haired flight attendant on his way out. The attendant nodded and quickly made her way over to Chloe with a "first flight" pin and an assortment of sodas for her to choose from. Chloe chose a Sprite, taking it from the woman with shaking hands.

"My name is Tanya, Chloe. I'm so happy you chose Rayon Air for your first flight. You just let me know if I can get you anything to make your flight more comfortable. Food will be served in about an hour, but we have snacks and more drinks available after takeoff," the pretty flight attendant assured her.

"Thank you, Tanya. I'm fine with my Sprite for now," Chloe assured her. Tanya smiled warmly and greeted the other passengers. Chloe congratulated herself for sounding very composed and older than her years.

Chloe's seatmate ended up being a very well-dressed man who reminded her of a white actor her mom would think handsome, a real George Clooney vibe. Unfortunately, she was more of an Adam Beach type of girl, if she was forced to crush on a handsome man over forty. The well-dressed, classically handsome white man gave her one passing glance before ignoring her completely. Chloe had hoped to have a much younger, much more companionable seat partner. It was only fitting for a heroine on her first plane ride to be seated by a handsome lead male, only two to three years her senior. Or at least one that spoke above two words to her. Determined to appear unconcerned and grown up, however, Chloe buckled her seatbelt and settled in to read her book.

Having only seen people fly in movies, Chloe was not quite prepared for takeoff, but did her best to not showcase the extreme terror coursing through her veins as the plane rattled noisily down the runway, shaking her to the core. She gripped the plush first-class armrests, digging her fingernails in for extra purchase. She looked out her window at the tarmac rapidly fading from view as the plane shot into the sky.

By the time the plane had leveled off and Captain Monica Fairway's voice assured the passengers that they had reached cruising altitude and could now use all electronic devices, set to plane mode, Chloe's fingers ached from gripping her armrest. She released it slowly, then turned to stare out the window. It was cloudy wherever they were above Iowa, but she imagined she could see her house.

She waved at her parents through the clouds, forlornly driving home, already feeling her absence, telepathically advising them to not worry. She was a sophisticated adult, now, graduating college and seeing the world. Opening her book, she intended to fall back into the world of *the Starless Sea* and to shake off the tension of takeoff. Her flip phone had limited internet usage, and it was extremely slow when it did work, so she had to depend on reading to take her mind off the fact that she was thousands of feet above the ground.

Chloe had to wake very early in the morning, and soon found that flying was not as exciting as she'd hoped. Her eyes grew heavy as she stared uncomprehendingly at the words in front of her.

She was jolted from a dream–one in which she'd been boating across the languid honey-colored waters of the Starless Sea and navigating Zachary to an unknown destination–by an uncomfortable jolt and lurch that made her feel as though she was back inside the vomit-reeking cage of the Zipper ride at the Williamston Fair.

"We are experiencing some slight turbulence," Captain Monica Fairway's entirely too chipper voice announced over the intercom. "Please return to your seats and buckle your seatbelts. We are flying through a storm system. Our flight attendants will also need to be seated and buckled for their safety. Food and beverage service will resume shortly."

Chloe watched, the terror rising inside her again, as Tanya moved past her, calm and smiling, and buckled her seatbelt. Her seatmate wore noise canceling headphones and was asleep even though the plane jolted as though it were an inflatable raft cruising at a good clip down a fast-moving river. Chloe's heart raced and her stomach plummeted when the plane dropped suddenly, then immediately jolted back into position.

No...this is much worse than the Zipper. The Zipper is only thirty feet in the air. If this plane comes down, we'd be falling for literal, terrifying minutes.

Chloe looked at her seatmate and was amazed to find him still sleeping, despite the jostling of the plane through the storm. Torrential rain poured down her window. She could see nothing but dark clouds and torrents of dark water. She stared out the window, transfixed and terrified. If only she had someone to talk to! She closed her eyes when a flash of distant lightning tore through the sky.

The plane dropped significantly. Her body rose against her seatbelt as the plane fell. She was horrifyingly weightless for seconds before she crashed back down against her seat and smacked her head hard against the window. Her vision danced with stars before darkness took her.

She opened her eyes to the dark, soulful eyes of Adam Beach. His long black hair fell in waves over his face as he leaned over her. "Are you okay? You bumped your head pretty hard there."

His graceful fingers cupped the side of her face gently. She blinked, stunned, several times before putting on a weak smile. "I'm feeling better now."

Adam Beach smiled knowingly. "Good. Here, sit up a little. I had the stewardess bring you a pillow."

Chloe sat straighter in her seat, thankful that the rocking of the plane had subsided. Her seatmate, Adam, placed a pillow delicately behind her head, then softly touched the bruise forming at her temple.

"That's a good bump you got there. Is there anything I can do? I sent the stewardess for some ice..."

Adam's hand remained cupped around her face. She stared into his bottomless eyes. "A kiss might make it feel better," she heard her possibly concussed, traitor mouth utter.

He laughed in a short, sexy way. He leaned down and placed a gentle kiss on her throbbing head. Her heart raced; their eyes met. Her blood pounded through her veins. He leaned in again, and...

Her seatmate unceremoniously poked her in the shoulder. She turned to him, wishing more than ever that she was seated by an Adam Beach and *not* a George Clooney. "Yes?" she answered, trying to keep the annoyance out of her voice. The man, not wasting even one word on her, gestured at Tanya, who was standing in the aisle, the storm having leveled off.

"We're doing food service now, hun. We had you down for a chicken caesar salad." Tanya passed her a tray with a salad, fruit bowl, bag of pretzels and another Sprite on it.

Chloe juggled the tray ungainly, not sure where it was best to put it. Her seatmate, possibly annoyed that her indecision was getting in the way of his meal, flicked a plastic lock on the back of the seat in front of her and her tray fell open, smacking the food tray she held and nearly toppling her soda. She righted the tray, and placed her dinner tray on top of the seat back tray.

"Thank you," Chloe automatically said, though she wished she'd taken it back right away, even though she hated to be rude. George had nearly spilled Sprite all over her salad. Why hadn't he just told her what to do? Movies and books had trained her to believe that handsome older men were generally charming. She was disappointed to see this was not the case. Perhaps this one was more the rascal, like Daniel in *Bridget Jones Diary*. Except that Daniel was not surly. A scoundrel and sleazeball, sure, but charming. Very disappointing. Yes, she very much wished she was seated next to Adam or even a charming, sexually deviant Daniel.

She contented herself with the fact that her salad looked expertly made, as if first class had its very own chef. She made a show of arranging her napkin on her lap and cutting her chicken into pieces before eating her salad carefully and properly, like rich people did in the movies. She didn't want to give George more reasons to scowl at her. Unfortunately, the salad looked better than it tasted. The chicken was dry and the tomatoes were pulpy. Chloe began to think spilling pop on it would only improve her dinner. And George, it turned out, ate with his mouth open. Handsome, wealthy men weren't supposed to eat with their mouths open! That was for the Tommy Tookers of the world! Chloe worried over his expensive looking tie. Adam, and even Daniel, would chew with their mouths closed, she decided.

~ Four ~

SHOPPING MONTAGE!

Though the plane ride had been more terrifying and decidedly less charming than she'd hoped, Chloe was not deterred from the hopeful excitement that the rest of her trip would be the most romance-filled excursion of her newly eighteen years.

She was determined to have a Jennifer Garner in *13 Going on 30* experience in the big city–shopping, parties, and sharing candy and kisses with a boy next door-type character. Only, the boys next door in Williamston were not the kind of boys she wanted to share her first kiss with, so she was very hopeful to run into a young Mark Ruffalo sometime over the course of the next week and a half.

All of this played through her head while she waited to deplane. Tanya handed down her suitcase and informed her that Tía Miranda was waiting for her just outside the gate. Chloe would have raced down the cramped, hot runway in her excitement, except that George deplaned first. George was determined to walk at as leisurely a pace as possible, while also taking up as much space on the tarmac as possible. So, our young heroine had to dawdle a little more than was properly romantic before starting her new adventure in the big city.

***

Boston was absolutely captivating to an impressionable Midwestern girl, more used to passing acres and acres of soybeans and corn than row upon row of buildings as far as the eye could see. The rideshare to Kendall Square was akin to a near-miss bumper car ride, as crowded as the streets were. The statues, ancient looking architecture and criss-crossing streets were all so different from anything our young heroine had ever known. She felt very small and somewhat anxious just riding past it all. And the buildings! Worn brick, gothic structures next to sleek, modern, shining edifices. Somehow, they all seemed to fit in just fine next to a dirty Duncan Donuts or 24-hour burger joint seamlessly. It was well curated chaos.

"Tía, what is that tall building there?!" Chloe pointed to a particularly tall skyscraper covered in rectangular glass windows that stuck out far higher than most of the surrounding buildings.

"Prudential Tower, mija. Where Tía Pheobe proposed to me," Tía answered with a swoon in her voice. "And it is our first stop before we hit the hotel. Our room won't be ready yet, and I promised you shopping."

"Tía proposed to you there! That's so romantic! Like, *Sleepless in Seattle* romantic!" Chloe sighed. "But please don't feel like you have to buy me things, Tía. You paid for first-class tickets here and back and you're taking me on this great trip. Being here is enough."

"You are becoming a remarkable seamstress, and I applaud your style, sobrina, but I promised you graduation and birthday shopping. And I keep my word! New city, new clothes, new Chloe."

Tía smiled at Chloe's expression. She could almost see the shopping montage roll behind her niece's eyes. She secured the deal by motioning to her own silk blouse. "You'll be doing me a favor. My wardrobe is sadly neglected. I can't go to my fifteenth reunion in a blouse I got three years ago! You'll just have to be resigned to spending my money. Can you manage that?"

"I'll suffer through, Tía," Chloe laughingly replied, very eager, indeed, to be apprised of what passed for high fashion in an actual city and knowing herself to be lacking in urban sophistication.

Prudential Tower's shopping center held more stores and fancy, classy people than lived in all of Williamston. When Chloe stepped into Tía's favorite store, Saks, she pictured herself as Jenna Rink–a successful fashionista with money to burn. In reality, the shopping trip was far less seamless. It turned out Tía's knee cart was not easy to manage in any of the narrow shop aisles. She rolled over a few toes of helpful sales associates in two stores before taking a break and simply watching her niece try on outfits in a shop that seemed to cater to more youthful frames.

Tía had to encourage Chloe–several times–to stop checking price tags. Chloe's eyebrows traveled higher and higher up her forehead the more she did and her Tía wanted her to try on the clothes she truly wanted. At the end of the shopping day, which was a tolerable three hours later, both women had at least four new outfits, two evening dresses, matching shoes, and a few new purses. Tía's pocketbook had been set back nicely, and they were both hungry and tired. Tía ordered a car, and the two exhausted travelers were able to put their feet up in the Kendall hotel surrounded by their day's loot.

After a late room service lunch, the two women prepared for the evening's alumni reception at MIT's Stata center. As the reception was only semi-formal, this gave Chloe the perfect opportunity to wear her new vibrant green, pleated, silk halter dress, quilted denim half jacket, magenta flats, and an adorable purse decorated in vibrant beaded citrus fruits. She put her mass of wavy brown hair in a messy double crown braid and went for minimal eye make-up and soft pink lips. She smiled at her reflection, and a classy, full-grown woman smiled back. Tía came out of the bathroom, where she'd been readying herself, and smiled warmly at her sobrina.

"Oh, Sobrina! Simplemente perfecto." Her Tía's shining eyes and the warmth of her tone made Chloe blush. Never one to expect praise when it came, but happy to get it all the same, she ducked her head prettily.

Chloe smiled nervously when Tía asked if she was ready to go, her stomach in an anxious tangle. Tía assured her it was only a little "check-in" and "mingle" for old people like her. Chloe had never been to a reception party, which meant that her imagination had free rein as to what might be in store for her.

Alas, Tía was not a prompt dresser, and was, what she called, "fashionably late" to almost every occasion. Her healing foot made this perpetual lateness more pronounced in this case. It was several anxiety-ridden minutes later, for Chloe, when Tía finally presented herself as dressed to her self-exacting standard. She looked very bright in a Barbie pink mid-length dress that hugged her moderately curvy frame, finished with a blindingly white blazer and white flats to match, all of which stood out nicely against her soft brown skin. Her lips were as pink as her dress and her ear-length hair styled in a perfect intentional muss. She hobble-twirled on her good foot once before taking up a white clutch and settling onto her orthopedic knee cart, a black scooter-type contraption that she was able to kneel on to keep weight off her foot.

"Time to make an entrance, sobrina."

Thankfully, the Stata center was extremely close to their hotel. In the two blocks they walked to the center, Chloe allowed her mind to wander, daydreaming that she was Mia Thermopolis, remade at Paolo's hands into a princess. Like Mia, she felt ready to have all eyes upon her as she presented herself, shined to perfection, to the world.

Making an entrance at an informal, busy meet-and-greet did not end up meeting Chloe's imaginative standard, unfortunately. There was no long, important staircase with hourglass balustrades and thick gilded rails to give proper attention to a coming of age woman making her grand debut. As a matter of fact, the Stata Center was beyond anything our heroine could have imagined, which is saying something for one whose imagination was working overtime almost constantly. It was very *interesting*, but it was not what one would call *romantic*.

Chloe stared up at the Picasso-like sharp lines and curves of the building in dumbfounded wonder. The inside of the Center was likewise astounding. It was geometric, metallic and mod. Nothing like the Greek-style architecture Chloe had come to expect from the postcards Tía sent her niece of MIT. It was not a bad difference. It simply jarred Chloe out of her lively imaginings, as it was so far from what she had imagined.

"This building is...*different*," Chloe mused aloud.

"It's fun, isn't it? It was completed a few years before I graduated. This is the place I most liked to do homework. My dorm was loud." Tía's eyes were far away, reliving her youth for a moment.

Inside, Chloe clung to Tía's purse, which she'd asked Chloe to hold, so she could have both hands for her knee scooter. Chloe found herself self-consciously apologizing for her Tía running over the tip of someone's polished shoe and ramming into the heels of a few people who stopped suddenly in front of her. Tía seemed unaware of the extreme embarrassment her niece was undergoing with each injured toe; she simply laughed an "Oops! Packed like sardines in here!" and looked around absently, searching for a familiar face.

Chloe looked past the frowning alumna who stopped in front of them suddenly and got heel checked by Tía's scooter. She was massaging her heel and throwing an impressive glower their way. They were in a longish line that ended in a table with young, friendly greeters wearing maroon shirts that read "Tech Baller," which Tía laughed at and Chloe didn't understand. The table wore a taut cardinal banner that read "registration table."

"Let's stay in this line. I think we have to sign in here, so they know we made it, and can give us our activity folders," Tía ordered.

Once signed in, Tía affixed a metallic pin to her collar that read "Dr. Miranda Mora, Course 6." There must have been levels of pins the alumni wore, as Chloe saw others affix less fancy plastic name tags on their shirts. Chloe got a metallic pin matching her Tía's, reading "Chloe Mora, Guest."

Tía wove her way through the throng of alumni, stretching her short frame to lay eyes on any familiar faces. She soon despaired of this tactic, as her knee scooter was hard to navigate in the crowds and increasingly more people were glaring over throbbing toes at them. They paused off to the side of a crowd. Tía massaged the calf on her right leg, which was working overtime with its friend out of commission.

"Maybe we should find somewhere to sit, Tía, since you're not seeing anyone you know," Chloe advised, worried about Tía getting overly tired but also worried about her injuring more people. Chloe was tiring, too, pushing past so many sharp elbows on rich-looking people who weren't used to being jostled.

"I wish Nate or Bev were here," Tía mused. "Or maybe some of my old friends from my dorm. I am sure Bev said she was coming…"

"Yeah, it's awkward not knowing anyone," Chloe agreed, wearied by the day's events and a little disappointed that they didn't quite meet her expectations. "Maybe we can just find a place to sit? I think I see some spots over there by the drink stand."

Tía spied the chairs and set her shoulder determinedly. "Oh! Yes, let's get there before they're snagged!" So saying, she began a bowling ball bee-line for the spot, jostling a woman into spilling her drink. Chloe hurried after her, apologizing constantly.

Chloe heard one petite alumna comment, "Ow! Who let Legally Brown in?"

Chloe glared at the woman as she passed, refusing to apologize to this particular alumna. Tía didn't seem to hear the comment and raced ahead of two friends who'd just spotted the vacant chairs in the refreshment area. Tía zoomed down a ramp at a clip, took a hard right turn just in front of the two seats and pulled her handbrake to a screeching halt, plopping herself triumphantly into one of the seats and flopping her purse on the other. She waved Chloe over, a victorious grin on her face and a mischievous twinkle in her brown eyes. The two friends who were headed toward the chairs grumbled as Chloe passed them, and turned around.

"Chloe, be a dear and grab us a couple of drinks and maybe an appetizer from one of the caterers walking around with trays," Tía said when Chloe got to the chairs.

"Do we have to pay? Or…" Chloe stuttered, embarrassed. She was sure her $45 would not go far for ritzy drinks and appetizers.

"No, no. Just tips for the bartender. Here," Tía rummaged around in her purse before shoving some singles and a five-dollar bill in her hand. "I just want an iced tea with lemon, if they have it. They probably have pop or lemonade or something for you. Don't be shy. Just ask for the virgin drink list."

Chloe's eyes popped, "Tía!"

Tía chuckled at Chloe's bright red face. "That's what it's called, mija. It just means non-alcoholic. It doesn't have anything to do with whether you've had sex."

Tía and Chloe had a good laugh at that. "Oh. I thought you were calling me one."

"You don't have to answer, but aren't you? That's not what I was saying, but now I'm curious."

Chloe blushed even more. "Yes, I am. But now I'm not going to be able to get drinks for us without laughing."

"Maybe I can help there." A tenor voice behind her startled Chloe into dropping some of Tía's dollar bills. A tall, broad shouldered, dark-haired young man in a "Tech Baller" shirt bent to pick the bills off the ground and handed them back to a now speechless Chloe. He had graceful, long-fingered hands, medium brown skin, deep brown eyes, and a full head of carefully mussed, slightly curly black hair. She guessed him to be of Indian descent, but he also looked a little like Miguel from Cobra Kai. Chloe was suddenly stricken with the fact that this hot guy had just heard her saying the word virgin several times. She looked around to find a good, quiet place to crawl into and die.

~ Five ~

TECH BALLERS

The young man must have read Chloe's embarrassment, and he moved to quickly recover her dignity. "Forgive me for intruding. It's my job to make sure every alumni and their guest feels at ease, cared for and, eventually, loose and free with their hopefully boundless pocket money," the cheeky young man quipped. "Please let me know if you'd prefer I get lost or if I'm not barking up a wealthy enough tree."

Tía, always tickled by impertinence, laughed heartily at this joke and extended her hand to him. "I'm Dr. Miranda Mora. This is my niece, Chloe Mora. She's helping her invalid auntie around town for the week."

He inclined his head at Chloe, like a slight bow, before replying to Tía. "Dr. Mora of ITfactor, I presume? That was a clever algorithm you created there. I *am* barking up the right tree, then. I'll collect some drinks and a few appetizers for you both. Be sure to note my helpfulness when the Big Give comes around. I'll be sure I'm your Tech Caller, or as my unfortunate shirt reads, 'Tech Baller.'"

"I just might answer the tech callers this year, then, you impertinent young thing," Tía replied, turning to her niece and sensing the question in her eyes. "But who am I to give the credit to when I do?"

The handsome student held out his hand. "I'm Michael Bath, Course 8."

"Well, we can't all be in Course 6," Tía winked. "But you're charming enough, so we will allow you to bring us a tea with lemon, at least two of those little shrimp appetizers I see people enjoying and..."

She turned to her niece and smiled over the stars in the girl's eyes. "Virgin..." Chloe started, then blushed, "Oh...I mean...Shirley Temple?"

Michael inclined his head, meeting Chloe's gaze with an assured, interested smile. "I can manage that."

Michael turned and sauntered off to the bar to grab the drinks. Chloe's eyes followed him, taking in the broad set of his shoulders, the perfect "V" shape his body made from behind. Tía nudged Chloe and lifted her brows. "What do you think of the student *body*, mija?"

"Tía!"

Michael returned shortly with two plates piled with various appetizers, including the shrimp skewers and their drink order. He set it on the long table next to their seat. Other people were chatting at the long table, sipping drinks, laughing, and reconnecting. The two women, not knowing anyone present, gave their attention to the charming Michael.

"So," Tía sipped her tea, and looked up at Michael. "Are you a fan of social apps like ITfactor?"

"Not nearly as much as my sister would like. She's much better at following trends than myself. Alas, Boston University is where she makes her home, so MIT will not profit from it."

"Boston University?! I've been thinking of that for my Chloe, here. Please, do convince her I'm right." Tía nudged the conversation to Chloe, seeing the eagerness with which her niece followed the handsome young man with her eyes.

"Boston University? But why not bring her wit and vivacity to MIT, Dr. Mora? She must be far too good for BU. We must convince her to come over to our side. Though I beg you not to tell my sister or father I said so."

Chloe laughed. "I'm going to have to disagree, even though I know you're making fun of me. I doubt BU would take me and I *know* MIT would not."

"Oh, no. The intelligence of your eyes led me to believe you much smarter than you are," Michael teased. Chloe smiled indulgently at the rogue. "I apologize. Perhaps you are perfect for BU, afterall. I'll have to introduce you to my sister."

Chloe laughed at him and shook her head. "You are a bit of a clown, aren't you?"

"You've found me out," he grinned. "Now you know our secret- MIT students can be just as foolish as anyone else. Perhaps more so, sometimes, when they are working towards something they want. I think you'll find most people here very *determined,* even if their goals *are* foolish."

"Oh, and what are *your* foolish goals?" Chloe inquired, amazed by the quick wit and vivacity of her speaking partner.

"I should think my current goal is quite plain..." He winked at Chloe.

Chloe, for her part, understood this to mean that Michael was unabashedly pursuing the fundraising scheme he said brought him to their side. Tía, on the other hand, had no reserved humility when it came to her niece and supposed the young man's true foolish goal was the affection of her lovely niece. As this goal could only solidify Chloe's attachment to Boston, Tía was not about to put a damper on it. She looked around for an appropriate excuse to leave the youth to their banter and found one in the tall frame of a recently arrived friend.

Tía rose from her seat, balanced unsteadily on her knee scooter, and clapped her hands. "Oh! It's Bev! Oh, Chloe, do excuse me for a moment. I see Bev at the registration table. I *thought* she was coming!" Tía pointed to a very tall, very brightly dressed, fit woman who was waving their way with perfectly manicured and very long neon purple nails.

"Michael, do me a favor and keep my niece company for a moment. The alumni association will be pleased you did." With that, Tía wheeled perilously fast upon her knee scooter, toward her towering friend and out of the way of the type of starry-eyed flirtations reserved for unjaded youth.

"Well, I think you are going about your duties very well. You've achieved the approval of the very best alumna you have if my Tía thought you good enough company to keep. She's kind, but she has a small circle and very little patience for talking about things that hold no interest for her. You might just have met your goal of securing access to her deep pockets," Chloe teased.

Michael's eyes brightened and his smile was genuine. "Hush, beautiful niece of our illustrious alumna. Procuring your Tía's good graces and donation is supposed to be a great secret and dance. Anyway, I don't think her dress even has pockets."

"I'll bet you're a very good dancer," Chloe replied, laughingly. She surprised herself with the comment, but Michael brought something out of her she never knew she was holding back.

"Abysmal and graceless, I assure you." His smile was too sly for words.

An awkward pause followed this revelation. Chloe's cheeks hurt from smiling up at the clever and extremely handsome Michael. She was almost afraid to break the silence and say something that would scare him away, so she took a long drink of her Shirley Temple.

Unfortunately, the stem of a maraschino cherry became dislodged from the cherry itself to make a fool of Chloe, causing her to hack and choke. Her classy, carefree manner was immediately called into question when she coughed the stem out onto the table. A group of chatting alumni seated on the other side of the table moved their glasses further down the table, eyeing Chloe's choking spell with distaste.

Michael patted Chloe on the back gently and offered her a napkin that seemed to appear in his hand out of nowhere. Chloe took the napkin in a mixture of awe over Michael's smooth grace, such a contrast to her embarrassing and unattractive sputtering. She dabbed at her eyes and mouth, and dipped her head, blushing furiously.

"I'm sorry," Michael intoned, trying not to laugh.

"Sorry for what? Did you de-stem the cherry in my drink in an attempt to sabotage me?" Chloe asked.

"I would never! I suspect the bartender." He gave the bartender a long, suspicious look. Chloe giggled.

"No," Michael continued. "I'm sorry because I've completely forgotten to partake in useless small talk." His eyes danced.

"I've always thought small talk a little boring, so you are excused," Chloe answered.

"Oh, no. No one can be exempted from small talk. It *must* happen. So, let me start." He paused to clear his throat. He stood straighter and wiped the grin off his face. "How long have you been in Boston?"

Chloe tried to copy him and pulled a serious face. "We got in only yesterday."

"And how long are you staying?"

"A little more than a week."

"Ah, hardly time to experience the season."

"Yes, we are embarrassed to not be here in time to catch a famous east coast snowstorm."

"Yes, that *is* a shame. And where are you from?"

"Iowa."

"I know nothing of Iowa except for a vague idea that they grow corn, so I will make an overall assumption and say, 'Ah! Iowa! Go Huskers! Which, I think, is some sort of sports team, but don't press me for details. Details are impolite and only showcase one's ignorance when one is engaging in small talk."

"I won't press, but only because I don't know anything about the Huskers, though I think they might actually be a Nebraskan team, and I want to seem smarter than I am on any subject that amuses you. So, I'll just ask where you are from, too," Chloe shot back.

"Salem. Now, you have to remark about witches or some descendant who was a witch and we can return to sane conversation again."

Chloe laughed heartily. "I don't have any East Coast descendants that I know of, and I'm sure my mom's side of the family, at least, were more likely to be oppressors of witches than anything else. Though, to be fair, my parents are much more open-minded than most Midwestern folks. Probably because my Tía and papa are first generation immigrants whose family failed to be properly Catholic."

"Oh, no. Am I talking to a protestant heathen?"

"Indeed, you are. And not a very good one. I often try to skip church unless it's a holiday. Our minister is very old and forgetful and not at all as interesting as my favorite show, which releases every Sunday."

Michael laughed heartily. "Well, then I don't have to feel morally obliged to be more upright than I am. Now, it's my job to smile stiffly and shuffle my feet..." On saying so, he performed the action admirably, "then we can, without guilt, speak freely again."

Chloe laughed at his ridiculousness and looked around her. "I have to say, MIT is nothing like what I imagined," Chloe said, motioning to the modern interior of the Stata center, all lines and angles.

"Oh, yes? And what did you imagine?" He smiled crookedly. "Are you disappointed that we are somewhat lacking in handsome genius janitors? Perhaps there should be more students roaming the halls muttering, 'Bazinga?'"

She searched him playfully, even more interested in him for referencing *Good Will Hunting* and *Big Bang Theory*, even if his tone said he was not impressed with either. "Having Matt Damon waxing the floors and solving math problems would be a great recruitment strategy. But I won't lie, I was leaning more towards the latter example."

Michael shrugged. "MIT students are *geeks*, which is much different from *nerds*. That's what that particular show gets wrong. All of them have some things they are maybe a little too passionate about. Take your aunt. She could have simply spent her time scrolling through political scandals and celebrity gossip, but she married the ideas in an insanely complex algorithm when she created her ITfactor app. That app is now one of the best indicators of who will be elected in campaigns at all levels, while also being the best indicator for which celebrity couples will hit it off. Don't get me wrong, *some* of us are awkward and incapable of understanding and following social morays, but, as you can see, not all of us are afraid of the opposite sex." He smiled at her meaningfully.

Chloe grinned back, her face warming. "Well, I've only been in Boston a few hours and only at MIT this once, so I'll have to take your word for it. I can really only judge the student body based on you and Tía, since you are the only MIT people I've met. But I do love my Tía. She's the coolest person I know. And you're no Sheldon."

"Sure, sure. Here I am trying to be the Indian Will Hunting, but I know it's all for naught. Tonight you'll post all about how some not at all handsome or likable MIT nerd who would not leave you alone to find better companionship." Michael feigned a hurt expression.

"I will not."

"Then, what will you post?"

"Who says I use social media at all?"

Michael narrowed his brown eyes at her in a playful manner. Chloe looked jestingly back at him. The locked eyes, just like in the movies, and the mood shifted. His face took on a more serious quality. Her stomach flipped and her knees jittered a little over that silly, slight change. She seriously considered that this encounter was just another of her vivid daydreams. Soon she'd be jostled out of it and this delicious Raymond Ablack meets Miguel from Cobra Kai fantasy man would be gone and she'd be alone and awkward in a strange place again.

Suddenly, his eyes shifted and took in something behind her. A slight frown crossed his face, only to be immediately replaced with his usual boyish grin. "Well, all good things have to come to an end, it seems. My supervisor is giving me the 'mingle and stop flirting' gesture."

"You flirt so much you need one of those, do you?" Chloe countered.

"I can't help if a little charm gets me better donation numbers than my rival, *Sandra*." He pulled a disgusted face when he said his rival's name. "But it's never before today been in earnest, I assure you. So, it is with great reluctance that I actually do my job rather than flirt with your beautiful person."

Chloe could hardly believe her good luck and didn't want to jinx it, but she also didn't want him getting away. Not having much experience with men, she was at a loss over how to approach telling him that she wanted to see him again.

"Have a wonderful evening, Ms. Mora," Michael said after a moment of awkward silence. And, like some dashing Jane Austen hero, he took Chloe's hand and bowed over it. His warm, long fingers gripping hers did nothing to make her think more clearly. It was all she could do to simply grin foolishly.

So, Chloe watched Michael walk away for the second time, this time a little heartbroken for not having secured any hope that she'd see him again. As she followed him with sad eyes, she suddenly noticed a very pretty blonde, green-eyed girl watching the exchange. The girl wore a shirt that matched Michael's in MIT's cardinal and gray, but it was about a size too small and stretched over her very bountiful chest in a way that caught the eye of every straight male and many gay women who passed her. She was the type of girl, Chloe thought with a sigh, that made one feel like an ogre no matter how long one had just spent flirting with a gorgeous young man.

To her surprise, the girl waved eagerly in Chloe's direction. Chloe looked from side to side, thinking the young woman must have spotted a friend. The girl shook her head and pointed at Chloe, then gestured for her to come over. Chloe, never having been made to feel welcome by anyone who looked so much like a living Barbie, was perplexed. She made her way over to the lovely young woman, who smiled when Chloe crossed through the packed bodies between her table and the railing of the stairs leading up to the second floor of the building.

When she finally stood in front of the young woman, it was clear she was as beautiful up close as she was from far away. More so, it turned out, as she had the most adorable dimples that deepened when she smiled at Chloe. Chloe immediately felt hideous next to her.

"Hey! Sorry, you probably think I'm a weirdo or something, but I just had to say that you look amazing! Like, there are so many old ladies wearing black sequins here that you just stick out like a unicorn in a herd of donkeys." The girl's eyes flashed wickedly, and she lowered her voice at the end of her diatribe against black sequins on middle-aged women.

"Oh, uh, thank you..." Chloe stammered, not used to such forwardness.

"You probably think I'm such a freak. I don't even know you, but that's just me. I have to say exactly what I'm thinking. No one can talk me out of it. My name's Lissa Thorne. What's your name?"

"I'm Chloe Mora. I'm here with my aunt, but she went to talk with a friend." Chloe surveyed the packed room. "Though, I'm not sure where they went off to. I should probably find her soon."

"I saw you come in earlier. I *thought* that was Dr. Miranda Mora. She's legendary. I *love* ITfactor. I *live* by it. You're her daughter, then?" Lissa's clever eyes sparkled.

"Oh, no, she's my aunt. She has no children of her own. But she's really awesome and always spoiling me. She's trying to get me interested in going to college in Boston, so we can be closer together. She lives in Nantucket, but she's in Boston for business a lot."

"Nantucket? Oh my god! So posh. I'm so jealous. Okay, that settles it. We *have* to be friends. I agree with your aunt. Boston is, like, so cool. There's bars and restaurants open twenty-four-seven. The shopping is killer and the men...well, maybe you've already noticed that there's a lovely *variety*? I saw you chatting with Michael Bath. He's good looking, I'll give you that. I work as a tech caller with him sometimes, but we don't talk much. Bit stuffy for me. Is he a close friend of the family? Or are you perhaps *intimately* acquainted?" Her dimples deepened in a conspiratorial smile.

Chloe couldn't imagine a less stuffy person than Michael and didn't read the implied euphemism her more experienced friend intended, so she simply answered, "No, not intimate at all. We just met."

"Well, I have to say I'm glad to hear it." Lissa looked truly relieved.

"Why is that?" Chloe couldn't imagine anyone not wanting to know someone as charming and clever as Michael.

Lissa motioned for Chloe to stand closer. When Chloe didn't get quite as close as Lissa thought the secret warranted, Lissa wound her arm through Chloe's and pulled her closer still. "I don't like to gossip," she whispered excitedly, "but I've heard the men in that family are all *bed hoppers*."

Chloe frowned. She was young to the world, but the meaning of this didn't go over her head. "Oh, I don't know. He didn't seem like that."

Lissa shrugged. "Honestly, I haven't heard the same about Michael, but my brother knows his brother and says he's *nasty*. I also heard that apple didn't fall far from daddy's tree. Their dad's a real creep, from what I hear."

Chloe's eyebrows shot up. "Oh?"

Lissa nodded knowingly. "I'm sure Michael's fine for a fling, but for serious thought, you might want to think of a man with a good family."

Chloe didn't like to judge people based on hearsay and was about to say so, but her thoughts were interrupted by a commotion at the entrance of the Stata Center. At first, it was hard to see what the packed crowd of annoyed alumni were grumbling about, but soon the crowds parted to allow a group of about fifteen young men in red, black, and white Harvard shirts chanting something in deep, booming voices. A blonde, stocky student in the front of the group held what looked like a fake beaver's tail above his tousled hair.

The rambunctious group was soon passing under the stairs where Lissa and Chloe talked. Lissa continued to hug Chloe's arm as if they'd been lifelong friends. Chloe found the closeness both a little endearing and a little stressful. The blonde boy waved at Lissa, who rolled her eyes and flipped him off, yelling, "Harvard drools."

The blonde guy chuckled and started a chant of "Beavers suck Pilgrims off" complete with rude gestures that made Chloe blush and frown. The gathered alumni couldn't stand for this and started throwing waded napkins and shrimp skewers at the group of frat boys. The chanters took this as their cue to leave, but the blonde boy stopped before going, waving the beaver tail at the stairs where they stood. His eyes fell on Chloe. He gave her what could only be called a leer before chanting again about beavers and waggling his eyebrows suggestively at her. She scowled and looked away, feeling as though she was more underdressed than she'd been only moments ago. She wondered how one such look could make her feel that way.

"Do you know that guy?" Chloe asked Lissa.

Misreading her interest, Lissa answered, "Oh, you have good taste, my friend. Even if he is a *Harvard* boy. You can't really go in with most Harvard boys because they are all pockets and no brains, but Xaiden has both. I should know. He's my big brother. And from what I just saw, he likes what he sees, too."

"Oh, no, it's not that, I just..."

Lissa laughed and slapped Chloe's arm lightly. "Oh, don't be all shy. Hey, what are you up to tomorrow? Wanna' hang? I'm done with finals after two."

"I am going on a tour of Boston tomorrow with my Tía, actually. She recently had surgery, so she needs my help."

"Oh, totally. If I had a cool, rich aunt like yours, I'd wanna hang with her, too."

"I bet you could come if you wanted to. I could ask, at least," Chloe offered. Though this girl was perhaps a little different from her usual friends, it wasn't every day she made new, sophisticated city friends. She didn't want to scare Lissa away by seeming more interested in hanging out with her Tía than her.

"Oh, no that's alright. I don't wake up till after noon, and I don't ever walk if I can help it. We went to the Sox game the other day, and I flat out refused to walk from the station. When you look as good as I do in a cropped Sox jersey, you don't have to walk, I told Xaiden. A rickshaw driver overheard and said he'd take me pro bono, or maybe pro bone. Disgusting, I know! I mean, the man had the gall to *ask for my number* instead of charging me. Of course, I gave it to him. Great calves. Anyway, I'm more interested in the night scene, if you know what I mean. Here, let me see your cell."

Lissa held out her hand in a familiar way, as though no objection could be made. It was strange to Chloe that this girl seemed so comfortable with her so soon. She *wished* she could be more like that. She handed Lissa her phone and the girl saved her data in it, typing faster than Chloe thought possible.

"I love how retro your cell is. You have the best style."

"Oh, well, it was just the cheapest one at the store. I don't use it for much."

"I mean, when you're money, you don't have to act money. That's why I like you. You're so real."

Chloe had nothing to say to that, as she wasn't sure what it meant. Lissa stared at her phone, typing furiously. When she looked up and smiled, Chloe's phone pinged.

"I just sent you the deets to a party. Please, please, *please* come. You *have* to meet my brother. He's a riot. It's a Harvard frat party, so it'll be tedious, but I just can't do it by myself anymore!"

"I'll ask Tía if she needs me. It'd be fun, though," Chloe answered, excited about the possibility of attending a real college party, even if that meant she would have to meet Lissa's brother, whom she'd almost decided was a little too rude for her liking. But she didn't like to form firm opinions right away. Maybe he was just acting up because he was with friends. Sure, he wasn't like Michael, our heroine mused, but so few men were.

"Let me know as soon as you can. I'm seeing this guy, Ashton. He'll drive us if I tell him to."

Chloe assured her new friend that she would let her know as soon as she asked Tía. Her vivacious new friend hugged her fiercely, as though two nights' time was far too long to wait to see her again, then sighed reluctantly about having to go make her rounds. Tía found Chloe not long after Lissa departed from her side. She introduced her niece to the tall, fit Bev whose height seemed, in large part, due to some very thin stilettos.

Bev wore the type of make-up that Chloe associated with drag, so she assumed Bev was transgender, though it was difficult to say for sure. She was a kind, vivid and laughing personality and she patted Chloe's cheek and told her what a gorgeous doll of a girl she was and how she would break every heart in Boston if she chose to stick around. Chloe had no idea how to deal with such silliness, so she just shook her head and laughed. Not long after the introduction, and too tired to continue to navigate the space, Tía called it a night and they went back to their hotel room.

That night, Chloe had the most interesting dream of going to a party with Lissa. Only they sported Regency dresses and hairstyles. Michael was there, but he refused to dance at such a party. He stood off to the side in a long-tailed jacket and tight breaches that made Chloe feel tingly and strange, too proud to notice her at first. Before long, Chloe was dancing with Lissa's brother, Xaiden. He looked dashing in regimentals, but his hands were too low on her back and his green eyes searched her too boldly. The only advantage to dancing with Xaiden came in the form of catching Michael's eye as they moved across the room. She met his gaze and he smiled, as if the whole party was a private joke between them. Everything else blurred and faded except that private smile.

~ Six ~

TWO BATHS ARE BETTER THAN ONE

The morning was quiet and a little subdued. Neither of the Mora ladies were very chatty first thing in the morning. They dressed in new outfits, more comfortable than last night's dresses, since the tour of the city promised a lot of movement. The air was cool, so Chloe chose her new purple corduroy dress jacket open over a white t-shirt and skinny jeans. She paired the outfit with her yellow and off-white paisley calf boots, which had a low heel and were very comfortable to walk in. She was admiring the color combination in the mirror and putting her long, thick hair up into a high ponytail when her Tía came into the bathroom behind her.

"You look so grown in that outfit, mija." Tía smiled. "Now, if you're done beautifying, it's my turn. We are supposed to meet in front of the student center in en una hora for the tour."

"I can do my makeup in the mirror in the room. Go ahead, Tía."

Chloe gathered her makeup bag and headed to the front room mirror. Before Tía closed the door, she called after her niece, "Oh, Chloe. I asked Bev about our friend Michael from last night."

Chloe perked up. His very name was a double shot of espresso. Tía continued, "She says she went to med school with his padre at BU after she got her bachelor's at MIT, and that they run into each other at Mass General. She was in biomedical engineering at MIT, but decided she wanted to try out doctoring. Anyway, Bev calls him standoffish and a bit superior, but she took a couple of classes with their mom, Sarah, who I guess was Course 8, mechanical engineering, at MIT. I didn't have any classes with her. Bev said she was very funny and kind and came from a pretty wealthy family. She died a couple years ago, unfortunately, so it's just Michael, his siblings, and their dad, now.

Chloe, eager to learn more about Michael but not eager to appear too eager, replied, "Oh, really?"

Tía mmmhmmed and closed the door so she could shower, and Chloe was left to think how tragic it must have been for Michael to lose his kind, funny mother. She applied her makeup in a thoughtful reverie about how enduring and brave her new acquaintance must have been to make it through such a hardship.

Tía, as predictably as ever, had them rushing out of the Kendall with hardly enough time to walk/roll to the Student Center, but she was looking very happy and fresh in a yellow blouse, white cardigan, and washed jeans. So much so that it was hard to be seriously vexed with her.

"So, you mentioned a party last night before bed. Tomorrow night, is it? Who'd you say invited you?" Tía asked.

"Um, Lissa Thorne. She goes to MIT, too, I think. She didn't say what she studied, though," Chloe answered, staring at the tall buildings in the bright fall sunshine.

"Course 14. Economics," Tía answered.

"Oh, so you were pretending to forget." Chloe smiled at her. "How do you know that?"

"Bev asked Pat. Pat manages the tech callers. When I saw you two talking, I asked Bev to do some prying. She's really good at prying. Even so, she couldn't get much information about the Thorne family last night. She sent me an article this morning, though."

Chloe and Tía dodged a group of students piling out of a drab-looking brick rectangle of a building. Chloe followed in her aunt's wild trail over nicely kept sidewalks and into the back of the building she recognized as the one on the postcard her Tía sent her a few years ago. It was a great neo-classical building with columns and an impressive white dome, iconic and grand. Chloe stared up at it for a minute before following Tía up the ramp. Tía sped on, thanking a student who propped open the door to allow them into the building.

"What was the article about?" Chloe asked her Tía, only half listening. She was gawking at the interior of the building. The floors looked to be marble. The walls were expansive and tall, and brilliantly white. She'd never seen architecture like this. She felt very insignificant walking through the halls of such a building.

"The article was about Trenton Thorne, their father. He put a lot of money into that cryptocurrency company that just tanked. And I mean *a lot*. I guess they had to downsize recently. Rough break. That's gotta be so hard with two kids going to such expensive schools."

"Oh, that's terrible," Chloe mused. Her heart dropped for her new, smiling, lively friend. She wondered if she'd had to take the job as a tech caller because her family wasn't doing well.

"Anyway, you're an adult now, Chloe, so I trust you to go to this party, but I do request that you come home by 11 p.m. I know that's pretty early, but we have a busy day the next day. And you must take your phone. And..."

Tía stopped for a moment. Waves of busy students and staff parted and walked around her as if she were a boulder in a river.

"What is it, Tía?" Chloe prompted.

Tía looked at her apologetically. "Sorry to ask, but are you on birth control?"

Chloe's face flushed. "No...no, I haven't needed it. Like I said...virgin."

"Well, some girls get on it just in case or for period related reasons, so I wasn't sure. If you're...that is, if you're thinking of sex, it might be prudent to bring protection to the party. You are my responsibility here, and..."

For a moment, a picture of a shirtless, serious-faced Michael popped into Chloe's head and caused her flush to deepen. "Tía, no! There's no one going I'd do that with. I mean, I'm sure they're fine, but...no."

Tía nodded nonchalantly. "I thought so, but I want you to know being prepared is nothing to be embarrassed over. I know my brother and your mother, and I doubt they brought any of this up. They were not particularly careful about babies. And a good thing, too, I suppose. As I am blessed with fantastic nieces and nephews, especially you, mija. It's just that I have high expectations for you. I'm sorry. I shouldn't put my own expectations on you, but I do hope you'll do other things first. Grow up a little. Be independent..."

Chloe felt a warmth not related to her embarrassment at talking about such intimate things. She felt...proud. Proud that her smart, capable, fierce Tía thought so highly of her. Her blush faded and she flung her arms around Tía. "Tía, I love you. I don't need anything for the party, but I promise to be responsible if I ever decide I do. Thank you for believing in me."

"Te amo, también." Tía held Chloe at arm's length, smiled fondly at her, booped her nose, then began to roll at light speed down the hall again.

They walked on for about four more minutes, passing under the great dome. The white circular ceiling seemed impossibly high. In just under 10 minutes, they were standing in an open courtyard in front of the Student Center, where a crowd of sleepy looking alumni and staff milled about.

The Student Center was a very geometric concrete building that looked like every building in the background of an 80s cop movie. It had the distinguishing feature of having a set of impressively long stairs on which sat students, MIT Alumni Association Staff and Tía's friend, Bev, looking fresh and happy in a gray t-shirt dress that hugged her fit frame and white jeans. An MIT sweater was tied around her shoulders. Her very straight hair touched her lightly muscled shoulders. Her makeup was more subdued around her almond eyes today, and she was at least an inch shorter in comfortable gray tennis shoes, though she was still very tall. Bev motioned them over and handed them both a huge iced coffee.

"Oh, you're a dear, Bev. We didn't get the chance to eat or have coffee," Tía informed her friend.

"Oh, I know all about how you operate. I brought donuts, too," Bev answered. She looked Chloe up and down and said, "Oh, Chloe, don't you look the picture of beauty? Those boots are amazing! Here, eat this donut quickly, before you get distracted."

Chloe took a chocolate donut that was filled with a delicious sweet custard, wondering at what Bev said. She took a bite and savored the sweetness before saying, "Why distracted? Are we leaving soon?"

Bev smiled wickedly at something behind Chloe, but didn't answer. Chloe, in the middle of a second huge bite of the donut, turned to follow her gaze and almost smashed the delicious pastry into Michael's lean, perfect midsection.

"Mmmsasham," she mumbled, chewing her giant bite as quickly as she could.

"Good morning, Ms. Mora," Michael smiled. *His teeth were so white and perfect!* He wore dark, fitted jeans, a cardinal MIT hoodie, and held a little yellow flag. "Dr. Mora, Dr. Ikeda," he nodded to the two women who were chuckling silently over the panicked look in Chloe's eyes.

Chloe swallowed the massive bite of donut, and said, almost breathlessly. "I didn't know you'd be working today! You work on weekends?"

"Not always. It seems I'm to be the personal chaperone of a smaller group of alumni. Probably because they would otherwise be too rowdy and ill-behaved."

Chloe looked confused for a moment, then sad. She'd been hoping if he was coming that he'd be able to hang out with her group, but if he had a specific designation, that would not be the case. Tía and Bev sipped their giant iced coffees and smiled at one another knowingly. They quite liked this quick trickster of a young man.

"My group consists of yourself, Dr. Mora, Dr. Ikeda, and a guest of mine. Less because of your troublesome nature, I admit, and more because of your aunt's injury. I thought she might need some extra help, so I volunteered to show your group around."

"Oh," Chloe laughed. "I see what you did there. Very clever. Well, now that you've embarrassed me for being slow in the morning, I promise you to be as rowdy and troublesome as possible. You'll have your work cut out for you. I hope you're prepared for a long day."

"Well, luckily, I'm a very prepared person." So saying, Michael pulled a napkin out of his pocket, as he'd done the night before, and offered it to her. "Your breakfast got away from you."

Chloe giggled and wiped her face where he indicated, then outright laughed when she came away with a huge dollop of cream, suddenly aware that she'd been trying to flirt with almost a tablespoon of pudding on her face.

She wiped the spot until Michael gave her a thumbs up. She laughed. "You could have said something before. And why do you always have napkins?"

Michael shrugged. "My dad is a neat freak. I picked up one of his tics. Let's just be happy I did, too, as you seem to need them a lot. Oh! Here's our last group member!"

Chloe turned. Coming up behind Tía and Bev was a beautiful young girl with caramel eyes and straight, dark hair that fell past her shoulders. She wore a rainbow sweater and sweater skirt combo that was somehow cooler on her than it would be on anyone else. The skirt came to just above her knees and hugged her slim frame. The oversized sweater fell off her light brown shoulder. Seeing Michael, she raced past Bev and Tía, who followed the young woman's progress appraisingly. The young woman flung herself at Michael, who laughed and hugged her as she wrapped her long legs around him.

Chloe suddenly felt not very well. She looked anywhere but at the two beautiful people. How could she have read Michael so wrong? She'd almost been sure he'd been serious in his flirtations. Though he seemed to like to tease. She cursed herself for being so naïve and foolish to think that a mature college boy from the East Coast could have actually been seriously interested in her. He was clearly just doing his job.

"Chloe...Chloe?" Michael's voice broke through her fog of misery.

Chloe shook herself back to the moment, as unpleasant as it might be to do so. Michael stood there with his arm casually slung around the beautiful girl's shoulder. "Can I introduce you to the final member of our party? This is Mindy, my twin."

Bev elbowed Tía, who was looking almost as put out as Chloe by this point. Chloe, for her part, was so thrown off by the change of feelings that overcame her she could barely stutter, "Oh...yes. Oh, hi. It's so nice to meet you."

"I'm going to go help Dr. Mora and Dr. Ikeda gather their donuts and coffee. I'll be right back," Michael said, giving his sister one last side hug.

Mindy looked delighted to meet Chloe. "Hey, Chloe! It's so nice to meet you. Michael told me all about meeting you last night."

"He did?" Chloe couldn't keep the smile from her face.

"Yes. He had a lot of nice things to say, which is abnormal. People aren't really his thing, as good as he can be with them."

Chloe looked behind her at Michael "helping" Bev and Tía with their final two donuts, shoving one in his mouth at their insistence and wearing the other like a pink sprinkled ring.

"I would not have guessed he didn't like being around people. He was so kind and funny when we met."

Mindy smiled knowingly over that. "He can please when he wants to."

Chloe looked from Michael to Mindy. "So, you two are twins? I wouldn't have guessed you were his twin sister."

Mindy shook her head. "Fraternal twins, yeah. I look a little more like my mom. Michael takes after our dad in looks."

"Michael tells me you go to BU. Do you like it?"

"I like the school. I'm not so sure I was meant to be a doctor, though. My dad wanted one of us to go into medicine. I sort of wanted to pursue music, but dad allows it as a minor. So, it's not all bad." She shifted uncomfortably and changed the subject. "I'm happy you met Michael yesterday, even if he did cancel our plans in order to chaperone your group today."

"Sorry about that." Inside, our heroine's heart sang. Rearranging one's day, after all, was a sign of great affection, in her estimation. But she said, "I hope you don't think it's too boring to go sightseeing with us. I'm sure you've seen all the sights. I can't wait! I've never been to a city like this before."

Mindy smiled warmly. "Not at all. I love Boston and we were just going to walk around and eat food, anyway, which I can do just as well with my brother's new friend."

"Meeting him was the high point of what promised to be an otherwise slow night. He's very quick on his feet and funny," Chloe said, feeling very pleased with the fact that Mindy seemed to be implying that Michael was giving her special attention.

Mindy smiled knowingly again and said, "Only when he wants to be. If he doesn't care to make someone's acquaintance or is displeased, he says very little. I've heard some dull, witless girls call him stuck up."

Chloe remembered what Lissa said about him being stuffy the day before, and wondered why Michael wouldn't want to make himself interesting to someone clearly as pretty as Lissa was.

She said only, "I don't know how witty I am, but I hope I'm not so dull that my company will become tiresome before the day's out."

Michael, on his way to give the pink sprinkle donut to his sister, overheard the comments and said, "Dull? You? I'll need sunglasses to avoid the glare of your brilliance."

Chloe shook her head but smiled up at him.

Mindy turned to her and said, "Looks like we're getting on the bus now." She gestured to a woman with a large flag that read MIT Tour Group. "I hope you're prepared for a walk. I think your aunt chose one of the more arduous tours, though we will be on the bus for large parts of it. Boston is one of the most walkable cities in the U.S., and your aunt stealthily charged my brother last night with convincing you it is the only city worth walking in." She threw her voice to Tía, who nodded her enthusiastic assent before turning to talk to Bev, who kept pace with her scooter. Mindy took an impressive bite of the pink donut.

"I love walking," Chloe answered earnestly. "I mentioned the tour to a girl I met yesterday, Lissa Thorne, and she said it wasn't to her taste. She said the nightlife is more interesting by far to her, but I don't think I can agree with her. I love long walks on a beautiful day, like today, and I have to admit, I'm already falling in love with Boston. I've never seen anything like it. So many people, so many bridges and buildings and old statues. It's very romantic."

"Romantic, huh? I never thought of it like that. You know, I know a little of Lissa," Michael replied. "Though we don't run in the same circles. She's been working as a tech caller for the last two months. My idea of nightlife is a good dinner in Chinatown, an early movie, and back to the dorm to study just while my roommate is vacating it. That way, I have the pleasure of dodging company for as long as possible. My roommate is more after Lissa's tastes and her tastes lean more...mature, from what I recall."

Chloe did not quite understand the implications of what it was to be mature in the way Michael meant, so her kind mind pursued only what she could say with certainty. "She is very beautiful and nice. And mature, I suppose, though I don't know her well yet. She probably thinks my fascination with walking is childish, and maybe it is..."

Mindy grabbed Chloe's arm and laughed, pulling her into line for the tour bus. "That's not what Michael meant at all. He is only being gossipy. He signed up for this tour to hang out with you all, of course, but also because he's just as thrilled looking at old statues as the day he came to Boston. Isn't that right, Mikie?"

Michael shrugged unashamedly. "It's a big enough city that I can walk for miles every weekend and still not see everything. I hope, if we convince you to come back, that I can put your walking acumen to the test and show you some of my favorite architectural haunts."

"Haunts? Like tours of ghosts in old buildings? That would be amazing!" Chloe exclaimed, not catching his meaning fully. Michael and Mindy chuckled.

"If that's your inclination. Though you'll have to excuse my sister if it is. Even though we live in Salem, she's dreadfully opposed to horror."

Mindy rolled her eyes at her brother. "Opposed to, no. Dreadfully sick of horror, more like." For a moment, her voice was not at all playful.

Chloe, not able to contain herself, chimed in, "I have to disagree there. I'm a huge horror fan. I would love to see Salem! *Hocus Pocus* is one of my favorite films. That and *Twilight*."

Mindy laughed. "Well, if we are classifying those as horror, then I'm on board. Though, you'll find my brother hard-headed about teenage romances, as he calls them."

Michael raised a playful eyebrow. "Not at all. I'm simply jealous of all the attention the moody vampire men and werewolves get. What about you, Chloe? Are you team Edward or team Jacob?"

With longer hair, Michael could pull off the Jacob Black look spectacularly. Picturing him without his MIT hoodie, on top of a motorcycle...She shook herself, blushing, and answered, "Don't think I don't understand that you're teasing me. I know most people don't think of either of those films as horror, but I'm more of a B+ Frankenstein and Dracula girl than I am a murder movie girl. I can't watch that, even if it is fake."

"Well, if you ever come visit us in Salem, we'll try to keep any horrors light, I promise. I'm going to ask the driver to lower the ramp for your Tía. Do the duty I signed up for and all that." Michael ran ahead to ask the driver for the accommodation.

Chloe looked back at her Tía and smiled brightly. "Tía, Michael is going to ask the driver to lower the back ramp for you."

"What a gentleman. Bev and I will wait back there. See you on the bus."

Once settled on the bus, Mindy and Chloe made their way to the back and sat next to the handicap seats by the ramp. Michael made his way back, parked Tía's knee cart next to her seat, and sat in the seat across the aisle from Chloe and Mindy. "First stop, Boston Garden!"

"Oh! I can't wait! Makes me miss my Pheobe. We used to walk the gardens every Saturday," Tía said.

Bev smiled at her. "You'll have plenty of opportunities to walk the gardens when Chloe decides to put you out of your misery and move closer. Now, Bath children, listen here. You are both in on the mission, I suppose? Mission keep Chloe? Say it with me, now. What's your mission?"

Mindy saluted and said, "Keep Chloe, mam!"

Michael winked and said, "Mission keep Chloe. I like that. I'm in."

Chloe blushed fiercely, and suddenly felt that this stuffy bus full of sleepy alumni was the most wonderful place in all the world.

"Speaking of our solemn mission, Mindy and I were hoping, if it's not a huge inconvenience to you, Dr. Mora, to show Chloe our favorite breakfast spot tomorrow, near Harvard Square. I was hoping we could walk there. It's a long walk, but we enjoy it. Or, if tomorrow's no good, Wednesday night they are showing *Interview With The Vampire* at the LSC."

"Oh! The LSC! I remember those days. Bev, remember that gorgeous guy you made out with during *Titanic!*"

"Remember? How could I forget? He was so delicious I had no eyes for Leo."

Chloe covered her face. "Oh, Bev!"

Tía giggled. "What?! You don't think we got up to mischief in college? Well, we had our fun. And, yes, Michael. I think breakfast and a walk would be fine if Chloe feels up for it. Bev and I were hoping to go to a lecture tomorrow that will only bore her to tears, anyway. As for Wednesday night, I don't see why that's an issue. I'll be ready to be in bed with a good book by then. I'm not twenty anymore! I will be fine with Bev helping me tomorrow. Of course, it's up to Chloe, not me. She's an adult now."

Chloe nodded enthusiastically at the twins, feeling like the luckiest newly eighteen-year-old in the world.

~ Seven ~

ONLY COLIN FIRTH WOULD MAKE THAT LAGOON MORE ROMANTIC

The bus let the alumni out at Boston Gardens. A woman with curly auburn hair and an Alumni Association sweater, who introduced herself as Pat, motioned for quiet and asked the tour groups to meet up in an hour by the Make Way for Duckling statue in Boston Commons. From there, the group would walk to the Prudential Center for the next portion of their tour. Pat advised them to always keep their student staff member, who carried their group's flag (red, orange, pink, blue, purple, and yellow), in sight and let them know if they needed help of any kind.

The group was dropped by an impressive bronze memorial of a regiment following a figure on horseback. Chloe, awed, touched the cold, metallic depiction and read the engraved words below it. She was struck by the three-dimensional nature of the figures and the way the artist captured bravery, death, and despair in such a moving way, and with such unforgiving material. A sigh escaped her lips as she ran her fingers over the hoof of a horse with a solemn bowed head.

"I wish I could see this for the first time again, like you're doing now. Isn't it brilliant?" Michael sidled up to her while Bev, Mindy and Tía meandered close ahead, smiling over a particularly lovely tree with vivid red and orange foliage, some of which slowly rained down upon the enchanted group.

"I hate to say that nothing we make today comes close to this kind of art because it makes it sound like there are no true artists left in the world, which I don't think is true, but..." Chloe looked into Michael's dark, smiling eyes. "It is true that this kind of work is rare now. I don't know that our fast-paced society can truly attend to the creation of work like this, with all the other easier distractions floating around. Or...I don't know. Maybe it's not as important to American society to capture such things. This, though...this makes me feel so, so sad, so proud, so invested in a group of men I never knew. Things like this make people larger than life. *Romantic.*"

She shook her head and blushed, embarrassed by talking so much, and worried that she was rambling and making no sort of sense.

Michael, though, looked at her in a scrutinizing, but not laughing, way. "You seem to like that. Romance, that is."

Chloe smiled. "You'll think me naïve and silly, I'm sure, but I do. I often wish life was as exceptional or as beautiful as books. As exceptional as this piece of art is. In reality, maybe this guy," she pointed to a man behind the horse, "smoked and drank too much. Maybe that man," she pointed to a guy in the front, "was daydreaming about eating bacon."

Michael guffawed. "Bacon?!"

"Well, maybe not. But you know what I mean. I want the moment I'm in to be as grand as I imagine it *should* be. As grand as this art makes it out to be. I don't think that's a bad thing. People scoff at romances and romantic people, but I think that's just because they've been disappointed in life. I'm sure, before long, you'll think me ridiculous for over quoting romcoms."

Michael waved the comment away. "I have to admit, I'm a sucker for a good romcom, so you'll never hear me complain about that. Those types of movies strip people of the things real people keep inside so we don't look foolish. They dare to be honest and foolish.

I like that. But it sounds like you know that they also set false standards."

Chloe shrugged. "For the most part, yeah. But I think some moments *are* the picture of romance. They feel exactly as they should. Though, I'll be honest. I haven't experienced much of them firsthand. I guess I'm just eager to be in the middle of a moment like that."

"What does *this* moment feel like?" Michael whispered conspiratorially, his eyes laughing.

Chloe thought about that. It was crisp but not cold outside. The tree's foliage was like a vivid fire against the baby blue sky. The laughter of her Tía, Mindy, and Bev carried over on a playful breeze. Michael's perceptive, always laughing eyes were locked on her, only her. *Only* her.

"It's one of those moments, I think."

Michael gave her a searching look, then, all too soon, looked away. "Well, I will do my best not to ruin that perception. There are plenty more statues and monuments here, if that's where your inclination runs. And, as our friends have figured out, the foliage is in the perfect moment between fall and winter, where the branches seem to be matchsticks on fire."

Chloe took in the expanse of the walks, trees, flowers, and perfectly manicured patches of grass that stretched out in front of her. "Such a poetic description. You're a bit of a romantic, too, aren't you?"

Michael dipped his head. "Not usually. I think it's catching."

"I can already tell I'm going to take a million pictures. I apologize ahead of time, but my friend, Amy, made me promise to post pictures. Let's go check with Tía. I bet she has some favorite spots."

"A million pictures, huh? Don't you think posting a million pictures will ruin the true romantic nature of the experience? Is the experience for you or is it for others?" Michael asked.

Chloe pursed her lips and eyed him. "Both, maybe? I don't know. I only just got on social media so I guess I'll find out."

"Fair enough." His mischievous smile reappeared, and he offered Chloe his arm. "Should we allow Dr. Mora to show us all the *romantic* spots?"

Chloe, even more sure this was one of her true romantic moments, took the offered arm, just as though she was in her very own Jane Austen book. Tía took the small group down walks past a sweet frog pond, remembering her own liaisons with Tía Pheobe and their picnic by this very pond. The noise of the city was all around them but felt far away. Lovers held hands under autumn trees and whispered despite the honking, yelling, and laughing that surrounded them. Intimate, quiet moments played out everywhere in the park, filled with stories in the making. Sure, there was also a moment when they had to walk around a very dirty and frantic looking man yelling at an invisible enemy, but, all in all, there was more beauty in this city than Chloe ever imagined.

Michael showed them the Soldiers and Sailors Monument–a tall, impressive structure that drew the eye ever upwards. They walked past a great gazebo, settled perfectly in the middle of walkways stretching out like spokes on a wheel around it. Mindy ran up and down a few of the spokes in wild abandon, pulling Chloe up and down two along with her. Chloe's heels clicked behind her new friend, her thick hair flying out behind her, Mindy's hand wrapped tightly around her own. But the true icing on the cake was the lagoon walk, somethIng both Tía and Michael insisted she see.

Michael led her toward a spectacular stone suspension-styled bridge, under which flowed the dark green waters of the lagoon. The water of the lagoon was still and filled the air with a swampy, but not unpleasant, scent. Michael walked to the edge of the bridge and motioned for the group to come up.

Tía turned to Bev. "Bev, dear, would you mind sitting with me on that bench down there by the lagoon? My scooter leg is getting sore."

Chloe, not at all interested in doing so, remembered her obligation to her aunt and said, "Oh, no. I can sit with you if you're sore, Tía. That's why I'm here, after all."

"I forbid it. You are to take in all of what Boston has to offer, so that by the end of the week you are fully convinced you should move here and put me out of my lonely misery," Tía shot back before turning to Mindy. "Mindy, my niece is a very good writer. I believe Boston University has several writing degrees, does it not? Maybe later you can talk to her about them." She winked at Mindy and rolled toward Bev, who'd run ahead to secure the empty bench.

Mindy laughed. "I like your aunt, and it's clear she *loves* you. She's right, by the way. Boston University has a great writing program. I have a friend in their screenwriting program. He loves it."

Chloe's eyes sparkled with interest. "Like, writing movie scripts?!"

Mindy nodded enthusiastically. "I'll give you his email, if you want."

Chloe nodded back. "Yes, please do."

They walked toward Michael, who was grinning as though he had a great secret. "Chloe, come here. I think you'll like this." He motioned that she look out toward the lagoon. Chloe sighed in admiration. White, long-necked birds glided across the green lagoon waters languidly.

"Oh! Are those *swans*?!"

Michael nodded. "Yes, and while I could be pessimistic and list the many reasons swans are actually just fancy geese, and just as stinky and pesky, I will refrain from doing so, since I think the way they move across the water with those long necks is sure to be just the picture of romance you were hoping for."

Chloe put her hands to her mouth. "They are so beautiful! Yes, you are quite right to almost keep your skepticism to yourself. Oh! Are those boats shaped like swans?!"

Mindy laughed and side hugged Chloe. "They are, indeed."

"This all reminds me of the countryside in England," Chloe mused, sighing.

"Oh! Have you been?" Mindy asked, sincerely.

Chloe shook her head. "Oh, no, never. Except for this trip, I really haven't traveled much at all. Tía took us to Disney once, but, well, my family can't afford to travel. But I've watched every Jane Austen remake ever made, and it puts me to mind the grounds of Pemberley–you know, the Colin Firth Pemberly? Maybe you don't," she smiled at Michael. "If Austen isn't your thing."

"You wrong me. Colin Firth will forever be Mr. Darcy in my heart." His tone was light, but his furrowed brow hinted that he had something else on his mind.

If Chloe had been watching the twins and not the graceful gliding of the swans, she would have seen the worried look that passed between them. As she didn't see the look, its meaning couldn't bother her, though the reason for the look might certainly bother her if she understood it.

"So, your Tía is a bit of an exception in your family, then? With her...lifestyle?" Mindy asked, her voice more serious.

"In more ways than one. She was the first person in her family to even go to college and she ended up at MIT! She got scholarships, of course, because she came from a very poor family. Then, well, you know about her app. She became the first wealthy person in her family for maybe ever. And...well, her parents didn't know she was gay until she brought Tía Phoebe home for Christmas one year. It wasn't unpleasant, though. My dad's side of the family is very loving and accepting, and Tía Phoebe wins everyone over."

Another mysterious look passed between Mindy and Michael. Michael broke the silence that followed. "I wish all families were like yours, then."

Chloe tore her eyes away from the lagoon. "What do you mean?"

Michael frowned and didn't answer for a while. Finally, he said, "Oh, nothing. You just speak of your family so well. It sounds like you all really love and support each other."

Chloe smiled and nodded. "My mama and papa are very affectionate. My papa's family is very close with us. Abuelo y abuela Mora are so sweet. We go to their house every Wednesday night and have a big, traditional family dinner. My mama's family...well, they had to get used to my papa. They were not as accepting as my other grandparents, at first. But, they love mama, and they have grown to love papa. And they are kind to us grandkids, especially come Christmas and birthdays."

"I'm jealous," Michael said, his eyes a little sad.

"Jealous?" Chloe asked.

Mindy broke in, as though she didn't want Michael to finish his thought. "Michael only means that we don't have a very big family. It's just us kids and our dad. Our mom passed away two years ago."

"Oh." Chloe looked meaningfully at Mindy. "That must be so hard. I can't even imagine." And she couldn't. Chloe had always been surrounded by the love of a big, sometimes hectic, often noisy family.

"Let's take a selfie here," Mindy encouraged, changing the subject to something less dreary. "Scoot towards Michael, Chloe." Chloe willingly obliged this command. "Good. Now Michael, you'll have to get cozier if we are gonna get all three of us in."

Michael gave his sister a knowing look but put his arm around Chloe. Chloe could have died happy right then. He smelled so good! He wore a sort of spicey smelling cologne that was subtle and lovely. And whatever shampoo he used was working. His curls tickled her forehead as he leaned his head towards hers.

Mindy flung her arm around them both and said, "Smile!"

They all smiled, and Mindy showed them the result. It was instantly Chloe's favorite picture of all time. While she and Mindy had pointed their best selfie smiles at the camera, Michael's eyes were locked on her and his smile was genuine.

"Hey, make sure to add me as a friend online, Chloe. I sent you a request. I'll tag you in this picture after you add me," Mindy said.

"Just a sec." Chloe quickly opened her flip phone and tapped the "F" icon to open it. She accepted the awaiting request from Mindy. "Done."

Mindy smiled over her enthusiasm, correctly assuming the reason for her enthusiasm was the look of complete adoration on her brother's face when he looked at the beautiful, sweet girl.

The three walked over the bridge and around the lagoon in silence for a bit before Chloe said, "So, do you really like the miniseries with Colin Firth, Michael? I never know if I should take you seriously. And you can't tell me this lagoon doesn't make you think of the pond he jumps in at Pemberley!"

Mindy smacked Michael playfully and said, "He's only making fun of me. I used to watch it non-stop as a teen. I was in love with Eliza, but pretended to watch it for Mr. Darcy, since I was not yet out. Though, honestly, I see the appeal. Colin Firth is wonderful."

"Honestly, I completely understand the Mr. Darcy fascination. Witty, rich, good looking, not suffering of fools. He reminds me of someone..." Michael feigned thoughtfulness.

Chloe giggled. He shrugged. "Seriously, I'm not like the men who like to berate the things women write. Why should I? How much better would the world be if men were as interesting as Austen or even Stephanie Myers seems to think they are?"

Chloe gave him a look that said she didn't quite believe him.

"You don't believe me?"

"You are a tease. But, if you don't believe men are like the way women wrote them, I can only say I hope you're wrong. I don't know enough of them to have a more informed opinion. I simply hope it because I'm a naive girl who very much wants to run into a Henry Tilney in my lifetime. Anyway, I'm not naïve enough to think that the world is either as good or as horrid as movies and books make it out to be. I despair of ever finding a romantic vampire in my lifetime."

Michael pulled a puzzled face. "Well, I have to admit. I have no idea who Henry Tilney is, but I agree with your other points. I think good books, shows and movies may exaggerate the good or bad qualities of people to entertain. I do agree, though, that real life is full of little kinds of horror on its own. I mean, even towns like your Whiteville have horrors, too. Don't you agree?"

"My town's name is Williamston, thank you very much, and I hope that's not true. I haven't heard of any," she answered.

"Oh, even your dear Williamston has its dark secrets. Just think of what dark secrets *Twilight's* Forks held," Michael countered. Chloe rolled her eyes at the example.

He smiled. "I hope your positive outlook rubs off on me. I could use a little sweetening." He looked at his phone and started. "Oh! Time to go find the ducks. Let's go collect Bev and Dr. Mora."

The trio of friends collected the women and met up with the rest of the group at the adorable duck statues, which Chloe took several pictures of, having been fond of the book growing up. The rest of the day was spent riding the duck tours past points of interest, taking pictures with a myriad of buildings and statues, and grabbing cannolis at Mike's Pastries at the end of the day. Chloe's mind was spinning with freedom trail facts, grand old buildings and the feeling of Michael's hand when he brushed hers, numerous times, as they walked side by side, touring the sites.

Around 7 p.m. the tour bus picked them up near Faneuil Hall, after the groups split to find food. By day's end, Tía was exhausted from using her scooter and fell into her seat on the bus with a relieved sigh. Bev, almost as tired as her friend, laid her head on Tía's shoulder. They both promptly fell asleep, as did many other alumni. The twins chatted about sites they still wanted to show Chloe and things they would see tomorrow on their way to breakfast.

Of all the sweet and endearing things Michael did for the women in the group that day, however, the thing that won Chloe's heart entirely was when he excused himself to talk to the bus driver for a moment, then came back with a smile on his face.

"What are you up to?" Chloe asked, eyeing him suspiciously.

"I asked the bus driver to drop you and your Tía off at the Kendall after the rest of the alumni pile out, so that she wouldn't have to wear herself out even more getting back to the hotel. It's on his way back to the bus station, so he said it wouldn't be a problem if I didn't mention it to anyone else."

Chloe's look of adoration was the perfect assurance to Michael that he'd understood "Mission Keep Chloe" and executed it perfectly. Michael, Mindy, and Bev said their goodbyes at the Student Center and the twins promised to collect Chloe promptly at 8 a.m. the next day.

The bus driver was awarded a hefty tip for his trouble in dropping them off at the Kendall, and the Mora women hauled themselves to their hotel room with tired feet and full hearts. Once settled into their pajamas with hot teas and facemasks, Chloe and Tía set down to their different tasks. Tía opened a book on the history of computer science, and Chloe set to adding pictures to her online profile. She immediately changed her cover photo to the photo Mindy tagged her in, catching herself getting lost in staring at Michael smiling at her. Not long after she uploaded the photos, she got a friend request from a "Lissa May," which she promptly accepted.

Almost immediately, Lissa messaged Chloe. "What'd ur aunt say 2 the party, Queen?"

"She said I could go. But I have 2 be back by 11."

"11?! Oh, well. Just so :) you can come! U have fun with the Baths today? I see u have a new cover pic. Looks like Michael had fun, from the pic."

"It was so fun. Michael and Mindy are awesome."

"Glad 2 hear not all the family r bad."

Chloe didn't really know how to answer that. Lissa didn't go out and say she didn't like that Chloe was hanging out with the Bath twins, but it seemed to her there was an undertone of jealousy. To assuage this, Chloe messaged:

"Can't wait 2 hang w/u tomorrow."

Lissa messaged an excited emoji and texted back, "Well, how bout we do lunch at 12, then. An earthquake won't wake me or Xaiden b4 12. I want u 2 get 2 know him."

"Sorry. Told M & M I'd do Zoe's for breakfast in the a.m."

"How cliche. I mean, I guess every1 has 2 try it, or so I hear. I haven't. 2 touristy."

"Maybe we can hang out when I'm done hanging w/the twins?"

"Yes! I can't wait!!!"

"Sounds great," Chloe messaged back, assuming this meant they would get together after 3 p.m. or so.

"K. XOXO. Night."

"Night. TTYL."

Chloe laid her head back against her plush hotel pillow and smiled. She wasn't used to people vying for her time and affection. It was kind of nice, even if it was a little tiring. She opened *The Night Circus,* having borrowed it from her library to read after *The Starless Sea*. She barely read a page of the beautiful prose before she fell asleep to very pleasant dreams that replayed the day's adventures, especially the feeling of Michael's hand brushing hers.

~ Eight ~

GETTING TO KNOW YOU

Chloe was in a tent at the Night Circus. Inside the tent, paper swans of every size and color were perched on the grass. Some were floating in the air of their own accord. A breeze stirred the swans. They moved across the grass at her feet, and through the air around her as if they were gliding across a still, green lagoon.

A voice behind her said, "Do you like the room I made you?"

She turned to find Michael looking gorgeous in a 1920s black suit, a red handkerchief tucked into his pocket. His dark hair was combed back in an old-fashioned slick. In his long-fingered hand was a shimmering, white paper swan. He was so close behind her that when she turned toward his voice, she was almost pressed against him. She took a step to close the gap and lifted her head. He blew at the swan in his hand, and it glided away. She watched its progress for a moment before turning back to Michael, feeling his warm body against hers. She looked up, breathless. He looked down, his dark eyes full of longing.

Chloe thought her alarm was particularly cruel this morning. It broke into her beautiful dream exactly when it was getting really good. But then she remembered that today was her day alone with the twins and she practically flew out of bed to jump into the shower.

Tía was lightly dozing when Mindy texted they were in the downstairs lobby. Chloe kissed her Tía goodbye and promised to text her whereabouts every so often before floating down the stairs. She'd dressed for cooler weather, since the forecast called for a chilly, partly cloudy day, but the outfit she chose was not chosen for modesty's sake. Her new, white, cable-knit sweater dress fell just above her knees and scooped wide at the neck, so that it draped off her shoulder. She wore it over yellow-orange tights and topped it with the boots she'd worn yesterday. Her hair was in a French braid down the back of her head and her makeup was light and soft.

Though the dress was a little shorter than she usually wore, and she worried that it clung a bit over her well-endowed backside, she still felt very confident entering the lobby from the stairs. And, this time, the entrance was all any young heroine could wish for. She was elevated on the grand, dusky rose carpeted staircase and lit by the romantic light of the lobby chandelier that hung above her like a shining crystal cloud. Mindy and Michael laughed about something at the bottom of the stairs, but Mindy caught her slow descent. Chloe nailed the entrance, looking the very picture of graceful Mia Thermopolis, princess of Genovia. Mindy elbowed her twin and he turned to smile at the descending Chloe. His expression upon seeing her solidified Chloe's confidence that she'd done well in her choice of outfit. His mouth dropped open a little, his smile slipping into something more stunned than amused.

Chloe hopped down the last step and was met by Mindy, who hugged her lightly and said, "Oh, Chloe! You look so nice. Here I am in my BU sweater and jeans, and you look like you stumbled off the runway."

Chloe dipped her head and shook it. "You don't need to dress fancy to look great, Mindy. Though I do admit to being a bit like my Tía in our love of fashion."

Michael shook himself and walked up to the girls, his eyes still stuck on Chloe. "You do look great."

Chloe blushed and looked him up and down. He wore jeans ripped above the knee, a well-fitting black band t-shirt from a band called The Gutter Twins, who Chloe had never heard of, and an open Pendleton sweater coat with black and white designs.

"You look great, too," she muttered shyly. "I've never heard that band on your shirt before."

Michael looked down. "Oh, yeah. Well, they aren't super popular, but their music was so good. I'll play some for you later."

"I'd like that." Chloe smiled, happy to have found something that made Michael want to connect.

"You two, ready, then? I'm starving and we still have a walk and a wait ahead of us," Mindy asked, turning from the lobby and leading the way out.

Michael sidled up next to Chloe and smiled down at her. "I hope you like Zoe's. It's one of our favorites. There will probably be a bit of a line, but I think it's worth the wait."

"I trust your judgment," Chloe answered back.

"Good."

***

The air was pleasantly crisp, and the clouds were heavier today than they were the day before. Chloe's legs would have been cold, except that the twins kept a good pace. Chloe stared in wonder at the sheer number of buildings they passed–bookstores, cafes, thrift stores, grocery stores, apartments, restaurants, bars, on and on as far as the eye could see. Most of the buildings on the walk were old-fashioned brick, which she was very fond of. They put to mind an Austeneque town, a Lambton. She ran her hand along a few walls to feel the rough surface here and there.

When they were about 20 minutes into their walk, Michael stopped in front of the window of a store with a sign in the shape of an old record hanging over a red door. The label on the faux record read "Retro Records."

"This is my favorite record store. It looks like they just opened. Are you both too hungry, or can we go in?" Michael's voice was pleading.

"I'm happy to go in," Chloe said, not caring as much about breakfast as about spending time with Michael.

"How about I go wait in line at Zoe's? It's just up the way. You and Chloe can stop in, then meet me in line," Mindy suggested.

"Yeah, that works. Thanks, Min," Michael said, pushing open the red door and motioning Chloe in front of him.

The floor dipped right in front of the door and Chloe tripped a little going in. Her heart jumped into her throat. She would have face planted had Michael not caught her arm and righted her.

She smiled at him, a little embarrassedly. "Thanks. That was close."

Michael still held her arm lightly and he smiled back. "I should have warned you. It's an old shop, so the layout is a little wonky."

Chloe shrugged. "No harm done."

Michael released her arm, almost reluctantly, and motioned her ahead of him. Chloe was astounded by the sheer volume of records in this shop. There were signed records all over the walls, hung in cases. There were broken records plastered under resin in the floor itself. Scratched records hung from the ceiling, with labels affixed that told the searcher what genre of music they would find down that aisle. And there were row upon row of records in tall wooden record bins running the length of the small space. The inside was somewhat dark, owing to the dark decor. Record lamps hung from the ceiling, illuminating the merch directly under them, a bulb sticking out from under the record, which sat flatly atop it.

It was one of the coolest shops Chloe had ever seen. Her family had a record player that had been her abuelo's, and they used it often. Her mama would have been especially impressed by this place. For a moment, her heart remembered her home and she missed her family.

"Wow, Michael, this shop is amazing!" she breathed.

He smiled fondly at her. An employee standing behind a glass case filled with rare records nodded to Michael and Chloe from atop a tall stool. Their head was shaved on the sides, a vivid green mohawk ran the length of the middle of their head. They had more piercings on their face than Chloe thought possible and a pretty cool zombie Ozzie tattoo that took up real estate on their chest and throat. Their badge read "Mo-they/them."

"Hey, let me know if I can help you find anything, Michael. You know where the players are, if you need to test them," Mo called out.

Michael waved at Mo. "Thanks. Hey, you have any Gutter Twins? Chloe hasn't heard them."

Chloe couldn't figure out how Mo would keep track of something like that with thousands of records to tend to, but they shook their head. "Nah, you bought our last one two weeks ago. I'll let Dino know you're looking. We do have one Twilight Singers. Should be getting a couple more Mark Lenegan's in next week. Aisle five, toward the back."

"Cool. Thanks, Mo," Michael said.

Michael took the lead and Chloe followed him down aisle five. Michael thumbed through the "T" section, but Chloe's attention was drawn to the "S" section where a very nice *Basement on the Hill* album stared back at her.

"Oh! *Basement on the Hill* is my favorite album!" she exclaimed. "Well, I don't have the *actual* album. I just listen to it on my computer!"

Michael studied the album. "I don't know that I've ever listened to Elliot Smith, though I've heard of him."

Chloe gave Michael a look of utter shock. "Mo said we can listen to these, right? I can play you my favorite song."

Michael smiled. "And we can listen to my pick after that." He lifted an album from the "T" section. It had a sexy picture of a woman's legs with black garters, holding up a white skirt or sheet to just below her thighs.

Michael saw Chloe's eyes rise and he laughed. "Don't judge an album by its cover. It's a good one."

They walked to the left back corner of the store. Chloe put her record on first, at Michael's insistence. She put the huge padded headphones next to her ears, then messed with the digital tuner until she got to her favorite track, "Twilight."

She motioned Michael closer to her, and he dipped his head to listen at the headphone. His cheek was against her hair as they listened to part of the song.

Elliot Smith sang a pleading ballad about forbidden second attachments and how it felt to be in the presence of a person who steals your heart.

After a minute, Chloe paused the song. "Well, what do you think?"

Michael furrowed his brow. "He sounds so mournful, but full of soul. His voice isn't really like anyone else I've heard, but it's in perfect harmony with his style. I have to say, I think you have pretty great taste. That's an awesome song. And if the other songs are as good or better, I'm won over. I'm actually a little surprised. I was terrified you might play something like Justin Beiber."

Chloe beamed. "Hey, don't bag on Beiber! He's got his moments." Chloe put a fake mic up to her mouth and sang, "My momma don't like you..."

Michael laughed. "Yeah, that one *is* pretty good. I was just trying to be cooler than I am. I actually like Beiber."

Chloe smiled. "Your turn now."

Michael replaced the album with his choice and adjusted it to find the song he was looking for. Before he started the song he said, "So, this isn't my favorite album with Greg Dulle because it doesn't have enough Mark Lanegan, but I think it might be a little serendipitous that this is the album they have here because it does have a song I want you to hear on it."

"Oh, yeah? Why's that?" Chloe asked.

Michael smiled crookedly. "Well, let's see if you can guess." He pressed play.

"Stay, baby, don't go away," the singer wailed in a plaintive voice. His voice was not classically good. It was strained and pleading, but not unpleasantly so. It worked, in an earnest, soulful way.

Michael bent his head close to Chloe's to hear the song as she did. He mouthed the words as they listened, and she could feel his lips against her hair. Chloe Mora had never before felt the kind of feeling that hit her in that moment, surrounded by Michael's scent, his lips moving against her hair, listening to a song she very much hoped was meant literally. Our heroine was certain her one great romance had come.

When they were done listening, Michael raised his eyebrows. "So, can you guess?"

Chloe blushed and looked at her feet. "I think you're doing a very good job taking the promise you made to my aunt seriously."

"Here's a secret." Michael leaned toward her ear. "I'm not really doing it for her."

Chloe looked up into his dark eyes and felt herself lean toward him, expectantly. Michael's grin fell away, and he stepped forward, too. A heroine, however, can never have exactly what she wants before the moment is perfect. It is this fact that led to the appropriate distraction that frustrated her desires. Both their phones broke out into different text tones, ruining the perfection of the moment and distracting the young lovers from taking the necessary next step in their romantic relationship.

Michael frowned at his phone but clicked on the text. "We better get going. Mindy says she's in the middle of the line and they try not to keep people waiting too long. I'll get these to go." So saying, Michael put the albums back in their cases and brought them to Mo at the checkout.

***

They made it to the line in front of Zoe's just as Mindy was only two groups away from being sat.

"Good timing, guys!" she called, waving at them from her position.

Michael and Chloe stood shoulder to shoulder next to Mindy, who was excitedly telling them all about some rude people who yelled at the host for not taking reservations. Michael, only half listening, nodded along with the story. He stretched out his right hand and brushed his fingers along the back of Chloe's hand. The touch was almost electric enough to shock her. Her hand tingled warmly in the wake of his touch. Chloe opened her hand, inviting him to grab it, when another fateful commotion halted the lovers in their tracks.

As is the case in most romances, the characters of a heroine and her intended must be tested. Lissa Thorne had come to Zoe's for just such a purpose, though her intentions were not necessarily bent that way. Had Chloe been paying attention, she could have prepared better for the surprise visit. As it was, all her attention was on willing Michael to take her hand and not wanting to presume enough to do it herself. There was almost no chance she'd been reading him wrong, but on the 1% chance she *was* wrong, she wanted *him* to make the first move.

"Chloe, do you know that guy?" Mindy asked Chloe. Michael dropped his hand away from hers, as if caught in some nefarious act. Chloe could have screamed in frustration.

Chloe, feeling the faint trace of Michael's hand against the back of hers, despaired but good-naturedly looked around. "Who?"

It wasn't long a mystery. She suddenly caught the too bold eye of a young, blonde man who was leaning across a brick building and peering at her over dark sunglasses. Due to the sunglasses, Chloe was not able to place the face that would otherwise have been vaguely familiar, if not entirely welcome.

She shook her head. "No, I don't think I do. Maybe I look like someone he knows," she answered.

"Or maybe you look like someone he'd like to know," Michael said, smiling in a way that looked more like a grimace.

Chloe frowned. "No, I don't think so."

"And why not?" Michael asked. "I thought the same thing when I saw you. At any rate, you'll have something to post about later. You can write: Today I went to brunch with a five and was stared at by a 9. It was a good day."

"I would never post something so silly," Chloe answered mysteriously. Secretly, she berated him. A five?! Hardly. The teasing flirt knew he was a ten and wanted to hear it.

The young man was soon joined by a very familiar face, however, and the mystery could no longer be hidden. Lissa waved enthusiastically from where her brother leaned against a brick building, leering Chloe's way.

~ Nine ~

HUEVOS RANCHEROS WITH A SIDE OF DISCOMFORT TO-GO, PLEASE!

"Oh, I see. I didn't know you invited other friends to breakfast," Michael said in a voice that sounded a little hurt.

Chloe shook her head. "I didn't. I told Lissa I was hanging out with you two today when she asked me to hang out with her. I *did* tell her that you were bringing me here, but she made it sound like she didn't really like waking before noon. She also didn't seem interested in the restaurant, so I told her I would hang out with her later."

Mindy eyed the approaching brother and sister. "I guess they were willing to make an exception for you."

Chloe's stomach felt strange at seeing her new friend approach the group, her brother at her heels. It did a nervous little flip, and it wasn't the same butterfly flips that she got when she saw Michael. She wondered at the sensation, and she wondered at Lissa showing up. Hadn't she said neither she nor her brother would ever wake up before noon? She was sure that she'd told Lissa she would hang out with her later...

"There you are! You should just see the look on your face! Surprised?" Lissa jumped up and down and clapped her hands.

Chloe wanted to caution her from jumping too high. The pink spaghetti strap tank Lissa had tucked into some very short white shorts was so low cut she worried that sudden movements could be very embarrassing for her new friend. Lissa looked as amazing as always, like she'd jumped right out of a Victoria Secret loungewear model ad. Her long blond hair was pulled into a high pony, and she wore crisp white shoes and high white socks. Chloe shivered a little just looking at the outfit, but she had to admit it worked to showcase all Lissa's considerable assets.

"Aren't you cold, Lissa?" she asked, in concern.

"Oh, this?!" Lissa gestured to her outfit. "I stayed at a friend's dorm on campus and didn't remember to pack anything but my pjs."

Mindy eyed the girl. "Didn't your friend have any clothes you could borrow? It's hardly above 55 degrees today. I would never send a friend out in this weather like that."

Lissa looked at Chloe when she answered. "Oh, well...my friend isn't really my size, so hi...*their* clothes wouldn't have been very flattering. I'd rather be cold than wear clothes that would engulf me."

Mindy looked at Michael, who scrutinized their visitors. Chloe was a little relieved to see that he didn't seem to be focusing on Lissa in his scrutiny. Instead, he eyed the yawning, bored looking Xaiden who studied Chloe from behind his sunglasses.

"Anyway, you're looking adorable, Chloe," Lissa continued, nudging her brother. "Isn't she?"

Xaiden took this opportunity to run his eyes over the full length of her body in a way that made his previous looks seem playful. He rubbed his hand over his unshaven cheeks and nodded in appreciation.

"She makes every other girl on this block look like shit," Xaiden answered, winking at Chloe.

Chloe shivered. She thought his comment was not very kind, especially in the company of two other beautiful women, so she was not feeling at all flattered by it.

"Oh, I don't think that's true. Mindy and Lissa are just as beautiful, if not more," Chloe said.

"Are you cold, Chloe? You can wear my sweater," Michael offered, noticing her shiver.

"No need, man. I run *hot*. She can have mine," Xaiden broke in, unzipping his slightly rumpled Harvard hoodie.

If Xaiden hadn't been there, Chloe would have worn Michael's coat if it was 100 degrees outside, just to be surrounded by his scent. Since Xaiden *was* there and he was hopefully and somewhat annoyingly shoving his rumpled zip-up at her, she shook her head. Whether she liked him or not, Xaiden was Lissa's brother. Chloe, being young to the game being played, thought only of the best way to not hurt anyone's feelings, rather than asserting her own desires.

"No, thank you," she held up her hands. "Thank you both. It looks like we're next to go in, and I'll just get too warm if I put anything else on," Chloe lied admirably.

Michael nodded and looked glum. "Well, just let me know if you need it."

Mindy, eyeing Xaiden's zip up with disdain as he shrugged it back on, said, "You two might want to get into line. We've been on the waitlist for twenty minutes."

Xaiden waved her comment off. "I'll just go tell the host to add us to your table. That way, Lissa won't freeze her skinny ass off."

Lissa, much more practiced in saying the right thing, gave her brother a stern look. "Xaiden, we can't expect to just push ourselves in on their breakfast date. We can wait."

"Why'd you wake me up, then?" Xaiden mumbled grumpily.

Michael, too gentlemanly to allow this, said, "It's fine. You can see if they can add you."

Xaiden smiled and slapped Michael's back in what looked to be camaraderie, though it was hard enough to make Michael lurch forward a bit. "Thanks, man. I knew you were one of those *nice guys*." The way he said it sounded more like a barb than a compliment.

Lissa shook her head, then sidled up to Michael, grabbing his arm. "That's so kind of you. Really. We only meant to surprise Chloe. We don't want to intrude."

Michael, ignoring her touch, simply said, "It's fine."

"If you're still offering, *I'm* a little cold. Would you mind?" Lissa gestured to his jacket.

Mindy narrowed her eyes at Lissa. "Why don't you wear *your* brother's dirty jacket? He runs hot, after all." Mindy did a perfect mimic of Xaiden's voice.

"Oh, he won't give it to me. He only said that so Chloe would wear his. He has a bit of a crush, I think," Lissa explained, smiling sweetly at Mindy.

Michael cut off Mindy's reply with a peaceable hand. "It's fine, Mindy. I'm not cold."

He shrugged out of his sweater, and Chloe watched with envious eyes as he handed it to Lissa. Lissa bit her lip and dipped her head before taking the sweater and pulling it on over her thin, shivering arms. She brought the collar to her nose and smelled it.

"I love your cologne! I bet you do pretty well with the ladies, Michael," Lissa purred. She buttoned the coat up to just under her breasts and pouted. "I'd better not button it up all the way. I think I'd stretch it out." She looked at her chest and smiled coyly.

A sudden surge of anger flushed through Chloe, seeing Lissa's large chest spilling out over the buttons of the jacket *she* should be wearing, but she let the anger go. Lissa was just one of those pretty girls used to flirting. Anyway, it didn't seem to faze Michael at all. Her comment fell on deaf ears, as he was looking past Lissa to the approaching Xaiden.

"Hey, they said the table will fit us all, but it might be a tight fit. I told them I major in tight fits." He looked at Chloe, lowering his sunglasses to reveal his reddened green eyes. Thankfully, Chloe missed any ulterior meanings in her innocence, which only made the comment uncomfortable to the rest of the party.

Mindy's name was called by the host, and she showed them to a round bench table in the corner. The restaurant was a cute 50s themed diner bustling with patrons. It had colorful checkered flooring and bright red bench seats and put to mind an era of milkshake counters and poodle skirts. The pleasant smells of bacon, pancakes, and syrup hanging in the air made Chloe more aware of her hunger. Mindy sat on the red pleather seat first and Michael scooted in after her, looking toward Chloe as if to invite her next. However, Lissa missed the very significant look and chose the seat next to Michael for herself.

"Come on, Chloe," Lissa patted the seat next to her.

Chloe sighed inwardly, but hid her frustration, smiled, and scooted in next to Lissa. Xaiden scooted in last. Chloe was put out by how close he scooted to her, so that she it was difficult to find anywhere to place her hands without touching him or his sister. Even more annoying to her was that Xaiden hadn't needed to sit so close to her, as there was plenty of room left on the end of the bench.

The one benefit of the entire awkward affair happening at Zoe's was that it was not made more awkward by there being a long wait. The server was quick and efficient and soon had drinks served and orders taken. It seemed they specialized in amazing food and quick turnaround here. Chloe smiled brightly when her hot chocolate was placed in front of her in a glass mug, towering with whipped cream. She loved whipped cream! It seemed that any feeling of enjoyment, however, could not be maintained with Xaiden nearby. Without asking permission, he swiped a stubby, rough finger through the whipped cream and sucked the cream off his finger in a lewd gesture. Chloe felt her face flush in anger, and she scooted closer to Lissa. Michael and Mindy shared a look of complete disgust.

"Xaiden, you brute. She doesn't want your fingers in her drink," Lissa scolded him.

"Here, Chloe, I'll swap you," Lissa scooted her perfectly coiffed hot chocolate towards Chloe. "You can have my whipped cream, brother dear. I'm watching my weight."

"Your loss. I love cream, don't you, Chloe?" Xaiden spooned whipped cream into his mouth with his finger, sucking his finger noisily.

Chloe looked across the table at Michael and Mindy. Her eyes screaming "help me."

Michael, taking pity on the cornered Chloe, said to Xaiden, "So, Xaiden. You're a second year at Harvard, right? What are you studying?"

Xaiden nodded and desisted his whipped cream frenzy to answer. Chloe smiled at Michael in appreciation. He smiled back.

"Yeah, sophomore. I'm studying business for now, like my dad did, but really, I'm there for the ball," Xaiden answered, "and the babes."

Mindy, with a devilish look in her eye, asked, "Oh, yeah. And which would you say is more your forte? Football or babes?"

Xaiden looked like he was considering this very seriously, but Lissa cut his answer off, knowing that nothing he said would endear him to Chloe. "Xaiden is really good at football. He's a defensive tackle," she interrupted.

Xaiden nodded and slurped his coffee, handing Lissa her now sad-looking lukewarm mug of hot chocolate, devoid of the whipped cream cloud. "What can I say? I'm good at sacks and good in the sack." He laughed heartily at his own joke, which fell flat with the rest of the table.

Chloe sighed and sipped her own drink, warming her hands on the mug, and looking anywhere but at Xaiden, who kept trying to catch her eye. Thankfully, the food came not long after this brilliant display of eloquence.

They ate mostly in awkward silence, except for the noise coming from Xaiden's part of the table. It seemed his eating manners were not much better than his manners in general. He ate as if someone were sure to grab it away if he stopped.

The food was delicious, however. Chloe got the huevos rancheros and was happy she'd done so. It turned out that Xaiden was very put off by spicy foods, which he so tactfully said "gave him the shits." The jalapenos were so spicy that the scent had him scooting to the far side of the bench, so Chloe no longer had to put up with his leg purposefully brushing hers. It was a great comfort to not have to succumb to his unwanted brushes, which made her feel unclean.

When everyone had their fill, a lull hung over the table, which Chloe broke by saying, "Oh, is it okay if I pay for mine with cash? They take cash, right?" Chloe had been surprised to see that many stores were going cash free in the city, which she was not sure was even legal.

Michael held up his hand. "Oh, no, Chloe. I intended to pay for yours. We invited you out, after all. That is, if that's okay? I can pay for it, if you don't mind."

Chloe, recognizing this as a sign that he had thought this was a date, was both happy and very let down by the way events had played out. She was just about to thank him when Lissa cut in.

"Oh, that is so sweet of you, Michael. We hadn't expected you to pick up the check. What a gentleman." Lissa leaned forward so that her chest and dimples were on full display.

"I think he meant that he'd intended to pay for Chloe, who he *invited*," Mindy said, her tone harsh.

Lissa put her hands to her face, as if embarrassed, but no blush was forthcoming. "Oh, God! Of course he did. I'm such an idiot."

Michael gave his sister a look and shook his head. "No, no. I'm happy to get the check. I'll just pay up front."

Mindy stood to let Michael out, her face cold. Lissa stood, too, and began sliding out of the bench on that side, so that Mindy had to stay standing.

"Well, I guess this is where we take our leave, huh, Chloe? You did promise to hang out with us today and it would be very unfair of you to go back on your word," Lissa said, loud enough to stop Michael in his tracks. He turned, frowning.

"No, well, that is I did say that, but I was sure you understood me to mean we were going to hang out later today, after I went out with Michael and Mindy," Chloe clarified.

It was a very uncomfortable misunderstanding, and she hated to hurt Lissa's feelings, but the uncomfortable breakfast had made it clear whose company she preferred. She was relieved to see Mindy smile at her and nod in encouragement.

Lissa pulled a pouty face. "Yes, well, we hadn't set a time, so I thought we were going to hang out after your little breakfast," then, reluctantly, "or, we could all hang out together. Since we are all here."

Mindy seemed ready to agree but Michael, clearly running low on patience, said, "No, no, don't let us keep you. I'd hate to be in the way of your *plans*. I'll just go pay for breakfast." His voice was icy, but his eyes, directed at Chloe, were mostly just hurt.

"Oh, Michael, that's so good of you. We *were* hoping to have her to ourselves for a bit. I wanted her opinion on a dress for the party we're going to at my brother's frat house tonight, and I'm sure that would just bore you. Thank you for understanding. Oh!" She unbuttoned his jacket and wrapped it around his shoulders. "Thank you for letting me borrow it. Sorry if it smells like my perfume," she simpered.

Michael removed the coat from his shoulder with a frown. "I guess we'll see you around, Chloe," he said, his face dark, before turning on his heel.

Mindy, looking very torn, glared in Lissa's direction, and whispered, "Don't worry, Chloe. I don't blame you for all this. I'll talk to Michael, calm him down a bit." She hesitated a bit before saying, "You can always call me if you get too uncomfortable." Her eyes drifted to Xaiden who was cleaning a gap in his front teeth with a butter knife.

Chloe realized, then, what a great friend Mindy was, willing to see her best intentions and understanding that the situation was extremely uncomfortable for her. She smiled sincerely, stood, and hugged Mindy tightly, who seemed taken aback by the display, but also touched. She hugged her back with feeling.

"Thanks, Mindy. I'll message you soon. Tell Michael I still want to hear the Twilight Singers, and that I'm so sorry about all of this."

Mindy nodded. "I will. See you soon."

Lissa, who'd grown impatient at not being able to overhear the girl's whispered confidences, sighed loudly. Mindy gave the girl a scathing look over Chloe's shoulder.

Lissa smiled back. "Bye, Mindy. So nice to briefly meet you."

~ Ten ~

FIFTY SHADES OF XAIDEN

Chloe, distraught over the look on Michael's face when he left and certain he would never want to see her again after such a fiasco, was very downhearted. She excused herself to go to the bathroom, where she allowed herself to take some deep, calming breaths among the retro framed posters and checkered floors.

She also immediately messaged Mindy, asking her to please give Michael her number, so she could properly apologize to him herself. Mindy sent a thumbs up and hug emoji back. Chloe met Lissa and Xaiden outside, trying and failing to not look too forlorn.

Lissa, noticing her friend's spirits, immediately put her arm around Chloe's shoulder. "Oh, Chloe, don't look like that! It breaks my heart. I just wanted to spend more time with you. You're here for so short a time. I truly thought you'd be happy about the surprise."

Chloe, hating to hurt anyone, was overcome by this display of sincerity. "Sorry, Lissa. I *am* happy to see you. It was just a misunderstanding. Don't mind me. I'd just hoped that Michael and Mindy would want to join us…"

Lissa pursed her lips, as if unsure of sharing what came to her next. "Let's walk and talk." She hung her arm through Chloe's.

When they were a little into their slow walk down the block towards Harvard Square, Lissa shared the thoughts that sat heavily on her mind.

"Maybe it's for the best that the Baths couldn't be bothered to be social. I've only heard more disturbing things about their family. A friend of mine and Xaiden's, Mira…" she looked at Xaiden to corroborate what she was saying, but he was busy texting, so she rolled her eyes and continued, "Anyway, Mira told me that Michael's older brother, Ryan, is a true slimeball. I guess he asked her on a date to see a movie. The entire time, he kept forcing his hands up her leg in the most disgusting way. She said he doesn't like to be denied what he wants. He made her catch the "T" home on her own after the movie, and acted all put out that she didn't, well, put out. He's a year above my brother, at Harvard, and in the same fraternity. Xaiden couldn't tell me much about him, other than the fact that he's good at poker, but if Michael's inclinations are anything like his older brothers, he only had one thing in mind for you."

"Michael has only been a complete gentleman to me. I'm sorry if that's true about his brother, but siblings can vary in their manners greatly," Chloe answered, though she did wonder at how they could be *so* different.

Lissa shrugged and said, "Then, he'll readily forgive any imagined offense and won't be too stuck up to be kind to you, should you happen to run into each other again, which is probably not very likely, since I intend to keep you all to myself. Anyway, girls can't be too careful. I'd hate to see you hurt. Looks can be deceiving, you know. I *am* trying to help."

Xaiden pushed himself between the girls, saying, "I hope you aren't thinking of keeping Chloe all to yourself, Lissa. I want a piece of her, too."

He finished this statement with a pleased glance at her backside that made Chloe feel sick to her stomach. She appealed to Lissa with a significant look, since Lissa had been so quick to defend her against Michael's imagined advances.

But it seemed Lissa didn't imagine her own brother to be a similar threat, as she simply shook her head and pushed him away, saying, "If you can't be good, walk back there."

"Walking back here is just as good a view," Xaiden called from behind them.

"Oh, don't mind him. He's a terrible flirt, but it's just his way of saying he's got a crush," Lissa assured her, which did nothing to actually assure her. "He's harmless, but a bit of an idiot with his feelings. I think the right girl could correct that, though."

Chloe, not thinking of herself as that girl at all, only said, "I hope you're right."

Lissa, reading this in a way that best suited her and her brother, smiled. "Anyway, I also talked to my mom about Michael's family. His dad works as a doctor for Mass General, where my mom works as a nurse. She said there is not a nurse there that doesn't hate him, either because he's an insufferable know-it-all prick or because he can't keep his comments about their bodies to himself. 'A real piece of work,' she called him."

Chloe didn't want this to be true. If it were, she thought it seemed likely that some bad habits might, indeed, rub off on his children, though she'd seen no proof of that. She chose to be silent on the topic instead of pursuing it further. Mostly because she wasn't completely comfortable with how one-sided Lissa's assessment of the Bath family was.

"Is there anywhere you wanted to go before we check out the dress store I want to visit?" Lissa asked, gesturing to the square opening up before them, complete with lovely cobbled sidewalks and power washed brick buildings trimmed around the openings in white brick. Just ahead of them, a sweet little French-looking information station with a green domed top sat staunchly in the center of the square.

"Oh, wow! This is beautiful! You are very lucky to go to school here, Xaiden," Chloe said.

Xaiden shrugged. "It's a little too touristy during the day, but yeah, it's cool, I guess. It's whatever to me, now. I see it all the time."

This blase attitude to his clearly privileged circumstances did not endear him to Chloe in the slightest. Having never had the good fortune to visit such lovely, rich environs before in her life, she couldn't take the view of Harvard and the well-manicured Cambridge itself for granted. She decided, however, that his nonchalance would not ruin it for her. She'd done a little research the night before on the local shops, hoping to visit them with the Bath twins, but she figured she might as well enjoy herself and visit them regardless since she was here.

"Now that you mention it, I would really love to see the Harvard Book Store. It's supposed to be really impressive and well stocked," Chloe answered Lissa enthusiastically.

"Oh, uh, sure. I'm happy to see you are as well read as you are lovely," Lissa gushed.

Chloe didn't want to comment that she didn't consider herself as particularly well read, as it would then lessen the secondary compliment, so she simply smiled. Xaiden yawned broadly, looking very put out.

"I mean, it's a bookstore. Seen one, seen em all," Xaiden added. "I'm not bookish outside of class. Reading for fun is whack. There's a pretty sick shoe store not far away, if you wanna go somewhere less lame."

Chloe, not interested in keeping Xaiden's company and even less interested in appearing to any advantage in his eyes, answered, "Yes, I *am* sure. If you aren't interested in seeing the bookstore, I won't be at all offended if you want to go look at the shoe store while I look at books."

Xaiden looked ready to agree to the arrangement, but Lissa, for reasons Chloe couldn't understand, seemed to want to encourage him to tag along. "No, Xaiden, we are here to spend time with our new friend. Don't be rude. We'll go to your store next."

Xaiden sighed loudly, but put up no further argument, and Lissa led the way. The bookstore had a grand double door entrance that bespoke its inner magnificence. Once inside, Chloe was a little speechless. There were two stories of wall to ceiling books on this floor alone, along with aisles and tables of books on either side of the grand room. Chloe's hands went to her mouth in wonder.

"Wow! I don't think I've ever seen this many books," she breathed.

Lissa nodded. "Yeah, there's even more downstairs, and upstairs there's a cafe."

"Really? There's a downstairs? Oh my gosh..."

Chloe started moving down the aisles of books, unaware of the brother and sister sharing looks of boredom behind her. After several minutes of wandering, Xaiden stopped in an aisle behind the fiction aisle she was pursuing and said, "Oh, shit, this book is raunchy. Hey, Chloe, I found a book I could get into."

Chloe dragged her eyes in a daze from the shelves she was scanning and distractedly said, "What did you say? Sorry."

Xaiden was holding a book called "Take One for the Team." It displayed a very muscular guy in a football jacket and no shirt holding a busty cheerleader pushed up against a locker, his hands not visible under her skirt. Chloe frowned at the book.

"His throbbing member pushed against the tight white fabric of his football pants. Carly tentatively lay her hand against it, feeling the impressive length of his..."

Chloe held up her hands in defeat. "Gross. No thank you, Xaiden."

Xaiden raised his eyebrows in what she was sure he thought was a very alluring fashion, but only made Chloe grimace. Lissa giggled. "You picked that book up because it had a football player on it. Be honest."

Xaiden nodded. "Yeah, but I opened it because of the title. I mean, it's pretty good writing. Really...descriptive." Again, he raised his eyebrows.

Chloe blushed and balked, but Xaiden, seemingly unable or unwilling to read her body language, stepped closer. "How about we take this to the corner over there and I read a chapter or two aloud to you?"

Chloe pushed the book away, disgusted. Lissa laughed heartily and punched her brother's shoulder. "Gross, Xaiden. Go read it to yourself, you perv."

"If we're gonna be here much longer, I will. At least I won't be bored," he countered.

Lissa looked at Chloe. "Whadya think, Chloe? Are we done here?"

Chloe, having only seen an eighth of what she wanted to see, but also not wanting to spend any more time being subjected to Xaiden's literary tastes, nodded. "Sure, yeah, we can go."

I'll just come back later with Tía, she thought to herself, *or with Michael, if he'll forgive me. He would never push that kind of book on me.*

However, it turned out the thought of Michael reading the book out loud to her was not as disgusting for some reason. She didn't exactly want him to do so publicly, as Xaiden had, but she couldn't say the idea of a private reading was as grotesque with Michael as the current narrator.

They stopped next at the shoe shop Xaiden liked so much. It was full of hightops that looked more popular with young men than anyone else, but Chloe tried to be polite in nodding and saying something positive every time Xaiden obsessed over a pair. Lissa called her boyfriend and asked him to join them soon at the dress shop she was eager to visit. He consented to this arrangement and Lissa led the way to the dress shop twenty minutes later. Chloe neither had the kind of money the dresses were going for, nor wanted the dresses they were selling. They all seemed to be made of the same clingy material, with purposeful cutouts in awkward places.

Chloe decided she had much better options of things to wear back at the hotel, but she played the dutiful friend and praised the dresses Lissa tried on while Xaiden snored on the purple velvet sofa next to the dressing room. He'd fallen asleep hugging the box with his new shoes in it and looked every bit like a toddler hugging a blankie. That thought, at least, was amusing, even if not much else was.

Lissa's boyfriend ended up meeting them at the dress shop about thirty minutes later. Lissa was taking her time deciding between four possible options that looked fairly similar to Chloe's eyes.

"Ashton, you have to be the deciding factor. Chloe and I agreed these are the ones that look the best on me, but I can't decide which to get."

In fact, Chloe hadn't had much to say about any of the dresses Lissa tried on, as none of them were to her taste, but she had told Lissa she looked very sexy and beautiful in all of them, because that was true.

"Well, I think red looks really nice with your eyes, but so does pink. So, I guess I'd choose those two?" Ashton answered honestly.

Ashton was a tall brunette with kind blue eyes and a slim frame. He also looked like he'd jumped right out of an L.L. Bean catalog, with his perfectly side swept hair, beige pants, navy blue collared sweater, and polished brown shoes. He was clearly very smitten with Lissa, though it was less clear that she was equally into him. Chloe thought he looked maybe a little too polished and proper for her friend.

"I just can't decide, and I didn't bring enough money for all four," Lissa pouted.

"Oh, well, if that's all it is, I can help you, babe," Ashton said.

Lissa, for the first time since he walked in, made her way over to Ashton and pecked him on the mouth. "You spoil me too much."

"There's no such thing as spoiling you too much," Ashton answered, allowing Lissa to pile the dresses onto his arm. "You're worth every cent."

"Good! Remember that when we visit the jewelry store, then," Lissa said, taking his free arm. "Chloe, dear, will you wake my lazy brother?"

Chloe reluctantly walked over to Xaiden and called his name several times before poking his shoulder. He started awake, a bit of drool on his chin, and smiled up at her, sleepily. "I was having a very nice dream," he informed her in a husky voice. "You were in it."

Chloe, not wanting to know any more about Xaiden's dream, hurriedly informed him they were moving on. Ashton bought Lissa's dresses, and they left the shop. Lissa wound them down a few cobbled streets to a pink brick storefront whose window sparkled with choice diamonds, necklaces, bracelets, and earrings. Chloe wasn't much interested in looking at things she could never afford and didn't quite understand the significance of, but she followed her friend into the store all the same.

In the jewelry store, Lissa attended Ashton with much more obvious care than she'd yet to bestow on him. She showed him rings that could stand in for promise rings, ran her fingers through his hair and whispered things to him that made him raise his eyebrows and blush.

It was surprising to see Ashton and Lissa together. They were both good looking and seemingly from rich families, even if Lissa's had fallen on hard times, but there the similarities ended. Lissa was vibrant and talkative. Ashton was quiet, thoughtful, and reserved.

Chloe had also noticed that Lissa's first concern was her own comfort, rather than those she was with. Chloe was trying to be companionable but was tired of the type of shops the brother and sister liked. Though Lissa was perhaps a little better at reading others than her clueless brother, who dogged Chloe in the store, pointing out ridiculously sized diamonds and saying things like, "Damn! That looks like a trophy wife's dream!"

Chloe, trying to be polite without encouraging, simply nodded at his comments. She checked her phone often, in hopes that Michael, having received her number from his sister, would text her anytime now, having forgiven her the offense she awkwardly stumbled into. After checking her phone for the hundredth time without luck, she sighed and slipped it into her pocket, feigning interest in a diamond skull charm bracelet in the nearest case, so she didn't have to feign interest in Xaiden.

A diamond skull charm bracelet? Just in case you want to be both goth and let people know you have money to burn?

Xaiden noticed where her attention was drawn. Trying harder to meet her where she was, rather than vainly interest her in his own amusements, which differed too much from her own to engage her, he said, "Cool choice. You're a bit of a bad girl at heart, huh?"

Chloe, almost at the end of her patience for Xaiden's innuendos, simply said, "Hmmm?" She hoped the question would give him time to consider a different line of conversation.

However, Xaiden had very few avenues he was willing to take, apart from innuendos, sports, and expensive finery. "I didn't know you were a goth girl. You like things dark and mysterious, huh? You know, the LSC is showing *Interview with the Vampire* this week? Lissa told me. I don't normally lower myself to hang out with MIT nerds, but I'd make an exception if you wanna go. I might even bring you a present, if you're very bad." Xaiden winked at her meaningfully.

"Oh, there's no need for bribes. I already told the Bath twins I was interested in going," she answered, intending to shut down his line of thought. She hoped the twins still *wanted* to meet her there. She would have to reconfirm with Mindy that she wanted to go with them, and hope Michael's feelings were not hurt enough to ignore the olive branch.

Xaiden, looking a little put out, shrugged. "Oh? Yeah, well, I'm glad you're going. I love vampire movies, especially that one. Has some really great scenes. Very sexy."

Having never seen the movie, Chloe nonetheless accurately guessed his mind was somewhere in the gutter and said nothing in return. Looking around the shop for Lissa and Ashton, she noticed them at the register.

"Looks like your sister is checking out. I should get back to Tía soon. She was hoping we would do lunch together today." Tía hadn't said that at all, but Chloe's enthusiasm for hanging out with

Lissa had waned. Since she thought it would be rude to back out of the party tonight, she wanted some time to herself to prepare for it mentally.

"Yeah, looks like she got ol' money bags to buy her something else. Wish I was a pretty girl instead of a pretty boy. Then I could bat my eyes at you and ask you to buy me something." Xaiden nudged her with his elbow. Chloe had nothing to say to that comment but gave a weak smile.

"Go on ahead. I'll meet you girls outside. I wanna look at a couple more things first," Xaiden told Chloe.

She very willingly left Xaiden behind and met up with Ashton and Lissa, explaining her need to meet back up with her Tía. Lissa, pouting a little, asked if she couldn't just spend the day with them, so they could get ready for the party together. Chloe, not minding Lissa on her own, suggested that she stop by the Kendall later in the evening, so they could get ready there. Lissa agreed to this arrangement.

Ashton, a more gentlemanly person than Lissa's brother, insisted that they drop Chloe off at the Kendall. They walked to the Harvard parking garage, which seemed a longer walk than the more convenient "T" station. Ashton had them pile into his BMW, and they dropped Chloe off at her hotel. Lissa blew kisses her way and promised to be there promptly at 8 p.m. so they could get ready. Chloe, feeling her social battery draining, waved goodbye and practically ran up the stairs to their hotel room.

Tía looked up from her cup of coffee and newspaper with surprise when Chloe entered the room. "Mija, I thought for sure I'd not see you all day. You look upset. Are you okay?"

Chloe, needing to vent, told her all about the mix-up at breakfast. Tía frowned at all the right parts and gave the most expressive "ay dios" to comfort her niece's proper embarrassment.

"Chloe, it all sounds like a mistake. Michael and Mindy seem like nice people. Message Mindy and let her know what you just told me–that you would have preferred that they stayed and that you are back at the hotel and feeling bad about how things went. If they are any kind of friends, they will reach out. If not, well, then it is better to know these things sooner rather than later. Too much pride is not ideal in friends or partners."

Chloe nodded over this sage advice, hugged her Tía and messaged Mindy right away, saying, "I'm back @ the hotel. My patience w/Xaiden ran low. I hope you-n-Michael still want 2 go 2 the LSC 2morrow. I still want 2."

Chloe's phone pinged and her heart leapt; it was a number Chloe didn't yet recognize. "This is Michael. Mindy thinks I'm being an idiot. I think she's right. See you at the LSC. We'll save you a seat."

Chloe immediately saved Michael's number in her phone. She texted back. "You are the least idiotic person I've ever met. I wish I could skip tonight and hop right into tomorrow night."

Michael texted, "Oh, but then you'd miss the frat bro's party."

Chloe texted back an eye roll emoji and, "I'm starting to think that wouldn't be 2 terrible. Alas, I keep my word."

Michael texted back, "That's good 2 hear. Be safe & careful tonight."

Chloe sent him a smiley face and messaged, "I will. SYS."

"See you soon." He texted back.

Chloe could have wished for more xo's or wink emojis, but she was beginning to see that Michael was the kind of person who played his cards close to his chest. She also began to see that she preferred that to Xaiden's lack of propriety and brashness.

"You look very happy. Am I to guess that text was from Michael and not Mindy?" Tía commented, sharp as ever.

Chloe nodded. "He said he was being an idiot and he will save me a seat at the LSC tomorrow."

Tía nodded approvingly. "Good. It is good to know your own worth, but not good to be unforgiving over silly misunderstandings. That shows good judgment. You know, Chloe, if you don't want to go to the party tonight, you don't have to. I can stay in or you can go to dinner with Bev and I."

Chloe shook her head. "It's okay, Tía. I'm feeling better about it now that Michael and Mindy don't seem upset. If I don't like it, I can come home anytime."

Tía nodded. "Yes, you can. And if you need me at all, you just call. It doesn't matter the time or the circumstance. I will always be there for you."

Chloe, feeling very lucky and extremely spoiled, jumped up and hugged her Tía fiercely. "You are the best Tía in the entire world.

Tía kissed her head. "And you are the best sobrina. But don't tell your sisters I said so."

"Deal," Chloe giggled.

~ Eleven ~

SOME BATHS ARE DIRTY

Chloe and Tía went to lunch on campus at a delicious burrito place in the Student Center, then Tía showed her around the buildings at MIT, which were fairly spread out and very different from one to the other. There were 70s looking concrete buildings, early 1900s brick buildings, more modern bright, geometric buildings like the Stata center, and then there was the neoclassical dome. MIT was a mishmash of interests and tastes, much like the student population itself. It lacked the continuity of Harvard and Harvard square, but it also seemed somehow more inviting. It seemed to say: anyone who is clever enough to come here is welcome.

She and Tía spent the rest of the afternoon in pore cleansing face masks, sipping tea and reading, as Tía's leg needed resting. Chloe set her alarm, then allowed herself a short nap. A message alert lit her phone and woke her just before her alarm.

It was from Lissa, and it read: "I'm a little early. I just finished my last final not long ago. Can I come up?"

"Sure. Second floor. 203."

"Good evening, sleepy head. Is that Lissa?" Tía asked.

Chloe nodded. Tía gave her a half smile and spoke in a rushed, worried series of cautions. "Before she gets up here, I just want to ask you some favors. I know what I'm asking will be a bit of a bummer, but I want to ask that you *not* drink tonight. You are still too young, and I'm supposed to be taking care of you. Of course, if you choose to, don't overindulge. One drink max, I think. And be careful to not leave your drink unattended. Some men are not to be trusted and might slip something in there...Oh, and please don't ride with anyone who's been drinking. I'll actually send a visa with you in case you need to catch a cab. And maybe you ought to bring some condoms, just in case..."

"Tía," Chloe interrupted, laughing. "I don't plan on drinking. I absolutely *do not* need condoms. Ick. I promise to be careful, and I will not get into a vehicle with anyone who has been drinking. I'll be home by eleven most willingly. As it is, I could forgo the whole thing, but I made a promise."

Tía smiled at her, reassured. "You are a smart girl, Chloe. Just remember to trust your gut. If something feels off, say something. Your safety is more important than other people's hurt feelings."

Chloe digested this piece of information and wondered at it. This morning, her stomach had done that little flip when Lissa and Xaiden showed up at breakfast and she'd ignored it. She'd then had to suffer through hours of uninteresting prattle and sexual hints from Xaiden, and shops she couldn't care less about instead of doing what she wanted. Was that what Tía meant about trusting her gut? Should she have said something then? Was she simply feeling nervous now, or did she really not want to go to the party? She searched herself but had a hard time finding the answer.

Her reverie was cut short by Lissa's knock, and it was soon swept away. Lissa had chosen her short, sparkly red dress with side cut-outs. She'd already styled her hair in a curly updo with side swept bangs, but her makeup was not applied. She carried a large, bright pink, bejeweled make-up bag in her hand.

"Finally! Girl time!" She met Chloe in a hug. She smelled of vanilla perfume and hairspray.

Chloe smiled, not as nervous about the night now that she was just hanging out with Lissa. Lissa eyed her. "I can't believe you're not even dressed yet. No matter. We'll start with your hair. I was thinking thick curls." So saying, Lissa brandished a curling iron like a sword.

Chloe giggled. "Curls it is. My hair is naturally wavy, so it will oblige. Come in."

Tía introduced herself to Lissa, then excused herself for the night, leaving a refillable card on the table for her niece. She was going to meet Bev for a lecture, dinner, and drinks. Lissa eyed the card, saying, "Your aunt really takes care of you, huh? I bet you do all sorts of amazing stuff with her."

Chloe nodded. "She's been kind to me. I love when we can spend time together. She really wants me to go to college here, so she can see me more often."

Lissa squealed her consent. "Yes, yes! You must! We would have such fun!"

She forced Chloe into the hotel chair and started on her hair with the curling iron. "I know another person who would be very happy if you stayed in the area."

Chloe raised her eyebrows towards the mirror, so her friend could read the implied question in them.

Lissa smiled. "My brother thinks you're the most beautiful girl he's ever seen. He was pretty smitten with you today."

Chloe's eyebrows drew back down. She didn't want to encourage Lissa's brother nor Lissa's clear hopes that Chloe would return his interest, but she also didn't want to be unkind. She settled for, "That's...sweet."

Lissa seemed appeased by this and spent the next half hour perfecting Chloe's hair. They both did their makeup before Chloe slipped into her dress for the party, which she was really excited about wearing. The dress was a newspaper print bodycon dress with an over the shoulder cowl sleeve on only one side and a sleeveless arm on the other.

Lissa eyed the dress with open adoration and envy. "That dress *slays*, Chloe."

Chloe grinned and pulled on her short, bright pink heels with little faux diamond bows on the sharply pointed toe and an electric lime trench that sat just below her dress. "Thanks. Tía took me shopping when we got in. She let me buy way too many things, but they all sort of go together, so I can mix and match them."

Lissa shrugged. "She doesn't have kids, right? Let her spoil *you!*"

Chloe shook her head. "She'd probably agree with you. I just don't want to seem greedy."

Lissa shrugged this off. "It's not greed if you deserve it, girl." She winked slyly. Chloe laughed this ridiculous answer away.

"Ready to knock 'em dead?" Lissa asked.

Chloe nodded eagerly, her interest in the party renewed by Lissa's bright smiles, kind words and miraculous talent with a curling iron.

***

Ashton picked the girls up at Lissa's request and parked at the student parking garage several blocks away from the party. This side of Cambridge was a little quieter than Harvard Square, but it was still plenty busy. Chloe was in awe of the number of people walking the streets, chilling at bars, eating very late dinners at restaurants that kept up with the pace and lifestyles of the people in the wakeful city. It never seemed truly dark in this city, either. Lights glared from every window, restaurant, phone and streetlamp as far as the eye could see.

Chloe could tell when they got closer to the party, however, as the pumping of music and ruckus laughter from early guests issued from a three story brick building sporting white columns and a flag with Greek letters slung across the entryway. Ashton, with a stunning Lissa hanging off his arm, looked back to where Chloe faltered more slowly behind them. She was feeling a little overwhelmed by the noise issuing from the building.

"Chloe, why don't you take my other arm? I'll be the envy of Harvard with two such lovely guests." Ashton's smile was kind and his eyes earnest.

Chloe smiled and took his arm. "Just a little nervous, I guess."

Lissa grinned at her. "We'll be fine if we girls just stick together."

Once inside, Chloe grew even more overwhelmed. Every surface of the floor, every beat-up chair, every sagging, mismatched sofa, and every windowsill were crowded with laughing, yelling, drinking college students. Some people danced near a loud sound system in a rounded turret room at the front left of the house. Others flocked towards the drinking station/kitchen at the back of the house.

Lissa spoke urgently in Ashton's ear. He nodded and released the girl's arms, turning to Chloe. "I'm going to get me and Lissa a drink. Do you want something?"

Chloe, feeling very childish, said, "Um, something non-alcoholic if they have it."

Ashton smiled reassuringly. "I'm not drinking, either. Designated driver. I'll get you a soda."

"Sprite, if they have it? Thank you so much, Ashton." Ashton nodded and headed toward the drinks.

Lissa grabbed Chloe's arm. "It's so loud up here! Let's go downstairs. That's where the gaming room is."

"What about Ashton? Shouldn't we wait for him?"

Lissa waved her concern away. "I told him to meet us down there."

Chloe nodded and allowed Lissa to pull her through barely dressed young girls and flexing young men, some dancing, some talking, some...otherwise engaged. She pushed past the sweaty, laughing masses all the way downstairs where a very angry sounding game of pool was being played out in the left corner of the room, an intense racing game was being played in the right corner of the room and an air hockey match was in full swing just to the side of them. It was a little less crowded down here, though that wasn't saying much.

The air in the frat house was close and stifling and Chloe began to get too warm in her lime trench. She untied the trench and hung it over her arm. A man watching the air hockey match next to them nudged his friend and pointed toward her and Lissa. They looked at the girls with huge grins on their faces. The red-headed man made a motion for her to come over to the table. Lissa rolled her eyes and pulled Chloe after her toward the group of men and women playing the racing game on a haggard, sagging cracked leather couch.

"Haha, you slow fucks! I win again! Pay up, bitches!" A blonde-haired, stocky man stood up from the couch and lifted his arms in victory.

Chloe's heart dropped. She'd recognize that voice anywhere. She'd hoped to avoid Lissa's crass brother for a little while. It seemed Lissa wasn't having that.

"Xaiden, look who's here!" Lissa shouted toward her brother.

Xaiden, wearing a red pullover with Greek letters and a pair of light-colored jeans, waved at the girls, vaulted the couch, and landed in front of them, sweating slightly with the effort. He eyed Chloe in his usual fashion, making her desire to be anywhere but under his detestable scrutiny.

"You look so fucking hot, Chloe...Damn, girl! I'm having a hard time not just snatching you up," Xaiden slurred.

He'd clearly started drinking some time ago and was feeling the effects nicely. Unfortunately for Chloe, this meant that he was even more uninhibited in his words and actions than normal. Not being particularly classy to begin with, this was not a good turn of events.

Chloe ignored his compliment and looked around. She saw Ashton making his way down the stairs with very full hands, and ran over to meet him, grabbing hers and Lissa's drinks from him. She hoped she looked helpful and not rude, but she dearly wanted to disengage from Xaiden's hungry eyes. She handed Lissa the only alcoholic drink–a bottle of something pink that smelled like cleaner –and sipped the lemon lime soda Ashton brought her.

"Wow, this place is packed," commented Ashton, in a tone that suggested being here was not within his comfort zone. "Um, Lissa, I have to make a call to my dad real quick. I'm gonna step outside. I'll be right back, okay?"

Lissa acknowledged her boyfriend's words by shooing him away and grabbing Chloe's arm. "Oh gross, Chloe. Pool table, almost black hair, blue eyes. He will *not* stop staring at me."

Chloe turned to where her friend indicated and saw a face that looked slightly familiar, though she couldn't say why. "Do you know him?"

Xaiden looked to where the girl's eyes were drawn and snorted. "You really know how to pick 'em, Lissa. That's Ryan Bath, dummy."

Chloe gasped. "You mean the twins' brother?"

Xaiden nodded. "Yup. Though Ryan's a bit more fun than those wet rags."

Lissa made a disgusted face but couldn't keep a certain hint of temptation out of her eyes. "Oh, gross, Chloe. Let's go upstairs, away from the *unwanted* leers of disgusting men." She spoke loud enough that her words carried to Ryan, who smirked in a secret way Chloe didn't quite like.

Lissa dragged Chloe back upstairs. Xaiden followed closely behind them, bumping against Chloe's backside a little too frequently for her to think it an accident. Her face burned with embarrassment.

"Come on, Chloe. We don't need men to have fun. Let's not let any of them tear us apart," Lissa commented loudly, drawing rather more glances and smirks their way from young men as they passed than she would have had she stayed silent about their plot.

Chloe followed her, however, hoping that staying right by Lissa's side would keep Xaiden away. Lissa dragged her toward the turret room where the music pounded out techno dance music that Chloe found kind of annoying. Lissa spun Chloe in a slow circle and danced in front of her, jumping and moving her body to the rhythm of the music. Men tried to step in, trying for either her or Lissa's attention, but Lissa pushed them away. Chloe shyly swayed to the music, setting her drink down and vowing not to come back to it after what her Tía had said about not leaving her drink unattended. They danced together for a few moments, Chloe loosening up and Lissa laughing, when someone tapped on her shoulder.

A deep voice followed the tap. "Mind if I cut in here? Your friend has been undressing me with those vixen green eyes since she saw me."

Chloe turned to reprimand whoever had cut into their girl's time, but stopped short when she noticed that Ryan Bath had followed them upstairs. She fumbled for something to say and settled on, "No, thank you. We are not interested in boys tonight."

The cocky young man laughed a short, disbelieving laugh. "That's not what your friend's eyes are telling me right now. Besides, I'm not a boy. I'm a *man*."

Chloe hated when boys said that. In her estimation, it was very easy to tell a man from a boy, and this one didn't pass. She stood firm. "I assure you, we don't mean to dance with anyone else tonight. Goodbye."

She went to turn away from the self-righteous jerk, but Xaiden caught her shoulder. "Ah, come on, Chloe. Let Lissa turn him down. She's a big girl. I want a turn dancing with the prettiest girl in the room."

With this, Xaiden grabbed her arm and drew her toward him, swaying his hips in time to the music. Chloe made to pull away, "I don't think so, Xaiden. Your sister was very firm. She wanted us to stick together tonight."

Xaiden half twirled Chloe. "Oh really?" He pointed at his sister, who was pressed against Ryan, her eyes locked on him in a very intense dancing session. Ryan looked at Chloe over her friend's head and smiled in a very annoying, self-assured way.

Chloe turned toward Xaiden, who pulled her next to him and started dancing again. "Shouldn't we stop that? Your sister is with Ashton, and I doubt he would like it that I left her to Ryan."

Xaiden laughed, his hand slipping lower down Chloe's back in a way that made her try to pull further away from him. "Like I said, she's a big girl. She knows what she's doing. It's not *our* fault if she does something stupid."

Chloe looked over and met Lissa's eyes. Her friend laughed and shrugged, as if things like dancing with men she detested were simply silly annoyances. Chloe wished she could feel the same way. Xaiden's hands were too free for her liking, running down her waist and around her back. He kept pulling her toward him, though she tried to keep a respectable distance. He kept saying things like, "God, you're so hot," which only made her feel queasy under his touch. The song ended and Xaiden's beer breath was making her nauseous, so Chloe pushed away from him, slipping out of his insistent, grasping fingers.

"I'm getting too warm. Would you mind getting me another soda?"

Xaiden looked a little put out but shrugged. "Yeah, I need another beer, anyway."

Chloe walked over to where Lissa was smacking Ryan playfully on the arm. "Uh, Lissa, did you want to join me outside? I need some fresh air. Maybe we could find Ashton?"

Lissa looked at Chloe and shook her head. "Oh, that's okay. I didn't bring a jacket, so I'd be too cold. I'll wait here for you."

Chloe was taken aback that Lissa wouldn't take the extended offer to leave someone she'd said disgusted her before she'd even met him. She frowned but said only, "Okay."

She pushed past men trying to grind against her as another song blared from the speakers and shoved her arms into her lime jacket. Once outside, she took a deep breath of the chilly fall air and let it out slowly. The air here was not as fresh as she was used to, but it was a serious improvement from the body spray and beer haze hanging over the heads of the partygoers inside.

She descended the few stairs leading to the door and sat on the bottom one, feeling confused and worn out. She fished her phone out of her pocket and texted Tía that she was doing okay and would see her soon. It was only 9:00, but Chloe wished it were later, so she could make the excuse that she had to return home before curfew.

"Hey, Chloe." Ashton walked up to her and sat on the stoop above her and to the right. "Some party, huh?" His voice was annoyed.

Chloe looked up at Ashton in his gray, zipped at an angle sweater. He seemed out of place on the stoop of a loud party in an expensive European zip up and perfectly pleated pants. "Oh, yeah. Kinda loud...I just needed a break for a minute. Thought I'd try to find where you went off to. How's your dad?"

Ashton looked at Chloe with sad eyes. "I didn't come out here to call my dad. I came out here to test a theory."

Chloe looked up at him. "A theory?"

Ashton nodded, sitting next to her on the stoop. "A friend of mine said Lissa only likes me for my money. Now, this friend is a really good friend. He's not the type to say something that will make me unhappy without reason. So, I figure maybe he sees something I don't. Anyway, I figure if I leave the party with Lissa looking like she does and she comes to find me after a bit, he's wrong. Or maybe she just stays with you, and that's okay, too. I mean, girls should look out for each other at places like this, but..."

"You came back in?" Chloe asked, seeing the pain in the rueful set of his mouth. "And you saw her dancing with Ryan."

Ashton nodded. "Yeah. Though, dancing is a loose term. Grinding might be a bit more accurate. I also saw how uncomfortable you looked dancing with Xaiden. I'm sorry I didn't step in. I...I was busy being selfish. I should have said something."

Chloe waved the comment away. "Or maybe I should have. My Tía told me to be more outspoken. I'm starting to get what she means. I just have to tell Xaiden I don't like him like that."

Ashton nodded his head, still looking very let down. Chloe sighed. "You know, it was just a dance. Lissa seems to like being the life of the party. That doesn't seem like your thing. Maybe if you texted her and let her know we want to do something else, she'd leave with us."

Ashton smiled at Chloe in a way that made her feel naïve. "Do you want to go, Chloe?"

Chloe nodded. "I'm gonna go let Lissa know. I'm sure she'll want to leave with us. Maybe we can go to a restaurant or something?"

Ashton's weak smile said he disagreed. "I'll wait here."

Chloe pushed her way back through the hot, gyrating bodies to find Lissa, but could not locate her on the dance floor. She went downstairs where Xaiden was back to playing the racing game he'd abandoned to dance with Chloe. He hadn't waited for her on the dancefloor, which pleased rather than upset her. She was happy to see he wasn't so into her that he couldn't be distracted by something he preferred.

When she asked him where his sister was, he said, "Don't know. Sit that beautiful ass down next to me. Don't worry about her."

Chloe declined this not very tempting offer and excused herself, saying she was feeling sick and Ashton was going to take her back to her hotel. Xaiden, a little too drunk to be clever enough to come up with a way to get her to stay, said, "Oh, alright. I'll see you soon, k?"

Once back inside, Chloe looked over the heads of the increasingly loud party goers to spot Lissa. When she'd almost given up hope, she suddenly saw a lush curly golden ponytail headed towards the third floor. Chloe almost called out to Lissa, but stopped herself when she saw who was leading her up the stairs by her hand. Ryan pulled a giggling Lissa upstairs behind him and through what looked to be a bedroom door on the third floor.

Chloe felt an array of emotions, but mostly she just felt disappointed. It was then that she realized that words said, no matter how sincerely, were not as important as the follow up action. Lissa, it seemed, was a girl of very sincere words and very insincere actions. Chloe slogged through the crowds, past the staring, hungry eyes of insatiable testosterone vessels and outside onto the landing.

Ashton looked up hopefully, but his face soon fell. "Couldn't find her?"

Chloe was not a dishonest person, but for a moment she wanted to lie. She pushed the urge aside. "I found her. She was walking upstairs and into a room with Ryan. I'm sorry, Ashton."

Ashton's eyes were momentarily angry, but it soon fell away. "I guess it's better to know now, before I get in too deep. Let me give you a ride back to your hotel."

Ashton was quiet on the drive back to the hotel, but he accepted a side hug from Chloe and her wishes for his future happiness with a great deal of class. Chloe couldn't help but think he'd be better off in the morning, and that he might even realize that already.

Having made it back to the hotel before Tía, Chloe opened her phone to check in and let Tía know she was back already, so that she wasn't surprised when she came back to the hotel. When she flipped the phone open, a message was already waiting for her, but it wasn't from Tía.

"How's your date with my rival?"

Michael! Her entire body felt pleasantly warm.

She answered, "Rival! I think not. It's over and it wasn't a date. I was there 2 spend time w/Lissa, but she was more interested in spending time with ur bro. Her bf is very upset. But was kind enough 2 bring me back 2 my hotel. I wish I had spent the day with u instead."

"After such a pretty text, I suppose I should forgive you for not being attentive to my needy ego all night, especially since you were suffering the prattle of an ignorant Harvard boy."

"You think you know him after meeting him once, then?"

"Not at all. It was an educated guess. How much *can* our Harvard boy drink?"

"I didn't count his drinks. Enough 2 not be 2 upset when I took my leave. It's weird, tho. He and Lissa talked a lot about ur family. I thought maybe u all knew each other before today."

"Hmmm...I'm gonna take a stab and assume none of what was said was to our credit?"

"Well..."

"Mmmhmm. I think you must be very patient to put up with Xaiden for long. I do not know him well, but after this morning, I don't wish to."

"Well, Xaiden's a little hard to take, but I think he tries to be kind to me."

"Kind to you? How shocking. I wonder what motivates that..."

"You think I shouldn't trust him?"

"Do you think I can possibly be unbiased in my answer?"

"I guess not..."

"I'm glad ur back safe. Sorry if the party was as lame as I hope it was."

"Lol. It was. But that's okay. See u 2morrow?"

"See you tomorrow. Sweet dreams."

"They will be now."

"Interesting..."

She lay her head down on the soft feather pillow on her cozy hotel bed and sighed in satisfaction. The night wasn't a total waste.

***

She was dancing most unwillingly with Xaiden. His hands gravitated towards her butt. No matter how many times she pushed them right, they explored her. She tried pushing away from him, but he grabbed her arms tighter, so tight it hurt, and his face darkened. Suddenly, she was very afraid. He was much stronger than her and his hands were on her again.

Just as suddenly, Michael was there, pushing his way through the crowd, and in between her and Xaiden. Michael grabbed her hand, pulling her into a different world–a simpler, less brazen world. There were no other dancers in this world–just an empty ballroom, glittering with candles in golden stands, a marble floor under her slippered feet, and a romantic fire blazing in a white marble fireplace. Michael bowed to her as a new song began, a classical piece with a slow, pleading violin melody. He was dressed like Henry Tilney in the early 2000s production of Northanger Abbey, long coattails and a cheeky smile. She wore a gown that reminded her of Catherine Moreland's first muslin gown, the very one Henry first commented on in his silly way. They went through the steps of a dance she had no idea she knew, a ritual that was proper enough to be right and intimate enough to be thrilling without being dangerous.

~ Twelve ~

THORNES IN CHLOE'S SIDE

Chloe woke to the loud ping of a text notification. She sat up hopefully, but sighed when she saw it was from Lissa.

"OMG, girl! Where'd u guys go last night? My phone died. I was crazy worried. Ashton won't answer my texts."

Chloe huffed and ignored the text. Tía greeted her with a "Good morning, sleepyhead. It's 10:30. You must be catching up from jet lag." Chloe nodded, thinking that must be it, as her head was still fuzzy, and her body heavy with sleep. Another notification pinged, and Chloe flipped open her phone.

"Chloe?! I know ur 2 good a friend to have left with my bf w/any bad intentions, but I'm really upset."

"Plz, plz, plz answer me. I just want 2 know ur ok."

Chloe took a deep, calming breath and replied, "I'm fine. Ashton took me home bcuz I was feeling overwhelmed. He went home bcuz he saw u with Ryan. I went 2 find u to ask u to come, too, but u were headed upstairs w/Ryan. I didn't want 2 bother u 2."

It took several moments for Lissa to reply. So long, in fact, that Chloe wondered whether she would. How could she possibly talk her way out of what Chloe saw as damning evidence of her lack of concern both for her boyfriend and her friend.

"That?! OMG, no wonder Ashton's pissed! But I thought @ least u might give me a chance, as a friend and fellow woman."

"A chance?" Chloe responded.

"A chance to explain what was going on. It must have looked bad, but nothing like *that* happened w/Ryan."

"Oh? Well, it *did* look bad."

"God! I can see that. I shouldnt've had another drink. They were so strong. He told me he wanted 2 show me some pictures from last week's game. I'm an idiot, so I agreed. He plays w/Xaiden on the Crimsons. It was all a front. He thinks he's God's gift to women. Had his hands all over me right away. When I finally got the creep 2 leave me alone, I ran downstairs 2 find u & Ashton. U both were gone. Xaiden was 2 drunk 2 drive, so I had to bum a ride from his awful friend Blake who kept asking 4 my digits. Barf. I hate men."

Chloe, picturing how scared her friend must have been, suddenly felt a crushing guilt overcome her. Lissa could have been hurt. If Ryan had been a worse kind of creep, she might have. And Chloe just abandoned her, believing the worst of her right away. She immediately texted back, feeling the weight of how Lissa must have felt.

"I'm so sorry, Lissa. I should've asked u. I hope u r ok? God, I feel awful."

"No, no. I was drunk and didn't keep my word. I left ur side. I'm srry."

"I need to get ready, but maybe we can meet @ the student center 4 lunch?"

"Yes! Meet me in front in 1 hr?"

"K. See u soon."

Chloe hurriedly explained why she was frantically getting ready, explaining to Tía that she would be back before they had to leave for the museum tour they were doing with the alumni association.

Miranda Mora looked on as her niece scrambled in an agitated way, so unlike her normally bubbly, calm self. She wondered about the veracity of what Chloe's new friend texted her this morning. Lissa seemed like a disingenuous girl to her. But she also knew that young people had to fumble with insincerity here and there, in order to learn and grow. She also didn't want to demonize the young girl, knowing that there were certainly many young men who took advantage of vivacious and lively girls, and she detested the argument that anyone asked for or deserved that kind of treatment.

This tornado of uncertainty swirled around in Tía's mind while she watched her sweet niece scramble to find her tennis shoes. She was almost glad, at this stage, that she was childless. The weight her words could have on her niece's life felt too heavy.

She said only, "Chloe, dear. Remember what I said about trusting yourself, okay?"

Chloe, pulling her handmade patchwork jacket over a white t-shirt and jeans, said, "Okay, Tía. I'll be back soon for the museum trip."

Tía kissed Chloe's head. "Bueno, amor."

***

Chloe rushed the 8-minute walk to the student center, cursing the tide of slow-moving students in her head. She could see Lissa waiting in front of the student center when she was across the street, in front of the crosswalk by the domed building. She cringed inwardly, when she noticed Lissa's stocky, hungover brother in tow. Did they go everywhere together?

They went to the food court in the upper part of the student center. Lissa and Chloe went to the Thai food vendor while Xaiden complained that he'd have the shits if he did that and went in search of pizza.

"I was hoping to talk to you alone," Chloe ventured when they were waiting in line for their food.

"Oh? To talk about the Ryan stuff? You can talk freely in front of Xaiden. I told him everything. Besides, he wanted to make up for being such an idiot last night. He feels badly for being too drunk to take you back to the hotel himself."

Chloe shrugged. "It's fine. He was having fun and Ashton didn't mind taking me. Did you talk to Ashton, by the way? Clear things up?"

Lissa waved the question away. "I tried to. He is still too angry, I think."

Chloe noticed that Lissa didn't seem too worried by her boyfriend's hurt feelings. They found a place to sit next to a window that had a peekaboo view of the Charles river. Chloe was feeling a lot less agitated now that she had good food and a nice view, and now that she could see Lissa was alright. In fact, Lissa was in pretty good spirits and hardly seemed bothered about Ryan when the topic was brought up.

"Maybe you should have called the cops or something last night, Lissa, if you felt like Ryan was forcing himself on you," Chloe suggested in between bites of spicy pad Thai.

"Oh, no. I had it under control," Lissa assured her.

"It must have been scary."

"What? Oh, that? No, not really. He wasn't too badly behaved, just presumptuous. He stopped with the grabbing when I asked him to, and I convinced him to leave off and let me rejoin the party in exchange for my number. Men are idiots, but they are easy to appease."

"You gave him your number?!" Chloe got that strange feeling back in her stomach.

"Oh, sure. But I haven't answered one of his obnoxious texts. He's really the most maddening flirt I've ever met." Her voice was playful, rather than angry, and Chloe began to get suspicious.

"So...he wasn't forcing himself on you, then?"

"What? No...no, nothing like that. But he did put me in an awkward position. He knows I have a boyfriend and lied and connived to get me alone. It was despicable. Mira was right about him," Lissa said, playing with her noodles.

"Well, I'm glad it was not as bad as I thought, then," Chloe said, feeling a little misled. She remembered what Tía said about trusting her gut.

She was just about to ask Lissa to elaborate her story more, when Xaiden sat down next to her with his pizza and said, his mouth full of half-chewed peperoni, "You tell her about Mr. Uppity, then?"

Chloe looked from Xaiden to Lissa in confusion. "Who? Ryan? I'm not sure I'd call him that..."

Lissa shook her head. "No, no. That's in regards to Ryan's dad. One of Ryan's best friends was hanging out with Xaiden last night. Xaiden did some recon to find out more about the Bath family. Turns out Ryan isn't all that fond of his father, nor are the twins, from what John said. He had some interesting insight, having been Ryan's roommate when the Bath's mom died."

"Oh?" Chloe asked, curious but cautious. Michael was right. Nothing Lissa and Xaiden said about his family was to their credit.

Xaiden nodded, chewing another big bite of pizza before saying, "Yeah. John told me some weird shit. I guess their mom was young and healthy. Like, he stayed at Ryan's house the week before she died, and she was fine. Then, all of a sudden, a week later, right before Thanksgiving, she was dead. No one knew how. And Cream, that's John's nickname, said Michael was super rude and secretive about it when he tried to console him and his older brother at the funeral. Their old man is a real stiff piece of work. Wasn't at all nice to her, from what I hear. Very possessive. And there were rumors she was straying, if you know what I mean."

Chloe gasped, but Xaiden just shrugged, chewing and talking at the same time. "You want to be careful with that lot. Some of the nicest seeming people are only out to hurt you. You gotta trust what's out there in the open; no secrets. Look, I know I'm no Saint, but one thing I got is honesty. I call things as I see 'em, and that whole family is fishy. Combine that with Ryan trying to get with my sister last night and putting her in hot water with Ashton. Well, it don't look good."

Chloe played with her food, frowning over it. The picture this painted was very strange and off-putting. It made Chloe wonder about Michael's reserve. Was he reserved because he was shy and polite, or was he reserved for other reasons?

Lissa nodded solemnly along with her brother's account. "Also, Ryan told me that Michael and Mindy are supposed to be going home tonight, that they couldn't be going to the LSC because their dad wanted them home right after they finished finals. From what he said, they're both done with finals and headed home today. That's part of the reason I was so eager to see you today. I'm worried that Michael is still angry that you chose us over him yesterday and is putting on this whole thing about meeting up with you tonight just to stand you up. I don't like to think that someone would actually do something like that, but, well, I was worried when Ryan told me that..."

"When did he tell you that?" Chloe asked, wondering why Lissa was so friendly and talkative with someone she clearly didn't like, and also hurt by the implications that Michael was so duplicitous.

"Oh, last night when we were dancing. He kept asking me on a date tomorrow. I said I was going to go to the LSC in hopes to hang out with you and that his brother and sister would also be there. He told me that wasn't possible, as their dad ordered them home right away. He said something like, 'I don't ask how high when dad says jump, but the twins do.'"

Chloe shook her head. "I don't believe Michael would do that. He seemed genuinely happy to talk to me when I texted him yesterday."

Lissa shrugged. "Well, just in case, we'll save you seats when we get to the movie. We're going a little early to get good seats. But, if I were you, I'd text him and call him to order. Playing games is not okay. Make him tell you straight."

Chloe excused herself not long after that, feeling uncertain and self-conscious. She'd never known being interested in someone would be so complicated. She had a hard time believing that Lissa and Xaiden weren't willingly mistaken about the twin's plans, but she figured it wouldn't hurt to message to be sure.

On the way back to the hotel, she texted Michael: "Hey, Lissa heard from ur brother that u guys might not be able to make it 2 the movies tonight. I hope that's not true. She said maybe your dad wanted u home? She and Xaiden are coming to the movies, I guess, but I told them I was meeting u guys. Anyway, I wanted 2 just confirm I'd see u there 2night."

Her mind was a knot of anxiety as she waited for a reply. By the time she had walked all the way back to the hotel, she still hadn't received a reply. She felt a growing sense of unease. *It's true. He's not coming...*Tía was doing her hair and makeup in the bathroom when she got back to the room, but he still hadn't answered her text. After Tía was done with her makeup and hair, Chloe arranged hers better, and they left to catch the tour bus that would take them on their alumni association trip.

The museum housed some of the most famous, infamous, and interesting art Chloe had ever seen, but she was almost too distracted to take it in, as wonderful as it was, due to the deafening silence of her phone. She half-listened to Tía's explanations and exultations over the art, but was more morose than she'd like to be.

Thankfully, Bev had tagged along and was better company than she was. On the bus back to MIT and the walk back to the hotel, Chloe was just as quiet. Bev accompanied them and kept up amiable chatter with Tía, which was good since Chloe only grew more and more morose with each passing hour.

Finally, after what seemed a lifetime, but was actually only a few hours after she'd first texted, Michael messaged back. It was a very long message, which immediately put Chloe on edge. Long messages were not often good ones.

"Sorry for not answering sooner. I was taking a final and left my phone in my dorm. I was a little offended by ur text & had to take time to think what to say. After how Lissa treated u yesterday, I'm surprised u place faith in her. If u still keep company of two such people, I'm not sure u and I should hang out. I did plan on being at the LSC tonight, but if u prefer the company of the Thorne's, I'll make myself scarce. I don't want to be around two people who harangue me & my family behind my back. I hope u enjoy the rest of ur stay in the city."

Chloe, in agony, could not think what to say to such a resoundingly final goodbye. Her question had been innocent, but Michael had not taken it as such. She tried replying several times, but it all seemed so hopeless. She realized she'd spent much of their short acquaintance accidentally offending Michael, and she wondered if someone who could not think better of her was worth the grief his words caused her. All the same, she could not keep tears from spilling out of her eyes, leaving tracks down her dark cheeks.

~ Thirteen ~

A GIRL CAN BUY HER OWN DAMN POPCORN!

Tía explained to Chloe how to get to the LSC, though she thought her niece seemed less enthusiastic about going than she'd been earlier. Chloe hadn't shared what was eating at her with Tía. She didn't want to ruin Tía's fun trip with silly teenage drama. Chloe might have even stayed at the hotel if she hadn't thought Tía would have stayed back with her instead of going out with Bev and a few of their new acquaintances from the museum visit.

She also didn't want Michael's opinion of her to keep her from having fun on this once in a lifetime trip. So, though she was not keen to have to put up with Xaiden's trying advances or even Lissa's probable half-truths, she was determined to enjoy the movie, and was even more determined not to let the moods or whims of other people keep her from enjoying the first trip out of Williamston she'd taken.

She walked the now familiar paths around MIT, looking for building 26, where Tía told her she'd find the LSC. She took a few wrong turns around the campus in the semi-darkness, though there was no real darkness in the city. There were always lights on–streaming through windows, pouring down from street lamps and shining from the ever-present vehicle traffic surrounding MIT.

She boldly asked a group of laughing young women where building 26 was, and they kindly put her to rights. She felt a strange sense of accomplishment walking into the building without a friend at her side, scanning the entrance for room 100, which was not at all hard to find. It was just off to her right, inside the building. A small crowd already streamed into the hall, faces glowing with eagerness, or turned down looking at their phones.

So it was that Chloe Mora found herself in front of lecture hall 26-100 ready for a night out. A movie poster for the showing was displayed on a plastic A-Frame floor sign outside the lecture hall. The movie poster was in sepia tones and displayed a grainy closeup of a young Tom Cruise with creepy intense blue eyes, holding what she could only suppose was a victim to his shoulder. There was also a man on a street bench, looking cold, alone, and forlorn. Having done some research, she guessed that the man was probably a young Brad Pitt. A strange doll-like girl stood near the bench, pale and intense. She knew this to be a young Kirsten Dunst, and was eager to see what she was like as a child actress.

She got into the ticket line, which fed into a popcorn and drink line. She bought popcorn and a drink from MIT students standing behind white fold up tables with the card Tía had left her for cab rides or snacks, which she hadn't used the night before. After thanking the Japanese girl who helped her pick the fullest popcorn, then topped it off a little more, she scanned the room for Lissa and Xaiden's golden blonde heads.

The hall wasn't that big, and she didn't notice the brother and sister. This annoyed her a little since the movie was set to start in five minutes and they'd said they were coming early. She was struck, again, with the inconsistency of the sibling's words as compared to their actions. She stubbornly did not look for the Bath twins, not even sure they would be there after the text she'd received earlier from Michael. Though still hurt by his unwillingness to believe her good intentions, there was a little guilt sprinkled in with the hurt. She chose not to examine that feeling for the moment.

Chloe was determined not to let the actions or thoughts of other people ruin her enjoyment of the show. She made her way down the rows to find a seat not too close to the screen, and sat in a hard-backed, wooden lecture chair near the middle of the lecture hall. She swung the armrest table up and set her popcorn and drink on it, feeling a little out of place, but also excited to be alone, surrounded by people she didn't know, about to watch a creepy movie in a strange city. She felt something stir inside her, the thrill of independence that she'd never known before.

She silenced her phone as a student welcomed everyone over the intercom. The lights dimmed and the huge, hanging projection screen came to life. The students first showed a few trailers for their fall-themed movie showcase–a lot of older Halloween and monster themed movies like the one they were about to watch, including some black and white wordless movies that piqued Chloe's interest and made her wish she could stay longer. If she lived close, she could make this a habit of her new, independent life. A third trailer was just playing when she felt a tap on her shoulder. She turned, expecting to find Lissa or Xaiden, but was surprised to see Mindy smiling down at her.

"Hi, Chloe! Is the seat next to you taken?" Mindy asked, her eyes apologetic.

Chloe smiled brightly, not at all upset with Mindy. Mindy hadn't *once* accused her of bad intentions. She'd been very empathetic and kind.

"On, no. Please sit. I'm so glad you came," Chloe said, indicating the seat to her right.

"We both came. Michael is getting popcorn. He showed me your text earlier, and I told him he was being a cad. Anyway, I hope it's okay if I want to be civil, even if silly brothers with big egos can't seem to be." Mindy winked.

Chloe smiled. "It's alright. I sort of understand. I second guessed him and made it sound like I was choosing other people's company over his, *again*. I really wasn't. I told the Thornes I was coming to spend time with you two. I can't seem to make everyone happy and I don't like to hurt *anyone's* feelings. I was just trying to be tactful."

Mindy nodded, but said, "Sometimes, we can't always help but step on toes in life. As long as you're not compromising your own happiness in the process, I wouldn't worry about it."

Chloe gave Mindy a searching look. "I guess I don't really know how to manage it all yet. I'm not used to having so many people want to be around me. It's not that I don't know my own mind. I guess I'm just used to *giving*. I have a lot of younger siblings and we don't have much. I've always had to be the responsible one, the peacekeeper."

Mindy patted her hand. "You'll find your way. Ah, there's Michael. Oh! And the movie's starting! Yay! I think you'll like it."

Michael nodded abruptly toward the girls, without meeting Chloe's eye, and sat on his sister's right, keeping a seat open between them. This choice screamed, "I am not sitting with you."

Chloe nodded curtly back and shared a private smile with Mindy, who rolled her eyes and mouthed "Boys!"

Three minutes into the film, a ruckus to Chloe's left announced the arrival of Lissa and Xaiden. People in the row behind them shushed and complained at the siblings as they noisily made their way down the aisle where Chloe sat.

Lissa explained in a loud whisper that they were at Xaiden's frat house and missed the train they wanted to catch. Chloe motioned that they should sit but said nothing. Lissa nodded and sat down two chairs from Chloe, leaving the seat next to Chloe for her brother. Chloe sighed inwardly.

Xaiden sat down beside her, glaring past her at Michael, who'd refused to acknowledge the siblings at all. Michael's eyes were so fixedly glued to the screen that it was painfully obvious he was trying to act as indifferent as possible. It was almost funny, except that Chloe couldn't find the humor in having to manage Xaiden's tedious company again.

For a while, Chloe was so sucked into the movie that she forgot about being in the middle of a conflict she never wanted. The world of Lestat and Louis was dark, disturbing, and sexy. She felt a little embarrassed to watch some of these scenes next to Xaiden, though. He kept raising his eyebrows at her and smiling every time Lestat manhandled a busty woman. Chloe pretended not to notice his suggestive glances.

She shoved her left hand under her leg after Xaiden's hand drifted over to her arm rest. She suspected he was trying to make an opportunity to hold her hand, and hoped he would take the hint, but he didn't seem very good at reading body language. She came up with the genius idea of offering her popcorn to him, in order to occupy his wandering hand, which distracted him for a while. Unfortunately, he devoured the entire bag, which left Chloe hungry, as she'd not had dinner.

Mindy looked at Chloe sitting on her own hand and shook her head. When the intermission screen came up for the movie, Chloe immediately stood, her hand numb, and asked Mindy to allow her past, so she could use the restroom and buy some more popcorn. Mindy followed Chloe, cutting Xaiden off from following right behind her.

"I'm going to use the bathroom, too. I'll come with you," Mindy said.

When Chloe got to where Michael sat, he stood and walked out of the aisle to allow her to pass, avoiding her gaze. Chloe's face fell, but she thanked him kindly. Mindy made a face at her brother that said she'd like nothing more than to smack him.

"Michael, would you mind buying me some popcorn? I'm going to the bathroom with Chloe. Actually, get her some, too, if you would. *Someone* ate all of hers," Mindy ordered her twin in a voice that broached no argument.

Xaiden followed behind the girls and heard Mindy's pointed remark. "Don't worry about getting popcorn for Chloe, Michael. I'll get it." He winked at Chloe. "I don't mind spoiling my favorite girl."

Chloe felt her face grow hot. "Please, neither of you bother. I have my own money and can buy my own popcorn after I use the restroom."

With that, she stormed past both impossible men, Mindy following in her wake. Lissa, oblivious to her surroundings, yelled after her brother to get her popcorn and a drink while he was up, and texted in a distracted, bored way. Mindy waited for Chloe outside of the bathroom and put a hand on her arm when she exited it, stopping her in her agitated tracks.

"Chloe, do you want to switch seats when we sit back down? I noticed how uncomfortable you looked sitting next to Xaiden. I promise this is not a ploy to get you to sit next to my brother. I apologize about the popcorn thing. You're right. You don't need anyone to speak for you. Women can buy their own damn popcorn. He can date his ego, for all I care. I just...I think you're very cool and fun and I'm sorry you are in such a weird position. This is why I don't date men! Though, honestly, dating women is almost as bad."

Chloe laughed in a relieved way. "I *would* like to switch seats, please. My hand is still numb from sitting on it. I wish I knew how to say what needs to be said in a way that won't hurt anyone's feelings. I just came tonight to watch a movie. I would rather Xaiden hadn't come if he was going to make it awkward. I don't have any plans for romance, and I just want to go somewhere without having to make myself small!" Her voice had risen a little, and she blushed. "I'm sorry. I'm frustrated."

Mindy patted her back. "Don't apologize for speaking your mind. Let's go get you some popcorn before Xaiden cleans them out."

Chloe laughed. "I'm so hungry."

"And candy," Mindy added, winding her arm through Chloe's.

"And candy," Chloe agreed.

When the girls returned to the lecture hall, they made immediately for the food line. Before they could get far in the line, however, Xaiden pushed past a crowd of students and shoved some popcorn into Chloe's hands.

"No need, girl. I told you I had you. I got you something else, too," Xaiden dug around in his pocket. Chloe dearly wished he hadn't bought the popcorn and was very much hoping he hadn't bought a candy bar and put it inside his pants pocket. Eating a partially melted pocket candy bar from Xaiden was where she drew the line. She would never be hungry enough to eat melted chocolate that'd been in Xaiden's hot jeans.

Instead, he shoved something onto her wrist after pulling her out of the food line. Xaiden didn't pride himself on being a clever person, but he was a doggedly determined one. He was used to getting his way. One sure way to win over the heart of a woman, he found by way of watching his sister, was through expensive gifts.

Without waiting for Chloe to react, he said, "Chloe, I know this is fast, but I really like you, and I want us to be more than friends. I saw you admiring this at the store, and I bought it for you, in hopes you would consider it a fitting gift for a boyfriend to give to his girl. I want you to be mine, and I want everyone to know it. What do you say?"

Chloe, shocked and embarrassed by the very public display, balked. She lifted her wrist to see the skull bracelet she'd barely glanced at in the jewelry store on her wrist. She felt a bit nauseous. Michael approached the group with his own bag of popcorn and handed it to Mindy.

"I was going to ask if you needed popcorn, after all, Chloe, but I see Xaiden has taken care of it." His eyes fell on the bracelet. He looked resigned rather than angry, as if his questions had at least been answered.

Xaiden's face was smug and confident. He put his arm around Chloe's shoulder in a familiar way and made to kiss her on the cheek, having assured himself before even waiting for a reaction that his gift would win him the heart of our heroine. Unfortunately, the tone-deaf gift and the attempted kiss were the last straws that toppled the patience of even our saintly Chloe Mora.

Suddenly, Chloe was very angry, angrier than she'd ever been. She shrugged out from under Xaiden's arm, shoved her bag of popcorn at him and removed the bracelet from her wrist.

She tried to keep an even tone, but it came out colder than she intended. "Xaiden, I am sorry if you felt misled into thinking I wanted more than friendship, but you are mistaken. That was never my intention. I hoped my disinterest was clear, but I see I'll have to be more direct.

Please return the bracelet. It's too nice a gift for friendship. I can't accept it." She handed the bracelet back to him.

Xaiden looked completely flabbergasted by this reaction, not having ever bothered to learn signs of disinterest that could not advance his desires. His face went through a volley of emotions before finally settling on anger. He shoved the bracelet back into his pocket, his green eyes blazing in indignation.

"I know why you can't be bothered to be more than my friend." He looked from Chloe to Michael, who Chloe had yet to acknowledge. "My gift wasn't *expensive* enough for your taste. Don't think I don't know what rich women are after. It's never enough with you rich bitches. Whatever. Chase the prize pig. See if I care." He pushed the popcorn back into her arms, and made a bee-line for his sister, yelling, "Lissa, let's go. I'm done with this shit."

Chloe was shocked and appalled by Xaiden's unfair insinuations and deeply embarrassed by the crowd of faces turned her way; she found herself speechless against such insanity.

Rich bitch? How had he ever gotten that impression? The man is completely blind.

She turned to Mindy and said, "When did I ever give the impression I was rich? Or even slightly interested in him?"

Mindy shook her head, bewildered. Michael's face was conflicted, but he managed to ask her, "Are you alright? Do you want to leave, or..."

"Talking to me now, I see? No! I came here to watch this movie and I'm going to finish it. Even better, I'm going to enjoy it now because I have popcorn and I don't have to sit on my hands until they're numb in order to avoid hurting an idiot's feelings! If I've accidentally offended you, too, feel free to make a dramatic scene and storm out. I don't exist to appease anyone's fragile ego!"

She walked past Michael, who was wearing a bemused rather than angry expression, and returned to her seat just as she saw Lissa vacate the row and slip out after her brother in a huff, her grass green eyes narrowed Chloe's way.

Good riddance.

Chloe chewed her popcorn and ignored the sidelong glances of a few people who'd seen Xaiden's embarrassing display. Mindy sat down next to her a few minutes later and slid a bag of fruit chew candies to her. She smiled at her friend and eagerly opened the bag, quickly locating all the pink ones while the intermission lights were still on. Strawberry fruit chews were the best remedy for her hanger.

"Thanks, Mindy," she murmured.

"You're awesome," Mindy answered back, smiling hugely.

The second half of the movie was even better than the first, made much more so by the absence of the Thorne siblings. It wasn't until they were gone that Chloe realized how on edge she felt around *both* of them. When the lights came up, Chloe smiled over at Mindy and noticed Michael had left. She wondered if he'd ever sat back down. She'd refused to look over at him at first, then forgot to as the movie intensified. Her heart dropped at his absence, but she didn't let it show.

"What'd you think?" Mindy asked, following Chloe out of the lecture hall.

"I loved it! It was a lot darker than I'm used to, but *really* well done. Sort of a grown-up *Twilight*," Chloe mused.

Mindy smiled. "It is, isn't it? I'm glad you decided to stay and finish it. I admire what you did in there, by the way. You really stood up for yourself."

"I should have done so sooner, I think. There probably would have been fewer hurt feelings," Chloe sighed.

Mindy smiled, revealing her agreement without saying anything that would rub salt on the wound. "You going back to the hotel now?"

"Yes, Tía will be back by now and expecting me. What about you? Are you okay getting back to BU? I see Michael left."

"Oh, no, he's here. Bathroom, I think. Do you need us to escort you back to the hotel?"

As much as Chloe liked the idea of spending more time with Mindy and even Michael, as stubborn as he'd been, she shook her head. "It's not far, and this place is never too dark or solitary. I thought the city would be scarier, but it's not so bad."

Mindy smiled. "Yes, I think you'll be safe from vampires roaming the city streets. But text me when you get there?"

Chloe promised she would and took her leave before Michael returned. She wasn't upset with him, really, but she had begun to wonder if bending over backward to impress a man she barely knew was really worth the effort. Besides, if she chose to come to Boston for school, she wanted it to be for the right reasons. She wanted it to be for *her*, not anyone else.

All the same, her dreams that night exposed her inner preoccupations.

***

She was on MIT's campus, but it was absolutely still, for once. A fog lay heavy under dim streetlamps, so that it was hard to see where she was walking. She couldn't even remember why she was out here. Going to a movie, maybe? She was looking for a different building, not the LSC, but her brain couldn't tell her why.

There was no friendly gaggle of women to ask along the way. The sidewalks were eerily absent of life. Chloe couldn't even hear the sound of traffic constantly humming through the busy side streets running parallel to the campus.

She did hear a sound, however-a clicking of shoes against the pavement. Every time she stopped, they stopped. She turned to see if anyone was following her, but met only emptiness-cold, dark buildings, and fog.

She swallowed, her heart pounding. "Is...Is anyone there? I heard you. Come out."

A figure wearing a dark velvet coat embroidered with scarlet flowers-an old, otherworldly fashion-stepped out from behind a brick building. Under his coat, his shirt was cream colored, flowing satin. The man stepped into the light of the streetlamps, the glow of which painted his golden hair almost white.

Chloe swallowed hard. "Xaiden? Are you okay? Look, I'm sorry if I hurt your feelings..."

Xaiden strolled toward her lazily, holding up a hand to silence her. "Not at all. You're not the only snack in the world. Though I admit you would have been a delicious conquest."

Chloe's stomach turned. She didn't like the way he spoke about her, as if she were something to be consumed. His green eyes were more vibrant, they almost glowed against the darkness. He'd been twenty feet away from her, but, inhumanely fast, he was there, at her side. She made to put distance between them, but he had a tight hold on her wrist. Chloe struggled against his grasp, like a vice around her wrist. It was no use.

"Let me go," she demanded, her voice cold. "I told you I'm not interested."

"A pity, I'm sure. I couldn't possibly just take what I want..." He ran a finger down her neck, and she shivered and pulled back. "But no. I see your heart, which is why I invited a friend."

A swish and a flash of motion behind her made her turn around. She was met by the figure of a second man, a taller, darker man. Xaiden pushed her toward the other man, who caught her in a loose, unwilling grip. She stared into the caramel eyes of Michael.

His eyes didn't used to be so light in color, but they were now. And they were achingly sad. Inside those eyes raged an inner turmoil-anger, hunger, grief, and disgust. Disgust and hunger seemed to be the two strongest emotions, and they played across his handsome features in a way that made Chloe pull away. Which emotion was he directing at her and which did he reserve for himself? Michael, too, wore a loose satin shirt over drawstring brown pants, but he wore no fancy velvet coat. His hair was longer than she remembered and pulled back into a ponytail away from the sharp angles of his face. He seemed thinner than before-starving.

"Michael? Are you okay?"

Michael flinched at his name and looked away from Chloe. He spoke to the ground, not daring to look at her. "Chloe, go away. Get out of here."

Chloe, hurt by the coldness in his voice, turned to go, but ran directly into Xaiden's linebacker frame. It was like running into a brick wall. He smiled in a way that made Chloe shiver. His feelings were not complicated. Hunger shone in his unearthly green eyes.

"You won't be going anywhere, Chloe. Michael needs you; he's chosen you. He doesn't know it, yet, but he has."

As fast as a viper striking, Xaiden ran a sharp nail down Chloe's neck. She felt a steady trickle of warm blood slide down her neck and onto her chest. Her head swam and the images of fog, Xaiden and streetlamps danced a slow, swirling dance around her.

She swayed. Xaiden took a step away from her. He was going to let her fall. But she didn't fall. Strong arms caught her up and wrapped around her like an embrace. Xaiden smiled, his eyes victorious. But it was not his arms that caught her up.

Michael held Chloe tight, meeting her gaze. His eyes were frantic, almost crazed. They ran from her eyes to the trail of blood trickling down her neck, between her breasts. Her ridiculously elevated breasts! A very tight rose embroidered under-bust corset boosted her chest so that her breasts were almost touching her chin. It would have been funny if Michael's eyes weren't so crazed, so hungry. He leaned toward her. Chloe let go of the fight. If she had to die under the lips of any man, he would be her choice.

His tongue brushed her neck and a thrill shot through her. "This is not who I am," he whispered fiercely against her neck, letting his grip on her go. He lay her gently down on the ground and walked away from her.

"No! Michael, no. Don't leave me to him. Take me, please!"

Michael didn't turn back, though. His back was rigid with raging emotions, but he would not turn to look at her. Xaiden swooped in over her. "Well, we can't say we didn't give him a chance, huh Chloe? Oh, well. Waste not..."

His green eyes turned red, and his fangs were the last thing she saw...

~ Fourteen ~

A POCKET FULL OF CONDOMS AND A HEAD FULL OF DREAMS

Chloe was startled awake by Tía hopping on one foot and flinging Spanish words about. Chloe didn't know the words, which is what made her sure they were curse words.

"You ok, Tía?" Chloe asked her cursing aunt, who sat heavily on her niece's bed, prodding her injured foot.

"I *would* kick the dresser with my injured foot," Tía replied. "Ay, Dios! That hurts!"

Chloe saw real pain in Tía's eyes. "Are you okay, Tía? Can you walk at all? Should I call someone?"

Tía waved the concern away and tried to stand, only to fall back down on the bed, her face contorted in pain. "Oh! Oh, shit...bad idea. No, no. I don't think I can. Maldito pie!"

Chloe, never having seen her tough as nails aunt in pain, felt very out of her depth. "Should I call an ambulance, Tía? Or see if the front desk has a wheelchair?"

"You know, that's not a bad idea. The wheelchair, that is. But, no." She grimaced and took a deep breath. "No ambulance. I'll call Bev, see if she's working today. The wheelchair would be good, if they have one."

Chloe threw on a hoodie over her pajamas and ran downstairs to the lobby, her hands shaking. Her frantic entrance roused the sleepy-looking receptionist. She raised a perfectly arched eyebrow over dark brown eyes. "Can I help you, Miss?"

"I know it's a long shot, but do you have a wheelchair? My Tía re-injured her hurt foot, and I think I need to get her to the doctor."

The receptionist ran her hands nervously over the shaved hair on each side of her head. The short, black afro on the top of her head bobbed as she nodded. "Actually, yes, we do have a wheelchair. Is she bleeding? Does she need an ambulance?"

Chloe shook her head. "She's not bleeding. Just in pain. I think she's calling a friend for a ride, but I'll let you know if we need anything else."

"What room are you? I'll bring the chair up."

"203. Thank you so much."

Chloe ran back up the stairs and found Tía on the phone with Bev.

"Thank you, Bev. I really appreciate it. Yeah...Oh! Ow!...No, no, just really hurts and is swelling. I don't know...an 8? Okay, see you soon." Tía hung up the phone.

"Chloe, dear. Get me a blanket, will you? I don't think I can pull sweats over these pajama shorts with my foot swelling like it is. Bev's coming to pick us up. She has a townhouse in Boston, so she's not far. Get ready, mija."

Chloe rushed to get Tía a blanket, her heart aching for her poor aunt. Tía's foot was badly swollen. It was twice the size of her other foot, with mottled purple bruising standing out against her brown skin. Chloe's heart raced. She tore off her pjs and replaced them with jeans, before hurriedly fixing her hair into a messy bun, and tying her shoes. By the time Chloe had her shoes tied, the receptionist had brought the chair to wheel Tía to the lobby.

***

Mass General was not a far drive, but traffic made it a lot longer than it should be, even with Bev behind the wheel. It seemed Tía's friend knew every side road and detour imaginable. When they finally arrived at the hospital, Bev was able to park in her parking spot, which was not very far from a windowed walkway that read Massachusetts General Hospital.

Chloe wheeled Tía, who was grimacing in pain, into the entrance under the massive white building. It was the biggest hospital she'd ever seen. Inside, much to her surprise, Bev passed the reception desk up completely and waved for Chloe to follow her.

The male receptionist said, "Good morning, Dr. Ikeda. You're supposed to be on vacation."

Bev turned around. She stood before a double swinging door and addressed the brunette. "Hello, Brian. My friend Dr. Mora wanted to make our vacation more exciting. I'll take her to my office. Who are our radiologists today?"

"We're a little low today. Dr. B is the only radiologist not currently occupied," Brian answered.

"Okay. I'm bringing Miranda to my office. Could you let him know I need his help with a scan on Dr. Mora's foot when he has a spare moment?"

"I will. Should I have a nurse come by your office to help with vitals and paperwork and all that?" Brian asked. "I think Sheila just got here."

"Oh, no. I know you're all busy. I'll take care of it," Bev answered, taking a clipboard from Brian with a nod of thanks.

Chloe followed Bev through the double doors, past several patient rooms to an elevator. They took the elevator to an upper floor with several offices and quieter, less busy patient rooms and halls.

The office Bev had them go to had the name badges of several doctors off to the side of the door on little metal plaques. Bev explained that this was just a temporary office that she and a few of the other doctors used for paperwork. She ushered Chloe and Tía inside and had Chloe park Tía by the window overlooking the city. A standing desk stood in the opposite corner, a large wardrobe stood on the far wall, and a black file cabinet sat stoutly across from them, next to the doorway. It was a sparse space with only two chairs and minimal decor.

"I'm going to go grab an ice pack, another blanket, and put in for a scan. I'll be right back. Fill this out for insurance, Miranda." Bev handed her friend the clipboard and patted her shoulder. "I'll snag you some painkillers, too. You're pale. How's the pain level?"

Tía shook her head. "Not great."

"Be right back."

Chloe took the clipboard from Tía and asked her the questions, filling out the long forms, so that her Tía could move as little as possible. When they'd almost completed the second to last form, Bev was back with a rolling IV, a blanket over her right shoulder, an icepack on her left shoulder and a stool in her free hand. Thankfully, Chloe heard her coming and opened the door.

Bev had blue doctor gloves on and had found a mask and jacket somewhere to wear over her yellow sleeveless blouse and navy slacks. She propped her friend's foot up on the stool, securing the ice pack around it and a pillow under it. Her black hair fell around her angular face while she worked, but she didn't seem to notice. She gossiped about people she and Tía both knew while she deftly slid the IV into Tía's inner arm. Tía laughed when she realized she didn't even feel the IV until it was in. Bev was, Chloe realized, a fantastic doctor. She was funny, kind, quick and efficient.

"I have you on a painkiller and anti-inflammatory, Miranda. It'll probably make you a little loopy. You just sit back and relax for a minute. I'm going to bring these papers to reception. Chloe, don't let her move."

Chloe shook her head. "I won't, Dr. Ikeda."

"Oh, stop that. Call me Bev, dear." With that, she swept out of the room, all efficiency and grace.

Minutes later, the door opened again. Chloe was readjusting Tía's warm, white hospital blanket and didn't look up when she said, "That *was* fast, Bev."

A deep, accented voice answered, "Dr. and Ms. Mora, I presume?"

Bev had a habit of speaking in a higher register than was natural for her, and she didn't have a posh English accent. Chloe turned toward the voice, blushing a bit. "Oh, sorry. I thought you were Dr. Ikeda. Yes, I'm Chloe Mora and this is my aunt, Dr. Miranda Mora."

The tall, thin doctor nodded. He had extremely blue eyes, a very symmetrical face, except for a slightly long nose, and had somewhat curly brunette hair, which was styled carefully away from his eyes. He was very handsome, apart from the permanent frown line in the middle of his forehead. That, and his eyes lacked the warmth you like to see in a doctor.

Chloe didn't have to ask who this person was. His son, Ryan, looked the very picture of him, apart from the fact that Ryan had a tad more melanin in his complexion.

"Dr. Bath? Oh, are you Mindy and Michael's dad, then?" Chloe asked. Dr. B from radiology, as Brian had called him, was Dr. Bath. Of course! Bev told Tía she worked with him, after all.

"Yes, Ms. Mora. I am very charmed to finally meet you both. My oldest son mentioned that you and Dr. Mora," he inclined his head her way, "were at the alumni events and that you've made the acquaintance of my twins. Ryan, I believe, said he met you in the acquaintance of some of his football friends recently."

Chloe didn't correct Dr. Bath. She wanted to say she'd met Ryan at a frat party where his liberal hands and wandering eyes had hurt a very good young man.

She simply smiled and said, "Yes, I've been to brunch and to the LSC with both Mindy and Michael. They also both accompanied us at an alumni association tour event."

Chloe smiled, remembering how happy that day had been. She thought fondly of how sweet and gentlemanly Michael was when he was not being forced in the company of those who mistreated him.

"The twins are more in their own confidences than mine, so I did not know you were so well acquainted. That said, I'm happy to hear it. Dr. Mora, you are renowned for your work. If your Chloe is half as hardworking and intelligent as you, I am very happy my twins made such a friend."

Tía, loopy on meds, did her best to keep up with the Doctor. "She is my most darling girl."

For some reason, this comment seemed to soften Dr. Bath's harsh features. His frown line disappeared, and some of his icy reserve melted away. "How about I take you for your scan? You can tell me *all* about her."

Tía seemed to think this an amenable idea, so she allowed Dr. Bath to adjust her foot and wheel her out of the room. Dr. Bath let Chloe know they'd be only a few minutes and that she could relax. Chloe sat on one of the vacant chairs in the nearly empty room and closed her eyes, tiredly.

She wasn't sure how much time had passed when the door opened again and Bev, Dr. Bath and Tía, a goofy smile on her face, came back into the room. Chloe stood and helped Dr. Bath get Tía into a comfortable position, while Bev elevated her foot once again.

Dr. Bath nodded at Bev. "It's settled, then. She'll need at least three days of bed rest if the swelling is to go down. No fracture, but the surgery site was aggravated by the blunt trauma. I do believe some of her wandering might also have exacerbated it. She needs someone who will make her be still."

Tía frowned, slurring a little when she said, "Lo siento, mija. I'm afraid I'm going to be rather boring for the last couple of days we are in Boston. I so looked forward to showing you a few more sights, too."

Chloe shushed her aunt. "Don't you worry about me. You worry about getting better. I can entertain myself, you know."

Bev looked at Tía and shook her head. "I think you both should come stay at my townhouse. It's not very big, but I don't get to see Miranda often and I can keep her company and ensure she's taking her medication and getting rest."

Tía smiled at Bev. "You are a good friend, Bev. I don't want to be a burden, though."

"Nonsense, it's settled. We'll check you out of your hotel today and into Hotel Ikeda."

Dr. Bath cleared his throat, which Bev took as an indication that he was asking to return to his other duties. She nodded to him. "Thank you, Dr. Bath, for your help running that scan quickly. We truly appreciate it."

"That is no trouble at all," the stiff man said, trying a friendly smile and just managing it. "I was thinking...I hope I'm not overstepping any bounds here, and please tell me if I am, Dr. Mora. What do you say to my twins inviting your niece to our house in Salem for a few days? That way, she will be cared for *and* entertained while you get the rest you need. She can see what lies outside of the city proper and my children can escort Chloe and show her around their hometown for a few days. She could have a little adventure and vacation with new friends, and you can have rest and time with Dr. Ikeda."

He caught the uncertainty in Tía's face, and held up his hands placatingly. "Of course, it's completely up to you, Dr. Mora. If you have other plans, please do not hesitate to say so. I also understand if you don't feel right leaving her in my care on such a short acquaintance. I have a couple of rounds I need to do. I'll leave you to discuss the possibility. Dr. Ikeda, you have my number, I believe. I won't bring it up to the twins until you've had time to talk it over." With that, Dr. Bath gave them a brief nod and left the room.

Tía looked at Bev. "Tell me about Dr. Bath."

Bev shrugged. "He's a bit of a stick in the mud, honestly. Not much of a sense of humor. Very hard-working, very meticulous in his looks and in his doctoring. Keeps the chit chat to a minimum at work, but is more direct than unkind. The nurses say he's a bit of a prick about lecturing them, but I've never heard any other unsavory reports."

Chloe remembered what the Thorne twins reported about Dr. Bath and thought maybe they'd added a few details to liven up the man's unlikeability. He seemed a little standoffish, perhaps, maybe a little intimidating, but not nearly as bad as they'd said. She found that to be the case with many of the things the Thornes said.

"Do you think he's trustworthy?" Tía asked.

Bev shrugged. "Honestly, yes. I think he's a bit conceited. The only reason I have to dislike him, really, is because he refuses to call me Bev. I suspect it's because he's not comfortable with trans folk, though he's never said that. Of course, he could just be one of those uber formal people. He would fit the bill, after all. But I can't really say. It's up to you, Miranda. I'm happy to have you both, if you don't think it's a good idea."

Chloe, having watched with quiet intensity this discussion between the two adults, decided it was time she spoke up for herself, just as she had last night. She had a very clear opinion on the topic.

Going to Salem?! It was too good to be true. She was a hardcore *Hocus Pocus* fan for life. She'd made seven *Hocus Pocus* themed outfits over her sewing career and had even brought one along.

Dr. Bath could be a complete ass and she'd put up with it all to see Salem! Even if Michael was still upset with her, Mindy was such a dear. She just knew this was one of those life changing, heroine making moments, and she couldn't keep silent any longer.

"Tía, I would never leave you, if you needed me, but if my opinion holds any sway, I'm absolutely *dying* to see Salem. They have a witch museum, Tía! *Hocus Pocus* was filmed there!" Chloe realized she was almost squealing and quieted her enthusiasm. "I mean, but only if you really, really don't need me. I'm happy to stay and help here. Really."

Tía and Bev looked at each other and broke out laughing. Bev put a hand on her friend's shoulder. "Let the poor kid go, Miranda. I do believe it would break her heart if you didn't."

Tía sighed and smiled. "If I hadn't met the wonderful twins, I would be more hesitant. They are good friends and good people. Besides, me and the twins have a deal, still. They are to get you to fall in love with the East Coast, so I can keep you here. If you message twice a day to check in, you can go."

"Oh!" Bev rushed out of the room in a flurry that made Tía and Chloe stare after her in bewilderment.

Seconds later, she rushed back in. "Chloe, as a doctor and a friend, I feel it's my responsibility to do this. I am sorry in advance, but I saw how you looked at Dr. Bath's dishy son and I feel it's necessary."

The right pocket on Bev's white coat was bulging a bit. She pulled out a handful of condoms. "There are several kinds here. Penises are as diverse as the people who wear them, so I got a variety. This is not me saying, 'You must have sex because you saw a good-looking young man.' This is me asking you to always be prepared for it, should you decide to. It's your choice, but my motto is come prepared."

"Bev, you made a pun! *Cum* prepared..." Tía laughed so hard she jostled her foot and cried out in pain.

"Let your own loins be your guide, love. Not his," Bev said, chuckling.

"Ay, dios, Bev, you old perv. Mija, Corazón y cabeza. Head and heart. That is your guide. Young loins are stupid. Believe me. If they weren't, I wouldn't have dated Daisy Rice."

Bev laughed uproariously at this. Chloe thought it very likely she'd turned completely crimson in embarrassment.

"How much sex do you think I plan on having, Bev? Jeez!" She took only four of the condoms if only to keep the women from making more sex puns.

Chloe shoved the condoms in her purse, her face scarlet, but her heart strangely warm. After all the *interesting* dreams she'd been having lately, she couldn't rule out any possibilities. And as much as she loved and admired her parents, she wasn't interested in being pregnant before nineteen. She had many things she wanted to do, and she wasn't sure parenting was one of them.

~ Fifteen ~

BATH TIME AT 5:20 SHARP AND NOT A MINUTE LATER!

Bev took care of checking Chloe and Tía out of their hotel room and setting Tía up in her spare room. Dr. Bath and the twins would be headed back to Salem by train later in the day. Chloe was to meet them at North station for the 5:45 train at about 5:20. Chloe texted Mindy immediately after Tía said she could go to check to make sure Mindy was amenable to the idea. The last thing she wanted was to be an unwanted guest.

Mindy texted back immediately with a happy heart-eyed emoji and exclamation marks. She must have texted Michael the plan not long after she received the news because Chloe got another notification after getting Mindy's approval.

Michael's text read, "I hope your Tía is okay? Sounds like my father was quite taken with you. He's normally very introverted and private. Whatever caused the change in his normal, standoffish behavior, I'm happy you're coming. It'll give me the opportunity to say I'm sorry for being an ass."

Chloe, smiling over the semi-apology, wrote back, "I don't know how charming I could have been. I was half asleep and still in my pj shirt, but I feel very lucky all the same. I've always wanted to see Salem. I'd suffer more moodiness if it meant I could walk the streets where *Hocus Pocus* was filmed!"

Michael texted back a laughing emoji and wrote back, "Hocus Pocus was mostly filmed in Burbank." Then finished it off with a cheeky tongue out emoji.

"You're off to a rough start on not being an ass."

"Lol. I'll promise to try harder. See you soon."

"SYS."

Tía, addled and sleepy, begged Chloe to take the pepper spray that was attached to her keychain and would not take no for an answer. "I can't be there with you, but I want to know you are as safe as possible. I don't suspect you'll need it, or I wouldn't agree to let you go, but take it anyway. And hold it out at arm's length and turn your head if you use it. That way, you won't get caught in the spray."

Chloe sighed and clipped the pepper spray to her beaded purse, looking at the fancy blown glass clock sitting on Bev's modern black pipe and white board fireplace mantle. "We should get going, Bev, don't you think?" she asked.

Bev nodded. "She will be fine, Miranda. You and I were younger than her when we left the nest. She has condoms, pepper spray, and money left on the card you gave her, right Chloe?"

Chloe nodded. "Yes, I have more than I need." She patted her purple bag. "Now, please rest, Tía. Dr. Bath said you needed to chill and Bev agrees."

Tía Mora smiled sadly. "Okay, go go. Call your mama and papa tonight and call me."

"I will. I promise. We'll be late if we don't go, though. I'll message every day," Chloe promised.

***

Bev pulled up to the station about three minutes after 5:20, but considering the traffic, that was a pretty impressive feat. She immediately saw Mindy, Michael, and Dr. Bath waiting by the station entrance. Dr. Bath paced and looked slightly jittery. The twins stood off from him and waved as she stepped out of Bev's car.

"Oh, good, you're here. We better hurry down, so we don't miss our train. The next isn't for a while." Dr. Bath was every bit as stiff and formal as he had been earlier, and his anxiety over missing his train kept him checking his fancy watch every ten seconds.

"It's my fault we are late, Dr. Bath. I wanted to be sure Chloe had everything she needed," Bev assured him.

He disassembled, "No, no, it was our fault. We should have driven you, so you would not have to inconvenience yourself, Dr. Ikeda."

Bev, not a huge fan of Dr. Bath's to begin with, grabbed Chloe's hand as she began to exit and whispered, "If at any time you don't want to be there anymore, you call me and I'll meet you at the Salem train station, okay? Doesn't matter when or why. Your Tía and I insist you let us know if you are ever uncomfortable."

"Thanks, Bev. For everything. You are a great friend. I'm sure it will all be fine," Chloe assured her.

Bev released Chloe, smiling. "Alright then. Have too much fun, okay?"

Chloe grinned. "Okay."

Dr. Bath sighed over the quiet exchange he couldn't hear and checked his watch impatiently. Chloe waved at Bev as she drove off. Michael grabbed Chloe's bag and Mindy wound her arm through Chloe's, smiling at her dad's already retreating back.

"Don't worry about dad. He's militaristic about time," Mindy assured her. "He likes to eat at the same time every night, so he's all hepped up about catching this train."

Chloe smiled and nodded at Michael. "You don't have to lug my bag around. I can get it, if you want."

Michael shook his head. "Don't you remember? I have to make up for being an ass. I must do my penance." He smiled cheekily, and Chloe laughed.

"Let's board soon or there will be no seats left together," ordered Dr. Bath, giving significant looks to his twins before turning to Chloe. "That was not directed at you, Ms. Mora. We are so happy you could grace us with your presence this weekend."

Chloe didn't know what to say to Dr. Bath, whose moods were so changeable depending on who he talked to that they were giving her a whiplash. She just smiled awkwardly and picked up her pace. They walked under the great industrial criss-crossing black bar overhang of North Station, wedged between brick and glass buildings like some kind of mod sci-fi scene.

The interior of the station was much like most of the T stations, housing self-checkout metro ticket stands and grubby homeless pedestrians in various states of lucidity. These sad people tugged at Chloe's heart, but the Baths avoided them without looking or stopping. The floor tiles were grubby off-white and yellow things, which had seen better days.

Dr. Bath rushed ahead so quickly that she and the twins were forced to rush along behind him, down sticky stairs into the station proper, which smelled like a strange mix of urine, hot dog cart, and various commuter fragrances.

They eventually exited the interior of the station onto a train platform outside and under some great awnings. The lights from the city shone on the metal exterior of the Newburyport/Rockport train. The train had a purple/pink and yellow stripe running the length of its metallic surface, with open doors set along the length.

Dr. Bath hurriedly passed out the tickets he'd pre-purchased for the train, and shooed them ahead of him, urging Michael to "find some seats together and stow Ms. Mora's bag."

Chloe, having never been on a train like this before, was relieved when Dr. Bath ushered her into a seat next to the window "for the best view," and gestured that Michael should sit down next to her. This arrangement endeared Chloe to Dr. Bath, even though she had to wonder at why he was so invested in delegating seats and arrangements. Dr. Bath made every moment feel like a tour with an over-invested, anxious guide.

His restless movements and stiff nature made Chloe feel jittery, which was not her natural state. However, once Mindy was seated across from her and Michael next to her, Dr. Bath excused himself.

"I hope I'm not seen as negligent in my social duties, Ms. Mora, but I have some work to catch up on. Michael, put your phone away and attend to our guest. I think I'll go to the drink cart and answer a few pressing work emails, if you all can spare me." He bowed his head in a strange formal way.

Chloe nodded. "Of course, Dr. Bath. No worries."

Dr. Bath smiled thinly and walked off with his laptop bag toward the drink cart. Michael pocketed his phone. "I was just checking to see if my final grades were posted."

Choe watched Dr. Bath depart into the next cart. The atmosphere in their train car immediately lightened. She nudged Micheal with her elbow. "You don't have to stop checking your grades. I'm a big girl and can entertain myself."

Michael shrugged. "They aren't posted yet. I have one more to take tomorrow, anyway. I can just wait until then to check."

"Oh, you have to go back tomorrow? Why didn't you stay in your dorm, then?" Chloe asked.

Michael met Mindy's eyes in a private, rueful smile.

Chloe caught the meaning. "Oh, your father wanted you to come home and help entertain me? Really, if you have to study or anything, I don't mind. I'm not high maintenance."

Michael raised an eyebrow. "Are you trying to get rid of me, *Ms. Mora*?" He stiffened his posture and imitated his father's formal way of saying her name. Chloe laughed.

"Not at all. Now that you've found your sense of humor again, I find you to be more than tolerable," Chloe answered.

"More than tolerable?" Michael said. "Glowing recommendation."

Mindy laughed. "You two are adorable. Want to play cards? I brought Uno."

They played a couple of rounds before Chloe began to get distracted, looking out the window at the passing landscape. It was not fully dark, and Massachusetts was so different from the flat landscape of crops broken by a small cluster of trees or cow pasture she was used to.

"Wow..." Chloe breathed in awe as they passed rolling hills littered with beautiful trees on fire with color–reds, oranges, yellows, and lime greens. A breeze blew a torrent of colorful leaves toward the train, and Chloe smiled in wonder. They passed through a few industrial and urban spaces before moving through this open country. Here, however, the houses that dotted the landscape were cape cod style homes with sweet little dormers and painted shutters.

"It's so beautiful..."she sighed.

Michael, looking not so much at the landscape he'd grown all too familiar with, smiled in agreement, his eyes all for the captivated and captivating girl next to him. "Breathtaking."

Chloe, noticing a change in his voice, turned and caught his full meaning in the way his eyes sparkled when she met his gaze. Michael smiled and shrugged. "The landscape's not bad either."

Chloe shook her head as if what he said was too silly for a response, but the grin that wouldn't leave her face was enough reassurance to Michael and his onlooking twin that the confusion of the past two days had not dimmed Chloe's feelings for him.

"How does Williamston compare to Boston and the surrounding environs, then?" Michael asked, watching Chloe drink in the darkening landscape.

"Well, I mean...I think Williamston is beautiful in its own way, especially in the spring when the flowers are in full bloom and the crick is high, but this...this is absolutely stunning. Boston is nice, and I think it might be fun to live in a city for a bit, but I'm not sure I'd always want to," Chloe answered.

Mindy nodded. "I have to agree. I love being able to leave my dorm and find a place to eat 24/7 and there's always something to do in the city, but I start to miss the quiet of home. Not that Salem is quiet in the same way Williamston probably is, but it's not as wakeful and busy as the city."

Chloe sighed. "I think I'm in danger of being overly romantic about Salem. I've always wanted to see it, and the quieter, slower life appeals to me. And I'm a sucker for witch stories, the history of oppression, and the gothic style architecture. I admit that my somewhat boring hometown might have relegated me to seeking drama out in books and movies. I promise I will try not to be insufferable, but I might fail."

Michael laughed. "I'm glad you're excited. We will try not to disappoint, though I think it might be inevitable. I imagine Salem, once you grow used to it, is just as boring and lame as any hometown, Williamston included."

"Oh, Williamston isn't too bad. Boredom was never really in the cards. I helped my mom with chores, the younger kids and homeschooling things. My parents are kind and loving. My home is small but comfortable, and we have cute animals to occupy our time and plenty of gardens and flowers and outdoors to roam around in during the nice seasons. Even during the harsh seasons, we keep busy-building snow forts, snowmobiling on Grandpa Jones' farm, caroling during the holidays in town. I hope it doesn't sound like I'm complaining about my home. It's just all so different here that it puts it into a new light. Mom and dad had a way of making what could be boring, not so."

She smiled fondly. "Mom taught me to sew and craft and can food. Dad taught me all about plants and mushrooms we could forage and about how to care for our fruit trees and our gardens. Every Sunday we would have ice cream Sundaes and a movie. I chose the movie Sunday before I left, even though it was my sister's turn. She let me because I'd be gone for my turn. It might not sound like a very interesting life, but I know how much I'll miss it if I leave. I already miss them–my parents and my siblings, and even Williamston. Salem isn't far from Boston, I know, but, well...wasn't it hard for you two, leaving home like you did?"

Chloe turned to each twin. Both Mindy and Michael wore guarded expressions. If they were excited about coming home or wistful in any way, it was hard to tell. Michael stood and excused himself for a moment, asking if he could bring either of them a drink. Both declined.

Mindy broke the silence. "Sounds like you've had a really lovely upbringing. I can see why having such a nice life back home might make it hard for you to leave. I can't necessarily speak for both Michael and myself, but leaving our house wasn't hard for me. I do miss *Salem* and some *people* in Salem," her face took on a somber expression, "but as nice a town as it is, I cannot miss our home. I'm glad you have that, though. Maybe that's why you're such a good person, and why you expect others to be as well. You're used to being surrounded by good people."

Chloe, seeing that she hit on a sore spot, was not at all surprised that a home that contained Dr. Bath would not be as warm as the one she was used to.

She changed the focus by saying, "Oh, I'm not always good. I've been having some very...*vivid* dreams lately." Chloe looked meaningfully to where Michael had been seated and blushed.

Mindy laughed and winked. "As to that...none of us are *always* good. That would be boring."

***

They disembarked the train at a station onto a quiet platform about a half hour after they departed Boston. The night was finally upon them, casting a shadow upon everything it touched. The air was cooler out this way, but also fresher. Dr. Bath waved them impatiently over to where he was standing, fifteen feet up the platform.

They followed him to an Uber pick-up area, where a black SUV stopped to load them. The driver, a woman in her 40s with wild brunette curls pulled into a very high ponytail, helped Chloe put her suitcase in the back of the SUV.

"18 Broad Street," Dr. Bath muttered to the woman as he frowned at his watch.

The nice woman nodded but said little to Dr. Bath, who stared at his watch or out the window with such dedication she could not mistake his unwillingness to talk. Driving to the Bath residence only took five minutes, but it was enough to fully psyche Chloe up.

The houses in Salem were one of a kind–many of them were painted in varying shades of black and gray, which intensified their old-world appeal greatly. Many houses were adorned with gables, dormers, and other gothic fittings. Chloe would have given anything to live in any of the enchanting homes she passed.

As it was just before Halloween, many residents had decorated their houses in orange lights, pumpkins, skeletons, fake spiderwebs, graveyards and, yes, witches. One modest-sized, nearly black gabled home was outfitted to look almost exactly like the Sanderson sister's house in *Hocus Pocus*.

Needless to say, our heroine was glued to her window, properly impressed by the way the dim street lamps lit the leaf strewn paths of the most wonderfully spooky town she'd ever seen. She grinned from ear to ear when Mindy asked her what she thought, but couldn't find the words to express her excitement.

They pulled up to a house that looked like two houses joined together by a wonderful, pillared entryway. The house was an intense tan color, almost brown, and the roof was dark gray. Small turrets stuck out here and there behind the double gable of the roof in front. An intricate stone fence surrounded the property and was painted the same almost brown color as the house. It sported a very interesting geometric pattern that reminded the onlooker of a squished shamrock. The house was the epitome of Salem. Chloe shivered in a mixture of awe and delight.

Night clung to the house, whose windows were dark and ominous. Chloe was sure she'd see a specter, looking back at her from one of the windows in the gabled rooms. For some reason, the picture of the specter in Chloe's mind looked like an older, more forlorn version of her friend Mindy.

Chloe knew it was wicked to imagine such things, but she wondered, still, about where and when Mrs. Bath had died and thought that such a house would be the perfect haunt for the tragic ghost of the twin's sad mother.

"Our home, Ms. Mora," Dr. Bath flourished his arm toward the massive gothic-styled structure.

Chloe, shocked out of her dire thoughts and back into the present, jumped at his somber voice. "Thank you, Dr. Bath. It looks like a museum," Chloe said, her mouth somewhat ajar.

Dr. Bath chuckled without much amusement. "Yes, well, it *was* at one time. When it went under, I bought it. Everything has a price; this one was a hefty price tag, but well worth it, I think. It must seem rather modest to someone used to the lifestyle Dr. Mora provides for her. It's the oldest house in Salem, however, and the most impressive, if I do say so myself. I had to have it."

"What? Oh, yes, Tía's house in Nantucket is wonderful. It's nowhere near this large and impressive, though. This is something out of a gothic romance!" Chloe answered.

"Well, I'm sure Dr. Mora's home is the perfect size for complete happiness," Dr. Bath added awkwardly. "Michael is getting your bag. Please, follow me, Ms. Mora."

Michael sidled up to her with her bag, smiling at the look on her face. "Well, will it do for the weekend?"

"It looks just like I pictured. Very gothic and old world."

"Are you prepared for all the horrors such a gothic establishment houses, then?" Michael's eyes were teasing, as usual.

"Is it haunted?" Chloe asked, almost seriously. She saw the ghostly lady in her mind again before she could shoo the thought away. A shiver ran through her at the notion.

"Only the attic. And the basement. And the dining room. Also, I advise against walking to the bathroom late at night, and not to stir from your bedchamber should you hear the clanking of chains," Michael's eyes danced. Chloe elbowed him lightly.

"I promise not to creep anywhere in your house after dark."

"Pity." Michael teased, raising his brows.

Chloe blushed and looked down. "I hope at least there are no monsters? No vampires, witches, or werewolves?" She smiled up at him cheekily.

Michael smirked, "Monsters? No werewolves or witches, I assure you. As to vampires..." Michael's eyes fell to his father walking briskly to the house. His teasing smile fell away. "Not exactly...not any vampires that drain blood, leastways. You're safe there."

Chloe frowned at the tone in his voice, no longer playful. The lawn in front of the house was small and perfectly manicured. Tall bushes grew just behind the fence to block out the road noise and lights. Topiary bushes were trimmed to perfection on each side of the house, very symmetrical. Their perfection reminded her of Edward Scissorhands. She could easily picture him attending such a house.

Everything about the landscaping was symmetrical to an unsettling degree. The unsettling perfection reminded Chloe of the home's owner, which drew her eye to him standing in the doorway of his house under a cast iron porch lamp.

Dr. Bath cast a very long shadow in the doorway, one that darkened the step considerably. "Ms. Mora, welcome to Pickering Place. Come in."

~ Sixteen ~

IT'S BLACK AND WHITE

The inside of the house was nothing like as romantic as the exterior of the house. For one, it was so clean Chloe worried about touching anything. The entryway was spotless, shining white marble tile flooring, which met a modern floating staircase made from black slabs of stone. Two metallic ropes created the railing which stretched across the length of the stairs. The walls in the entryway were covered in some sort of strange black, white and gray brush stroke wallpaper.

There were stark black and white photographs framed on the wall, images of graffiti covered alleys and worn boots discarded in a gutter. The rest of the house, from the left to the right, seemed to carry on this theme of stark lines and blacks, grays and whites.

The carpets to the right, in the room that looked to be the unlived-in living room, were so white they shone like snow on a sunny day. Chloe decided she was never going to walk into that room. She didn't even trust her clean socks on a carpet so white.

"I'll have the twins give you a tour of the house later, Ms. Mora, but I like to have dinner directly after getting home and getting changed. I'm going to go change and clean up, and we'll have dinner promptly afterwards." He smiled in his strained way. "Mindy will show you to your room. Make yourself at home." He walked off to the left, through a dining area and beyond a very modern kitchen, where she assumed his room was.

Chloe followed Mindy up the staircase. Chloe took the stairs slowly, as she worried about dropping off the side of the flimsy metal ropes that served as rails. She inwardly thought this was the last place in the world she could ever feel at home. It contrasted so differently from her own.

The walls in their mobile were painted a lively yellow and were cluttered with family portraits and children's art. Their second-hand floral sofa was covered in at least three colorful patchwork quilts from Grandma Jones, who made them as gifts regularly. Their floors were fake wood linoleum covered in a huge, bright rag rug mom taught them all to make one year for a homeschool art project. There was color in every corner of her house, stacks of books on and around various sized bookshelves and neat piles of clutter in every nook. If ever there was a house the complete opposite of her house, it would be Pickering Place.

The stairs opened onto the second floor, where black wood floors and black geometric wallpaper were surrounded by spotless white trim. Professional black and white photos of the twins and Ryan from babyhood to now hung in a perfectly straight line of white frames down the length of the considerable hall. A white table held a black vase of white sticks of some sort. Mindy turned to the left and stopped in front of the second door on the right.

Mindy walked very quietly in her own house, almost tiptoeing. She pressed down on a black door handle that almost blended into the black door and waved Chloe inside. Once inside the room, Mindy let out a great sigh. A faint smile spread across her face and she gestured Chloe into a room so unlike the rest of the house that the contrast made Chloe a little dizzy.

"This is where you'll stay. Ryan's room is right next to this one, but he won't be coming home soon, so you don't have to put up with his noise. I'm across the hall from you, and Michael is across from Ryan's room." Mindy smiled, looking a little self-conscious for some reason.

"This room is beautiful," Chloe answered honestly. "There's so much color! Can I take it home with me?"

Mindy laughed. "It was my mom's room."

Without thinking, Chloe said, "Oh, your mom and dad had separate rooms?"

Mindy, looking slightly embarrassed, nodded. "Yes. My father and mom had different styles, as you can see. My father said my mom's taste gave him a headache and that the busyness would keep him awake. Most of the house is my father's taste, but this room...this was all hers. It was her oasis. Ours, too, really..."

"What a lovely oasis," Chloe said quickly, trying to cover for her social misstep.

Mindy nodded, a faraway look in her eyes, as she scanned the room. The walls were covered in teal and gold peacock print paper, the ceiling was a deep marigold yellow, and the trim was a brassy antique gold color. The curtains were a burgundy-pink, teal, and gold sari fabric, vibrant and warm. A four-poster bed was painted to match the trim, with the duvet in the same burgundy color as the curtains.

Pillows in various vibrant shades of pink, orange, and teal decorated the bed, a deep purple velvet wingback chair, and even the wooden chest at the foot of the bed. A beautiful gold patina Indian lantern hung from the ceiling, a modern bulb resting behind the pink glass inside. A bedside lamp on a teal and gold table was made from another such lantern sitting on a little patina holder. The glass inside that lamp was orange.

Mindy shook herself, remembering her purpose as delegated by her father. "Oh, you should get ready. If you want to clean up for dinner, there's a bathroom down the hall to the left. There's actually two up here. Um..." Mindy looked uncomfortable saying the next thing. "If you could be quick about settling in, that would be good. Like I said, my dad is very militaristic about time. He likes to eat at 6:15 every night."

Chloe thought this a very strange habit, as she was used to eating anywhere from 4:30 to 7:30 at night, depending on the dish served and who was cooking. If it was her father, they ate later. Her mother liked to eat earlier. If the kids made the dinner, it varied. But she just smiled and looked at the little golden clock settled on the wooden dresser under the window. It read 6:10.

"I'll be out in a minute. I'm just going to change out of my sweater for dinner," Chloe assured her friend.

"Okay, I'll go wash my hands, then I'll show you to the dining room," Mindy said, leaving the room.

Chloe set her purple suitcase against the far side of the dresser and eyed a little goddess figurine next to the golden clock on the dresser. It had four arms and was holding what looked like a musical instrument. The twins Indian descent came from their mother's side, it seemed. She thought this must be a Hindu goddess and wondered who the goddess was and what she signified. She'd have to ask the twins.

Taking in the vibrant warmth, Chloe walked around the room and smiled. She liked it up here and wished the entire house was so wonderfully bright and welcoming. Sitting on the bed to remove her Hocus Pocus hoodie, she noticed a section of the wall behind a lovely orange and purple silk screen was not covered in wallpaper. She stood, crossed to the screen, and peeked behind it.

There, behind the screen, was a wooden door. It was unpainted and looked very period specific. It was the only thing she'd seen in the house that looked like it belonged to a Salem home. The door had a very gothic peak at the top, and it was very short, shorter than her, and she was not known for her height. Its antique handle was brass.

She put her hand on it and it was so cold she pulled it back. Shivers ran up her arm. A cold breeze seemed to come from the cracks around the door and through the keyhole. Chloe dropped to her knees to investigate the keyhole before opening the door, unsure of what she would find. The hair on her neck stood on end as she closed one eye and leaned in. A knock sounded on her door and she stood, almost toppling the silk screen.

"Come in, Mindy!" Chloe turned to the door in time to see it open. Michael stood in the opening, his button up shirt unbuttoned to reveal a tight white t-shirt underneath.

"Hey, my father wanted Mindy to help set the table. He sent me for you. Are you ready?" Michael stood just outside the door, as if crossing the threshold was forbidden.

"Oh! Sorry. I got distracted. There's a little door over there, and...Well, sorry. I'll grab a cardigan from my bag and I'll be ready."

Chloe fumbled through her suitcase to find her pink and white striped cardigan to wear over her pink spaghetti strap tank top and lime green t-shirt skirt. She pulled it on, smiling toward Michael. Michael's eyes, however, were locked on the far side of the room, on the door behind the screen, as if he could see through it.

"Michael, are you okay?" Chloe asked.

He shook himself out of his daze and smiled. "Oh, uh, yeah. Sorry. Just...that door is locked. We don't know where the key is. Our father doesn't want it opened, so he hid the key. Just so you know. He uses it for storage. Things he doesn't really want laying around the house get shoved there. It's his dirty little secret..." Michael's smile was not at all happy.

"What is?" Chloe asked, wondering what things Dr. Bath would want to hide from the world. She shivered, a little, a creeping suspicion forming more solidly in her colorful imagination.

"What? Oh, just stuff he doesn't want to get rid of, but that doesn't fit with his...black and white theme. You might have noticed?" Michael asked with forced lightness, which Chloe didn't quite believe.

"I did, yes. It's very...modern," Chloe hazarded.

Michael laughed. "That's a nice way to put it. Shall we? We will be a minute late as is, and we can't have that..." That smile that wasn't a smile came back. He seemed to wear it a lot here.

She met him at the threshold of his mother's room and put her hand on his arm. She didn't know why she did it, only that he seemed lonely for a moment, and she wanted to comfort him. He looked at her hand resting against his forearm and smiled a different smile, a genuine smile.

"Let's not be late, Mr. Bath," Chloe said, mock formal seriousness.

Michael turned into her touch and put his hand on top of hers, looking down into her eyes. "Your eyes are like the sky on a fall day," Michael said in a hushed voice.

"Yours are like a warm cup of black coffee," Chloe answered back, a flush creeping into her cheeks.

Michael leaned down, keeping his coffee black eyes locked on her storm gray eyes. Chloe's heart raced and her knees became soft and insubstantial.

A thump, thump, thump of feet almost running up the stairs broke their heated moment, and Chloe dropped Michael's arm.

"The doctor's got his stern face on, Mikie," Mindy said, somewhat out of breath. Her eyes went from Michael's annoyed expression to Chloe's flushed cheeks, and she bit her lip. "Oh, uh, sorry, but it's time."

Michael nodded and offered Chloe his arm in the way that made her feel very much the Austen heroine. She took it and they made their way down to dinner.

Dinner was an awkward affair, starting with the annoyed click of Dr. Bath's eyebrows when they reached the bottom of the stairs at 6:18.

"I apologize, Ms. Mora, for keeping you waiting to eat so long. The twins are usually much more punctual, but I suppose having a guest has made them forgetful of common courtesy," Dr. Bath said, shooting pointed looks at the twins.

Chloe made to argue that she had, in fact, been the reason for any delay, but caught Mindy shaking her head in an almost frightened way, and kept her reply to herself. Why was Mindy frightened of her father? She'd never seen children more obsequious to a parent's needs. It made her wonder about some of the things the Thornes had said. She shook that thought off. The Thornes, she had to remind herself, had not been honest during most of her dealings with them. If Dr. Bath was her father, she'd probably be obedient, too. His commanding air made people listen. She would do her best, in their place, not to be the subject of his hard looks or words.

Dr. Bath turned on his heel like a drill sergeant and led the way to the dining room to the left of the foyer. The black slab wood table in the middle of the embossed white wallpapered room was very long. Dr. Bath stood by a white upholstered dining chair until Michael showed Chloe to hers and remained standing, very formally, until Chloe sat.

Chloe sat quickly, not liking the undue attention. She noticed that Michael stayed standing until she sat, too. Both twins were very stiff and formal around Dr. Bath. The conversation was stilted for this reason. Dr. Bath's attempts at conversation were forced and monotone, and, unfortunately, mostly directed at Chloe, who grew nervous and unsure under Dr. Bath's exacting blue stare.

She fumbled to put her napkin on her lap, as Mindy did across the table from her, and it fell to the floor by her feet. Michael, sitting next to her, reached down and retrieved it, placing it on her knee in a graceful, swift motion. His hand lingered on her leg for a moment. She met his eyes, and he smiled quickly before pulling his hand back. Her leg tingled after he withdrew it, as if the ghost of his hand still warmed her.

The few second contact was enough to make her feel a little more comfortable. She watched Mindy choose a small fork for her salad and copied her, not wanting to eat with the wrong silverware, but feeling a little overwhelmed by the many options laid out before her. She waited until Michael started his roast with a large fork from the middle before she did the same.

He winked when he realized her confusion and continued the rest of his dinner with purposeful and helpful gestures to the correct piece of silverware for each dish. Chloe took a bite of her roast and smiled. It was a tender and flavorful roast; better than anything she'd ever eaten before.

"This is a delicious roast, Dr. Bath," Chloe said when the clinking of forks and the downcast eyes of the twins grew too awkward.

"Perhaps a little dry, but Anya does a good job making sure our dinners are well rounded and healthy," Dr. Bath replied. "Anya is our cook and our maid."

"Oh," Chloe said, not sure how to respond to that. *A cook and maid?* Some of papa Mora's cousins did work like that for rich people, but she'd never actually met anyone who hired a cook and maid full-time before.

"Yes, I'm sure she is not half as good a cook or housekeeper as Dr. Mora has, but she is affordable and efficient," Dr. Bath said with a forced smile before taking a small bite of roast and chewing it for a very long time.

"Oh, Tía only hires help for cleaning and cooking *sometimes*. Tía Pheobe likes to cook and clean in between making art. She says it calms her. Besides, their home is large but not huge, and they don't have children, so it stays pretty clean," Chloe answered.

"I see. Well, I see she spends her money and efforts on more important things, like caring for her niece," Dr. Bath responded.

Chloe, feeling uncertain about what to say, answered, "She is very good to me and my siblings."

Several awkward minutes later, when everyone had eaten their fill, Dr. Bath stood. "Michael and Mindy, please remember to take Ms. Mora's plate into the kitchen for Anya. She'll be back in an hour to clean up. Ms. Mora, I regret that I cannot be a more attentive host, but I have some work to do in my office. My children, however, have been tasked with entertaining you until curfew." The last word was directed at his children, and both twins nodded soberly over the reminder.

Curfew? Weren't the twins adults, now?

It was strange that they still had a curfew. Chloe nodded at Dr. Bath, thanking him for dinner and his hospitality. He smiled his strained smile and left the dining room. Across the table, Mindy watched until her father walked out of sight, then met Chloe's eyes across the table and smiled mischievously.

"I hope you didn't eat too much, Chloe. Michael and I have a surprise for you. We couldn't say in front of our father."

"Surprise?" Chloe asked, looking from one twin to the other. She pictured the twins unveiling a hidden key, unlocking the forbidden upstairs door, a forlorn ghostly apparition gliding towards her...

Michael stood and took Chloe's plate. "Yep. Our father wanted us to give you a tour, but most of the house looks pretty much like this. We do have one room, though, we think you'll like..."

Chloe's mind raced with possibilities. The most embarrassing of which was the picture of a boy's room, dimly lit by candles, and Michael standing in front of her, not as fully dressed as he currently was. She blushed and pushed that thought away. "Let's see this surprise," Chloe said, smiling up into Michael's eyes. The laughter and life in them had returned.

~ Seventeen ~

THE MYSTERIOUS STAIRCASE BEHIND A BOOKSHELF

Mindy grabbed Chloe's hand and pulled her through the living room with the so-white-it-hurt-your-eyes carpet into a very impressive study with floor to ceiling iron pipe and black wood bookshelves.

Mindy crossed to one of the bookshelves and pushed a small button on the wall behind the shelf to her left. The shelf to her right made a hissing/clicking sound like a spaceship door in a sci-fi movie. It separated from the rows of shelves next to it, sliding forward several inches along a well-hidden track in the burnt wood flooring, then off to the side. Mindy stepped into the darkness and began to descend concrete stairs.

"Oh my god! That was the coolest thing I've ever seen," Chloe gushed, psyched out of her mind to find a real secret doorway in the library of Pickering Place.

"Just wait till you see inside," Michael's voice said, from behind her. "Here," Michael gently spun Chloe so she was facing him. "Close your eyes."

Chloe lifted her brow suspiciously and Michael laughed. "Trust me. Close your eyes. I'll lead you downstairs. Come on, I thought you were all for romantic adventures in spooky old houses."

Chloe smiled. "Okay, fine, but if there's a dungeon down there, I'm out."

Michael grinned mischievously. "This isn't Phantom of the Opera."

"That's too bad."

"Close your eyes."

Chloe rolled her eyes but closed them. Michael grabbed one of her hands and led her carefully through the open bookshelf. The air was immediately colder above the stairs. For a moment, Chloe imagined she was Christine and Michael was the reclusive Phantom of the Opera, sweeping her off to his lair.

"Put both of your hands on my shoulders, so you don't trip down the stairs," Michael said from the step below her, placing the hand he held onto his shoulder.

A shiver of pleasure crept through our heroine as she lay both hands on Michael's firm, broad shoulders. The cold air coming from below swept past her and brought with it Michael's scent-clean laundry and a subtle, earthy cologne. He was warm under her hands, which was good because as they descended, it grew cooler.

"Careful, we are coming to the last step and it's a bit of a drop to the floor." He stopped, turned, and grabbed both of her hands. "Okay, step down."

Chloe kept her eyes tightly shut, even though everything in her wanted to see where she was going. She was a sucker for a surprise. Carefully, she took a step down but was still not prepared for how far down the floor was, and fell forward a little. Michael caught her and righted her.

"Can I open my eyes before I break my neck?" Chloe asked, but, in reality, the thrill of Michael's hands steadying her was worth the scare.

"Just a second. Mindy is just finishing something up."

Michael released her hands now that she was steady. She immediately wished he'd take them again. She took a deep breath, trying to picture the surprise before she opened her eyes. The air smelled strongly of salt and butter–popcorn! The room was cool, but it didn't smell dank like a basement or cellar usually did.

"Okay, open your eyes," Mindy called excitedly.

Chloe opened her eyes and met Mindy's smiling form holding a red tray with a red and white striped popcorn bag, a bottle of Sprite and three boxes of movie theater candies covering an array of flavors–fruity, chocolatey, and sour.

Behind Mindy was a screen the size of the entire far wall. The sides of the walls down here were covered in red sound-proofing panels, like a real theater. A small popcorn machine sat in the upper right corner of the room, giving off that lovely buttery smell. A see-through glass refrigerator was on the other side of the room, next to a little glass display case filled with theater candies.

"Wow!" Chloe exhaled and took the tray of goodies Mindy offered her. "Thank you! This is insane! You have your own theater?"

Mindy nodded enthusiastically. "Yeah, when we were little, we used to raise money for things we wanted by selling tickets and snacks to a small group of friends at school. We'd have movie nights at Pickering Place once a month, when father was staying in Boston. You can imagine over ten kids in his house at once were too much for him. Mom would be the usher and we'd handle the snacks. It was fun. It was super popular. The tickets sold for $20, for a ticket, drink, popcorn and candy."

Michael held out his hands for Chloe's tray, which she gave him, and he led her to the sunken seating area, where two rows of five comfortable looking red recliner seats faced the screen, the back row slightly more elevated than the front. There were also seats set above the sunken area for visibility. It looked like it would hold about fifteen people in the seats. They also passed bean bags in the back by the door, where extra people could sit on the red carpet behind the recliners and chill.

"Where would you like to sit, miss?" Michael asked, standing formally in the aisle between the rows of three and two recliners.

"Uh, I guess in the middle row?" Chloe asked, unsure where the best viewing was.

"Wonderful choice," Michael commented, walking to the seat in the far right middle. He opened the cushy arm rest on the right of the seat and unfolded a little table from the arm, which he set the tray on. Chloe's mind was blown.

"That is amazing!" she said, heading toward the seat. "What are we watching?"

"To set the mood for your stay in Salem, I say we pick a witch movie," Michael answered. "We have a big collection of DVDs, which is what we project onto the screen."

"Very old school," Chloe said. "I agree with that request. What witch movies do you have?"

Mindy laughed and came forward. "What don't we have?"

Michael put a thoughtful hand to his chin. "What do you think, Mindy? Should we go for the historically inspired *Salem Witch Trials* miniseries with Kirstie Alley?"

"Ooooh! I like her," Chloe clapped.

"That one is pretty long. We won't be able to watch it before curfew," Mindy cautioned. "It's already 7:30. We better stick to movies."

"Like the *Blair Witch Project*?" Michael supplied.

Mindy gave him a look. "That's what you want to show her? In a new house, in a creepy Halloween town? She won't be able to sleep."

"Fine, I suppose you're going to say something like *Hocus Pocus*," Michael teased.

"No, because I know she has good taste and has already seen that. Though I suggest we watch it another time."

Chloe nodded. "I've seen it more than I care to admit."

"Oh! What about *Practical Magic* or *Witches of Eastwick* or *The Craft*?" Mindy offered.

"I will die of boredom if you make me watch *Practical Magic* again," Michael groaned.

"I've seen that one. It's not boring. It's sweet." Chloe gave Michael a side eye. He held up his hands defensively. "But I haven't seen the others, so maybe one of them?"

"*The Craft* is my suggestion, but it's rated R," Michael said, raising his eyebrows and grinning. "Can you watch R-rated movies, miss?"

Chloe laughed, though she was a little hesitant. "I *have* watched rated R movies before. With you, last night, for instance. Ring a bell? Is it very scary or gross?"

"Not too scary nor particularly gory," Michael assured her. "A little ridiculous, at times, but a classic witch movie. Eastwick is funnier and more my style, but I have a feeling you might appreciate the teen angst of *The Craft*."

"Okay. *The Craft* it is."

"I'll get us popcorn and drinks, Mikie. You start the movie."

The twins got their snacks and settled into recliners. Michael asked Chloe if it was okay if he sat in the recliner next to her, in the middle, as that was his preferred seat. She said that of course it was fine, elated to find herself finally seated next to Michael without the interference of the Thorne siblings.

Mindy sat in the far left seat in front, her preferred seat, she said. Chloe suspected she might also be giving her and her twin space. The recliner was fairly big. The air was still a little chilly down here, which Mindy was prepared for. She gave Chloe a fluffy white blanket, taking one for herself, too.

Chloe was sucked into the film from the very first few minutes. She instantly related to the awkward new girl in town, Sarah. She'd been feeling that way since she stepped foot in Boston, after all. As the movie progressed, she noticed Michael leaning toward her more and more. He wore only his white t-shirt, and she noticed him rubbing his arms, as if he was cold.

"Want to share?" she whispered, offering him part of the big fuzzy blanket Mindy got her.

"Thanks," he smiled, immediately thrusting his arms under the blanket. "That's better." He leaned toward her more, so as not to pull the blanket away. She snuggled into the blanket, warmed by their mingled heat.

The movie intensified, revealing Nancy and her friends for who they truly were. Nancy was a real piece of work. Being one of two brown girls in a white town, Chloe had met with negative and mean people, but she'd been mostly sheltered from negativity in her life. She never had the school bully or clique experience. She wondered if that's why she'd been homeschooled. Maybe her mother had been protecting her from the brunt of other people's small-minded meanness, their whispers about whether her family were here legally.

This movie made her feel very naïve, but also curious about what it was like to go to school with other people her age. Were a lot of people more manipulative and evil than she'd thought?

She couldn't imagine someone as truly bad as Nancy. The actress was amazingly creepy. Chloe unintentionally got closer to Michael as Nancy's evil nature progressed. She became very aware of Michael's proximity when the scene between Nancy seducing Chris in the form of Sarah came up.

She looked at Michael, who noticed her attention shift. He looked back at her, a little shyly. Always the gentleman, he shifted his body away from her to give her space, so that she didn't feel pressured by the intimacy of the scene. That gesture solidified her feelings immediately. She grabbed his hand from under the blanket and leaned into him. His laughing eyes danced, and he smiled, squeezing her hand back.

Much can be said for the first bold, intentional romantic touch between two people with mutual affection. It was so powerful, that the rest of the movie seemed to speed by in between moments of Michael's thumb caressing the back of Chloe's hand, Chloe resting her head on Michael's shoulder, Michael breathing in the coconut scent of Chloe's hair. Every breath was thrilling, every moment was drawn out to infinity. Even so, the movie ended too quickly.

"Oh, crap!" Mindy said, when the credits rolled. She looked at her phone, noticing the time, and stood, turning to them.

"What is it?" Chloe separated herself from Michael, a little shy about affection in front of his twin.

"It's five after," Mindy said.

Chloe couldn't imagine why Mindy's voice sounded so somber. She was certain they didn't abide by a curfew when they weren't home, and she couldn't imagine Dr. Bath would insist that two 19-year-olds keep to such a strict curfew when they were entertaining a guest. It was just after 9:30, after all. Hardly late.

Unfortunately, Chloe's own upbringing ill prepared her for the reality of oppressive parenting that many others in the world had to endure.

They climbed the dark stairs quickly. Mindy pushed the button to open the secret door into the library. As they exited the room, a low, stern voice connected to a shadow in the doorway of the library said, "Did you forget the time?"

The dark library felt more ominous with Dr. Bath's stiff frame and cold demeanor radiating into it. The library was dark and the room behind it had only one light turned on, so that she could only see his outline rather than his features.

Chloe imagined him as just his shadow, imagined his shadow growing and spreading out over the entire library, over them, pushing down upon them. That's how it felt to her when Dr. Bath was around. He was a man of slight build, pale and not very tall. He shouldn't take up so much space, but he did. Mindy tried to excuse their behavior, but Dr. Bath held up a hand to silence her.

"Ms. Mora, I am sorry, but the twins *know* that I am very strict about getting enough sleep. I do not function at work without the required minimum hours of sleep, and Michael has a final tomorrow. Otherwise, I might be more lenient."

Chloe swallowed the lump of anxiety in her chest. "Oh, no, I understand. I'm tired, too." This was not a lie. Tía's foot injury had woken her very early and she was starting to feel it. But she also wanted to keep the tentative peace, even if she was thinking to herself that this house felt like a dictatorship when Dr. Bath was around. Peace did not last long in dictatorships.

Dr. Bath nodded once and walked toward his room, not turning as he said, "Lights out in ten minutes, so Ms. Mora can have time to prepare herself for bed."

Mindy looked at her twin and rolled her eyes. "Sorry about that, Chloe," she mumbled after her father had left.

Chloe, worried that Dr. Bath was lurking within earshot, just shrugged and followed the twins upstairs. Mindy showed her the bathroom she could use to brush her teeth, then said goodnight.

Chloe quickly brushed her teeth and changed into her pajamas, not wanting to run into Dr. Bath checking whether his "lights out in ten" command had been obeyed. For some reason, she was afraid to meet him in the hall alone. This thought spurred her speed, and she was ready for bed in five minutes. She almost collided with Michael, who was headed to the other bathroom when she was exiting.

"Oh, sorry. Just trying to hurry, so you guys don't catch grief again," Chloe said.

Michael shook his head, glaring down the stairs. "I'm sorry about my father. He can be...really hard to deal with. I forget how much when I'm at school. Then I come back and it's like I'm five all over again." He sighed, then looked at Chloe and his face softened. "I'm glad you're here. You make being here bearable."

Chloe put her hand on his arm. "Don't worry about it, Michael. I'm having a great night. Really." She met his eyes and stumbled on her words. "It's been...really nice."

He smiled at her, lifted her hand from his arm, and kissed it. His lips were warm and soft. She felt her legs melt a little under her. "Good night. I'm going back to Boston with my father tomorrow, but I'll be back fairly early. I was thinking, when I do come back, maybe we can spend some time alone tomorrow?"

Chloe wanted to spend time alone with him right this moment, but she nodded eagerly. "That sounds fun."

Michael released her hand. "It's a date, then."

Chloe didn't remember getting back to the guest room, so she must have floated back, her mind and body buoyed by the promise of time alone with the hottest, smartest, kindest man she'd ever met.

Once in the room, however, her eyes were immediately drawn back to the door behind the silk screen. She wondered where Dr. Bath kept his key and what secrets he wanted to hide from the outside world. The more she was around the man, the less she wondered at his wife having slept in a separate room. Was she unfaithful like the Thorne siblings had hinted? Chloe couldn't blame her if she had been, though she disapproved of unfaithfulness in general. Maybe his wife had been afraid of him. Maybe she had reason to be.

Chloe started to walk to the door when she heard heavy footsteps on the staircase. She immediately shut off her light and jumped into bed, pulling the cold silk duvet up to her ears, her blood pounding in her chest so loudly it sounded in her inner ears.

The sound of footsteps came down the hall, closer and closer to her door. They stopped just outside her door. She watched the door, wishing she'd locked it before jumping into bed. The light under the door from the hallway revealed the long shadow of Dr. Bath. It sank under the door and stretched across the foot of her bed.

Then, suddenly, the light in the hall clicked off and the footsteps turned and made their way back down the stairs. Even after she couldn't hear Dr. Bath's footsteps anymore, she kept her eyes on the door and the foot of her bed. She could still feel his oppressive shadow in the pitch darkness, as if it stayed behind to keep watch over her in the night.

***

Sleep came to Chloe the moment she lay her head on the pillow, but it was a heavy, strange oppressive sleep.

She stood on the threshold of Dr. Bath's spotless white carpet. Tall, red flames blazed in Dr. Bath's black marble fireplace. In front of the blaze stood Dr. Bath, warming his hands on the red flames.

Chloe stepped foot on the too white carpet of the living room, carefully, aware she was not wearing shoes, but worried all the same that her feet would mar the perfection. She went to take another hesitant step forward but frowned down at the ground. Her foot stuck to the carpet as if it were a living, sucking thing.

She frowned and tugged at her foot until it was free of the sticky white carpet. The tug felt like removing skin with a bandaid. She winced silently, tucking the pain inside. Her foot came loose, only to stick again to the floor, as if the brilliantly white carpet was made of super hold fly paper.

She fought the pull and walked toward the dancing red flames. Dr. Bath stared so intently into the flames she was not sure he knew she was even here. She didn't know why she was even walking toward Dr. Bath, whom she could not like. His stiff, rod straight back was turned toward her. She could back out now, and she was sure he wouldn't notice. She looked behind her and gasped in horror. The snow white carpet was now covered in blood red footprints where she'd walked.

The gasp drew Dr. Bath's attention. He turned slowly, every movement deliberate and formal. "Ms. Mora, you're finally here. Please, come closer. Don't be shy. We haven't got all night."

Chloe, not wanting to offend the twins' father, fought against the suction of the floor, painstakingly putting one foot slowly in front of the other, all the while thinking he would be so angry with her for getting blood on the carpet, instead of worrying about the injury she was causing herself. Every tug tore at the skin of her feet, but she knew it was dangerous to keep the doctor waiting, so she kept on, trying not to fuss.

"Come, come. We have a very strict schedule to keep, Ms. Mora."

Dr. Bath's handsome but cold face was strained with the effort it took for him to be polite. His ice-blue eyes narrowed at her slow steps. When Chloe finally made it to him, he regarded her with a calculating expression.

"I'd have thought Dr. Mora could provide better attire for her near-daughter. But perhaps this is a traditional dress for your culture? Anyway,

I'm quite sure Dr. Mora knows best about formal attire. I would have thought something designer was in order, but this will do. Why waste money on the wedding, when there are so many important expenses in life after marriage, after all?"

Chloe looked down at herself for the first time. She was wearing a simple lace maxi dress, much like the one her mother wore in her own wedding photo. It had been made from a tablecloth mom found at the thrift store. Her head swam. Why was she wearing this dress?

"Marriage? I'm sorry Dr. Bath, but there's been a mistake. I'm not old enough to be married, yet. I'm very flattered, of course, but I also think you may be too old for me." Chloe struggled to stay polite. How could Dr. Bath, as handsome as he was, think she would be interested in marrying someone her father's age? Gross.

Dr. Bath shook his head, amused. "Of course not, dear girl. That would not be proper. I was speaking, of course, of your marriage to my son." He turned his head as footsteps approached from the library. "Ah, here he is..."

Michael walked into the room in a fitted tux that looked absolutely phenomenal on him. It hugged his broad shoulders and waist perfectly. He looked like a magazine model. He looked so good in the expensive suit that Chloe felt underdressed and awkward in her mother's old lace tablecloth dress. While he looked immaculately dressed, however, his usually laughing eyes were rimmed in dark circles and his smile was placating, rather than true.

"You look beautiful as always, Chloe," he said, reserving a sad smile for her.

"Oh, Michael, you look so nice, too, but I was just telling your dad I'm not sure I'm ready for this. It's too fast. I'm really honored that he thinks so highly of me, but I don't think we should marry," Chloe explained, hoping that saying so would not hurt him too badly.

"Chloe, I understand, I really do, but given the other options, maybe we should just do what he wants..." Michael trailed off, looking defeated and worn.

"Other options? What, going to college, getting to know each other better? Making sure we are a good match? I don't understand..."

Dr. Bath looked at a ridiculously large wristwatch on his arm and sighed impatiently. "I thought of all eventualities, Ms. Mora. If my son Michael is not to your taste, you may choose from my other children, but let's make it quick. We really do need to keep to a schedule. I'll give you two minutes to decide, but then we really must get on with the ceremony." He turned to the library and shouted, "Mindy! Ryan! Stop dragging your feet. Get in here, if you please."

Mindy walked in wearing a lovely black designer dress and veil. Her eyes were sad, but she smiled and waved at Chloe. "It's fine, Chloe. If you choose me, we'll make it work. I know you aren't particularly interested in women, but we are good friends, aren't we? We could make it work, if we have to..."

Chloe put her hand on her forehead. "Have to? Mindy, you don't want that! You deserve to choose what and who you want in life."

Mindy just hung her head and hugged herself. Chloe was baffled to see her strong, smart friend so kowtowed by her father into making a decision that went against her own free will.

Dr. Bath waved an impatient hand and Mindy dropped her head and stared at the floor, as defeated as her twin. "Two minutes are up. If it's not Michael or Mindy, it will have to be Ryan."

Ryan walked in wearing a suit identical to Michael's, only his white shirt underneath was unbuttoned down to the waist, showcasing his vanity—his well-managed physique. "Let's get this over with, then," he said in a bored way. "I have a date with Lissa tonight."

Dr. Bath rolled impatient eyes at his eldest son. "Really, Ryan, you'll have to postpone. You must keep your honeymoon engagement to your new wife."

Ryan shrugged. "Lissa and Chloe are good friends. I'll just invite her along, eh Chloe? That actually suits me better. Two girls at once. What could be better?" He raised his cold eyes, so much like his father's, to her.

Chloe shook her head. "No. I'm not okay with that. I'm sorry, Dr. Bath. I'm not okay with any of this. This is a decision I have to make for myself, and your children are adults now. You can't just make them marry to please you."

Dr. Bath stalked toward Chloe, whose feet were stuck so firmly to the floor that she couldn't move. "Time's up, Ms. Mora. I'm afraid I'm not used to being told no. Just ask the twins. You will choose now. I have been more than patient." Dr. Bath's blue eyes then changed and became as red as the flames in the fireplace. "You will do as you're told, like anybody in this house, or there will be consequences."

"What?! Mindy! Michael! You can't let him do this. You can't be okay with this?!" But Mindy and Michael only hung their heads defenselessly.

Dr. Bath grabbed her wrist and pulled her forward, toward the red flames. "No! No! I want to go home, please! No!"

"Too late." Dr. Bath flung her into the flames.

~ Eighteen ~

DEAD MAN'S TOE, DEAD MAN'S TOE!

She woke up, heaving, her borrowed blankets askew and tangled around her feet. She took a few deep breaths to orient herself, feeling out of sorts after such a dream. It was a minute later that she realized someone had knocked on the door lightly.

She untangled herself from her sheets, smoothed down her hair and opened the door a crack, not wanting to be caught in only her overlarge Hocus Pocus sleep shirt if it was Dr. Bath knocking on her door. Thankfully, it was not. Michael stood in the hall, awkwardly playing with the cuff of his Pendleton sweater.

"Hey, Michael. Wow, you're up early," Chloe said, opening the door a little wider.

Michael's eyes dropped for only a second to her bare legs, before they shot back up to her face. His cheeks flushed adorably, and he stuttered a little before saying, "Sorry, Chloe. I didn't mean to wake you up, but I just wanted to say goodbye before I left. I have my last final today. If you don't mind coming downstairs soon, my dad wants to say goodbye, too. He said he might be very late coming home tonight and didn't want to be complacent about his host duties or something. I don't remember exactly. Sorry to wake you so early."

"Oh, no, that's fine. I'm glad you did. Just a second. I'll pull on some pants and come down," Chloe said, smiling at him warmly, and turning back to the room slowly, in the hopes he watched her.

Chloe pulled some jeans on and put her hair up in a ponytail, then left the vibrancy of Mrs. Bath's room. Michael waited for her at the top of the stairs. He led the way to the dining room, where his dad sat in his chair at the head of the table with a black cup of tea and a half-eaten piece of toast.

"Oh, good. Ms. Mora, sorry to disturb your slumber, but I wanted to be sure to say goodbye before I left. It is likely my work will keep me away late tonight. We are short staffed at the hospital lately. Mindy will show you around while Michael is finishing his final, but he should be back fairly early. I hope to return with my eldest son, Ryan, late this evening, which will prevent me from being present for dinner. Michael and Mindy said they will take you out tonight, so I know you will have a nice time visiting our little town."

Chloe, still sleep deprived and reeling from the strange dream she had, marveled at how Dr. Bath planned out every portion of his and his children's days as if a minute of downtime would be the end of them all, but couldn't get her brain working fast enough to take it all in.

"I'm a very easy to please guest, Dr. Bath. I am sure everything will be fine. Have a nice day at work," Chloe managed.

Dr. Bath assured Chloe that he would and he and Michael, who looked sleepy and less than enthusiastic about sharing the commute alone with his father, left. When the door shut behind them, Mindy sprang up from her position at the dining room table, where she'd been watching the exchange over a cup of hot tea.

"Are you awake, or do you need to sleep more?" Mindy asked her friend.

"I don't fall back to sleep well. I'm awake now," Chloe said, yawning.

"If you want to shower and stuff, we can go to my favorite cafe for breakfast. It's called Witch's Brew Bakery. I want to introduce you to the owner and manager, Kira." The way Mindy said the name Kira, drawn out meaningfully, her eyes dancing, left Chloe in no doubt about why she wanted to go to the cafe.

"Kira, huh?" Chloe teased.

Mindy smiled, blushing. "So? What do you think?"

"I'll get showered and changed. I hope they have cinnamon rolls and a *gallon* of coffee," Chloe answered.

Mindy nodded enthusiastically. "Their cinnamon rolls are to die for. And their coffee is the best in town. I'm not just saying that because I'm biased."

"Alright. Give me a few minutes." Chloe could see that Mindy had woken up, showered and changed when her father and Michael did. She wondered if Dr. Bath had made her rise early, or if she'd risen on her own. She wouldn't put it past the man to keep Mindy on his schedule just to be demanding.

***

The walk to Witch's Brew Bakery was the very definition of charming. Salem's sidewalks and lawns were covered in orange, yellow, gold, brown, and red leaves. The houses ranged from white to black, but many were the traditional New England cape cod style homes in various sizes. Most houses were decked out for Halloween decor. Smiling pumpkins and witches flying from the trees greeted them at every turn. She guessed it was probably a very busy time of year for the town.

It was a cold, somewhat misty morning, but Chloe was wearing a black sweater over striped purple and black leggings, on top of which she wore one of her handmade purple and black witch skirts. She'd finished off the ensemble with the quilted denim jacket Tía bought her, so she managed to keep mostly warm. It was about ten minutes to downtown Salem, where the shop was situated, and Chloe grew more and more excited the closer they got.

She was walking the cobbled sidewalks towards downtown Salem! Only a couple of blocks from the Salem Witch Village! She smiled as the breeze lifted her hair and fake spiderwebs danced on fences and bushes. The shops downtown were either tall old wooden shop buildings, skinny and smushed together, or they were brick edifices matching the color of the cobbled streets. Mindy led her past closed tourist shops and towards the smell of rich coffee, sugar, and butter.

Kira's shop was a tall, skinny building painted a purple so dark it was almost black. The shutters were green and the sign hanging above the matching green door was in the shape of a black cauldron bubbling over with a green witch's potion.

The inside of Witch's Brew Bakery was even more interesting than the outside. Black cotton spiderwebs crisscrossed the ceiling in the downstairs area. Giant black spiders sat inside the webs, staring down at the customers. Fake but realistic bats hung from old rafters. Old fashioned stick and hay witch's brooms hung from invisible strings from the upper floor where cozy black and purple loveseats and cushy chairs welcomed visitors. The witch's brooms were decorated with "dripping" electric light candles. They glowed dimly above the second-floor seating area.

There was a glass case to the right that welcomed customers with creepy treats–deadman's toes (shortbread cookies), graveyard dirt (mousse of some sort with sprinkled cookies on top of it), intestines, BATlava (baklava in the shape of bats), and charred children (gingerbread children decorated with burned clothing and little X eyes). To the left was a coffee station. An old schoolhouse chalkboard above it listed the specials, drinks with names like "Oil of Boil", "Life Potion", "Newt Saliva", "Glenda's Good Witch", and "Polyjuice Potion".

The young woman at the cash register had a pierced septum, tight, smooth black curly hair, dark freckles on light brown skin, and a smile that took up half of her face. Her light brown eyes sparkled when they landed on Mindy, whose face lit up in response.

"Hey, you!" the woman practically squealed, before launching herself over the counter and into Mindy's arms.

Mindy half-lifted, half-hugged the lovely woman, giggling. "Kira! I brought the friend I was telling you about." She kissed Kira lightly on the mouth, then gestured to Chloe. "Kira, this is Chloe. Chloe, this is Kira, my girlfriend."

Chloe tentatively held out her hand, and Kira took it in both of her warm hands, squeezing them. "I've heard lovely things about you from Mindy. I'm so glad you could come visit! I just know it will make Michael and Mindy's break so much nicer."

Chloe smiled. "I'm so happy I could come, too. I hope I'm not ruining your girlfriend-time by visiting, though."

Kira dropped Chloe's hands and put her arm around Mindy's shoulder, her smile fading a bit. "Not at all. I'm not exactly welcome in Dr. Bath's home. If anything, your being here gives Mindy an excuse to visit downtown, which I'm sure would not be possible if you were not visiting and needing to see the sights."

Chloe frowned, contemplating such a revelation, but Mindy broke in before she could say anything about what Kira revealed. "I'm starving, my sweet. You have any fresh intestines for Chloe?"

"Intestines?" Chloe giggled. "I have to admit, I was hoping for cinnamon rolls and a mocha."

Kira nodded sagely. "Intestines and Mouldering Mocha for you and Life Potion and Deadman's Toes for the love of my life?"

Mindy kissed her girlfriend on the nose. "You got it. We'll sit upstairs." She handed some bills to her girlfriend. "Keep the change, goodlooking."

Kira eyed the two twenties. "That's a big tip."

Mindy raised and lowered her eyebrows. "You have to put up with quite a lot to be with me. I promise you, it falls short."

Kira kissed Mindy again, this time a little longer and more thoroughly than before, then winked at her and told her to sit down and she'd bring the treats and drinks soon. There were only a few sleepy looking people typing away on computers or staring at phones on wooden chairs next to live edge coffee tables.

The downstairs seating area had a fireplace with a huge black cauldron hanging over a pretend, electric fire that gave off minimal warmth. The walls were unpainted brick near the fireplace and foggy, spooky forest wallpaper on the rest of the walls. Spooky local art with little paper price tags hung from the dark walls going up the stairs. Chloe noticed a near-naked nymph covered in well-placed fall leaves that looked very much like Mindy. She blushed a little when she saw that the artist was Kira. Clearly, it *was* Mindy. Chloe pointed to it.

"That's you. Kira is really talented. It's kinda haunting, but also really good. You kinda mesh into the leaves that are falling from the trees, like you are a part of the nature around you. Your arms are like the branches of the tree there."

Mindy smiled proudly at the painting. "She's so talented. She owns and runs this place, plans the menu, trains her bakers and baristas to make new monthly treats and drinks, and finds time to paint."

Mindy led her past several more paintings. One of which was a faun that looked very much to be half Michael, half goat in a winter landscape. Chloe laughed when she saw it. "She really is good."

Mindy laughed at the painting, too. "Michael would hate that you've seen that. Best not to mention it."

Chloe shook her head as they headed toward the seats upstairs. "I won't be able to help myself."

Mindy laughed knowingly and chose two cozy black armchairs near a little round window that overlooked the shops behind the coffeehouse. The cobbled brick square with fall trees shedding leaves was idyllic. In only a few minutes, Kira climbed the stairs with a black tray laden with two steaming cauldron mugs and two gray stone plates. She handed a twisted, red-tinted cinnamon roll mass that dripped with a red glaze frosting to Chloe and some grayish green-tinted very realistically shaped toes with yellowing almond slice nails to Mindy.

The intestines might have looked hellish, but they smelled divine. Chloe breathed in the cinnamony sweetness and sighed. "This looks absolutely disgusting, but I can't wait to eat it."

Kira chuckled and put her steaming cauldron on the stump and glass table in between the plush chairs. "Happy feasting, my lovelies. I'm getting a small commuter rush downstairs, but I'll come back up in a bit." She planted a kiss on Mindy's cheek and hopped down the stairs.

Mindy watched her walk away, a faint smile pulling the corner of her mouth up. She dipped a toe in her matcha latte before biting it. "Are those shortbread cookies?" Chloe asked.

Mindy nodded. "Yes. Very buttery. Dash of nutmeg. Life Potion, you probably know, has to be green, like it is in *Hocus Pocus*. Hence, matcha."

Chloe cut a soft piece of gooey cinnamon intestine and sampled it. She mmmmmmed for much longer than she intended, but it was soooo good. "I've never had intestines, but I don't think I'll ever eat better," she said.

Mindy laughed. "Yes, Kira is *truly* magical. I'm very lucky to have her."

Chloe took a sip from her mocha, which was not overly sweet and had a nice rich dark chocolate taste, before saying, "Your father doesn't like that you're a lesbian?"

Mindy took a sip of her matcha and stared out the window before answering. "I don't think he's thrilled that I'm a lesbian, but I think if Kira were from a rich family with glowing prospects, he could overlook it. But she's not. She was a poor girl from Roxbury who worked her ass off to afford her dream, which, for two years, looked like it might fail. But not now. The cafe is doing great. She's almost saved up enough for a small down payment on a house outside of town, here. Fixer upper, but it has promise. She's done a lot more in her twenty-five years than most people do in their whole lives. She is the type of person who never takes no for an answer and always finds a way to get what she wants. She would have to be, to put up with our situation."

Chloe shook her head. "I'm sorry, but I guess I don't understand. You're 19, almost 20, right?"

Mindy nodded. "Two months I'll be twenty."

"So, why do you have a curfew in your own house? Why do you let your father tell you where you can go and when you should go there? You and Michael seem so...restricted for adults," Chloe said. "I'm sorry. I know that's forward, but I guess I just don't understand."

Mindy shook her head. "No, you're right. It's weird and it's controlling and it's infuriating."

"So, why do you deal with it? Why do you come back if he's not kind to you and if you feel so stifled? I mean, I get why you come back here; this is where Kira is, but...why back home?"

Mindy took a deep breath. "It wasn't always so bad. I mean, father's always been who he is, but it was tempered a bit when my mom was alive. The house had splashes of her art here and there. I mean, it still had to be absolutely pristine. My dad has a form of OCD, you see. You might not notice his ticks because he hides them and pushes them down, but he does so by controlling his environment very strictly."

She took another sip of her matcha. In a somber voice she continued. "My mom used to take the brunt of it, I think. But...she's not here anymore, and it's gotten worse since she died. But, besides that, my dad was raised to think very highly of "the American dream." His parents insisted he marry well. They moved to America after college and were both doctors. My mom's grandpa owned a pretty successful tea business and chain of stores in England. Her dad and mom moved to America to pursue an education, but he oversaw the acquisition of his father's business to a huge corporation, which just made the family richer. My mom, by extension, was very wealthy. My father's family was moderately well off, but he had his sights on being rich."

"Okay, Kira isn't rich. Doesn't her making you happy have any sway? I mean, he must have loved your mom, too. He didn't just marry her for money, right?" Chloe asked.

Mindy frowned and picked at her dead man's toe. "Honestly? I don't know. I think he thought her beautiful. She was. There were rare moments where he would look at her in a way he never really looks at anyone, and I thought, yes, he must love her. But..." she sighed, searching for the right words.

"I don't know if my father is capable of loving the same way she loved him. And she did, at first, though I think she was very unhappy toward the end of her life. She tried to hide it, but some of her sparkle faded those last three years before she died. And when she did die, she took all that sparkle, all that vibrancy with her. And father only grew more controlling, more insistent that we get an education that would set us up and jobs that would see us wealthy. As long as I am using his money for college and living expenses, we are to abide by his wishes for our future. He threatened to cut me off when he found out about Kira."

"Oh my god! Really? So...he doesn't know you're still with her?" Chloe asked.

"I think he suspects we might be, but we are careful. I have learned to be very careful and secretive, and he's gone a lot. Kira visits me in Boston on her days off. We make it work, but...I sometimes think she's right. That I should just say fuck it and be done with him. Let him cut me off. It's hard, though. He has a way of making me feel indebted to him, and, well, it might not sound like it, but I love him. He's my father, after all, despite his faults. I've already lost one parent..."

Chloe had a hard time understanding how anyone could feel particularly affectionate toward such a person, but she understood that children loved their parents, no matter how bad they were. Tommy Tookers' dad was an addict who sometimes got abusive, but he was constantly talking about the loser like he was a great guy who just made a few mistakes.

Chloe then understood what Mindy had been saying about her being blessed and cursed with a very loving childhood. It did make it hard for her to understand how kids from unloving homes could want to connect or stay around such terrible parents. She sipped her mocha in silence for a while, before asking about what really bothered her. It was stupid. She knew it was. But she couldn't get the idea that Mindy's mother's death was somehow connected to having a husband like Dr. Bath. Young, vibrant mothers simply didn't die at a young age, in her mind.

"Mindy, you can just say you don't want to talk about it, if I'm asking too many hard questions, but how *did* your mom die?"

Mindy sighed. "I wasn't there. I only know it was sudden. My father refused to say much. I mean, he's a doctor. He could have explained it if he wanted to, but he just...he couldn't talk about it. I think it's the first time I've seen him truly ruffled. I was called home after it happened. I immediately asked him what happened, and he just shook his head."

Mindy's eyes were far away and glistened slightly. She relieved the day as if it were yesterday and spoke in a pained hush. "It was like he was in shock, only he never snapped out of it. If he catches any of us talking about mom, he freezes up and gets angry. Michael thinks it was a hemorrhage or tumor. It made it really hard to accept that she was gone, not knowing, but I had to. I got used to not talking about her, honestly. If I ever miss her, I just sit in her room and I smell her clothes, still in their drawers. I've always been surprised that my father doesn't touch her room, that he keeps her things. I mean, you've seen him. He's not sentimental. Her room is one reason I give for staying around, for following his ridiculous rules. It shows me that he loved her. That, somewhere deep down, he misses her. And her room gives me comfort even when the rest of the house feels like a prison."

Chloe ate her intestines in quiet contemplation. The buttery dough melted in her mouth and the cinnamon lingered on her tongue. It was pretty gross-looking on the plate, but it was actually one of the best things she'd ever eaten. She thought about Dr. Bath being sort of like her treat, but in reverse. He was pleasing to look at and seemed to be polite and welcoming, but inside she wondered if he wasn't really just a truly vile person.

She didn't ask Mindy any more about her parents. She understood that her friend wanted to think the best of her father, but something ate at her about this situation. Chloe couldn't help but think that Dr. Bath lacked the kind of emotional maturity that Mindy gave him credit for. What really happened to Mrs. Bath? Did Dr. Bath keep her things around out of love or out of guilt? What was that door in her room hiding?

She and Mindy left the cafe two hours after they got there. Kira visited with them on and off and Chloe marveled at how in love the two were. She felt for her friend, who couldn't be open about her relationship.

She began to worry for herself, too. It had become clear to her that Dr. Bath couldn't know about her being poor. She didn't like to be dishonest, but she knew, eventually, she would have to come clean about that. She wondered whether he would be as kind a host as he had been once he knew. His demeanor towards her truly didn't make sense. He never asked about her family, apart from her Tía. She suspected that her Tía's celebrity, to him, might make up for her own lack of fortune.

None of these thoughts were pleasant, but they were pushed aside in favor of the appeal of fantastic treats in the company of wonderful people in one of the coolest towns she'd ever visited.

~ Nineteen ~

SALEM SIGHTS

The girls hung out at the cafe for a bit longer with Kira, then said their goodbyes as shops started to open. Mindy was kind enough to buy breakfast, which relieved Chloe, although she was embarrassed to need the help. Tía had given her money, but she wanted to spend it on the promised souvenirs for her siblings.

They visited a few touristy shops with Salem and witch-related goodies. Window displays hung with spooky spider webs, mannequins wore full witch costumes in windows, pretend potions settled atop cauldrons, and smiling jack-o'-lanterns glowed from storefronts.

For a girl whose favorite time of year was fall, the setting felt absolutely magical. Chloe used some of her dwindling money to buy a "witch and warlock" mug set for her parents, which she knew they'd love. She carefully picked each sibling out a fun souvenir, mentally tabulating the fact that she could not spend much more money on her trip in Salem. She assumed she would have to pay for her return ticket on the train home, after all.

Around eleven o'clock, Chloe got a text that read, "I'm back in Salem. Final was not too bad. Where can I meet you girls?"

Mindy grinned over the smile that lit her friend's face. "I see I'm no longer the first girl to get my twin's texts. Tell him to meet us at the Witch Museum. It's open now, and you can't come to Salem without visiting it."

Chloe nodded enthusiastically over the plan and messaged Michael, "Meet us at the Witch Museum! (witch emoji, happy emoji)" Michael texted back a thumbs up and a witch emoji.

In minutes, Chloe and Mindy stood in front of a grand pink brick building with arched windows, trimmed with lighter colored tan bricks. Next to her was a statue of a man with a pilgrim style hat and flowing robe. He was mounted upon a boulder, putting his impressive statue at an even more impressive height. He was an imposing, frightening figure. The statue's plaque stated that he was Roger Conant, "founder" of Salem.

Chloe rolled her eyes a bit at the stuffy looking man. She imagined that founding was a kind verb for setting up camp in already occupied territory. She struggled internally knowing that much of what gave her a thrill about this town came at the cost of the lives of indigenous people and martyred women.

Most tourism of any town in any country was probably filled with hard history, but she couldn't help but be brought in and thrilled by the prospect of being here. As a young woman of color, she understood that history was not kind to people like her, to brown people and to women, especially the combination of the two. But she was also a thoroughly romantic, Americanized teen and she couldn't help but dance with excitement standing outside of the museum, her eyes searching for Michael's tall figure.

He didn't keep her waiting long, strolling up waving, about fifteen minutes later. They were soon inside the imposing structure. A kind cashier with bored eyes gave Chloe a brochure and suggested they visit the Old Burying Point as well. The trio thanked the bored man and set off through the museum, which was hokey but extremely entertaining. Chloe was impressed by the honesty of the history that the museum displayed and enjoyed the new section on modern day witches.

The twins insisted on showing her the Witch Dungeon museum, too, as well as the Burial Point, where many of the historical women and men put on trial for witchcraft met their fates. The dungeon was Chloe's favorite stop, with the reenactment of the witch trials and the spooky, dank cells underground taking the cake. She loved the dark, spooky atmosphere and the dreary history that hung over the building like a shroud. She also loved that Michael pulled her close in the chilly dungeon when she shivered from the chill.

Around noon, Mindy excused herself to spend lunch with her girlfriend, who had the rest of the day off. She kissed Chloe's cheek and smiled at her twin with a cheeky, knowing grin before almost skipping off to see Kira.

"Won't your father be upset if we don't check in some time today?" Chloe asked Michael.

"Actually, father just messaged Mindy and I a few minutes ago that he won't be able to make it back tonight. He is doing a double and will stay in Boston. He and Ryan will head back together tomorrow, so we are free to do as we wish without his...direction tonight."

Michael's proper but easy persona seemed to fall back into place, with the thought that his father would not be darkening their doorstep tonight. Chloe smiled to see it.

She was a little taken aback to hear that Dr. Bath was not keeping his promise to Tía to be present to oversee them, however, and she excused herself to check in with Tía to be sure it was still okay that she stayed over, even with Dr. Bath not present. For a moment, she contemplated not bringing up the subject to Tía, but quickly dismissed it. She had always been honest with Tía, and there was no reason to start being dishonest now.

Michael assured her that she was right, which made her more enamored of him. He could've asked her to lie, but he supported her doing what would make her most comfortable. Tía, to her joy, was so happy with how responsible her niece was that she assured her she was okay with the arrangement.

She asked Chloe to please call at any time should she feel uncomfortable or unsafe and to make use of the "gifts" Bev gave her should she be *too comfortable* with Michael. Chloe blushed upon reading Tía's message and was mortified when Michael asked her what her Tía said about her staying.

"She says I'm an adult now, and she trusts me. I figured she would say something like that. She's very cool," Chloe answered.

"She seems cool. Hungry?" Michael held out his hand.

Chloe took his outstretched hand, smiling so hard her cheeks ached. "Very."

~ Twenty ~

BEWITCHING MR. BATH

They had a quick slice of very tasty pizza before Michael steered her toward a shop a block down from the pizza place, informing her he'd made a secret reservation at a shop one of his friends from high school worked at. She grinned in wonder at such a romantic gesture and congratulated herself on achieving "true rural heroine meets city boy and falls head over heels status."

The shop they stopped in front of had a very cool black and teal broom hanging above the doorway. The window of the shop had a witch's broom standing upright surrounded by the words "Witch's Stitches and Broomery."

Inside the shop, they were greeted by a cute, smiling red headed girl wearing a black apron over a teal Wednesday Adams type dress. The apron sported the emblem of the shop and her name, Katie, on it.

"Hi, Michael! This must be your lovely date, Chloe?" Katie said, waving at the two of them from across a tall, massive table surrounded by wooden stools.

"Hi, Katie. It is. She's visiting from Iowa, and I thought I could hardly let her go back without her own broom from Salem."

"All the way from Iowa? Wow! Michael said you're here with your aunt, but that you're also considering colleges in Boston, when he called to make the reservation. What do you think about the

East Coast, so far?" Katie had a bit of a Boston-eque accent, Chloe noticed, which neither of the twins seems to have.

"I love it. So much to see and do. I'm especially fond of Salem, though," Chloe admitted.

"Yeah, my folks live in Dorchester, but me and three other girls rent an apartment here. We love it, too. One of my roommates owns this place. I'm the manager. Did Michael tell you what we do here?"

Chloe shook her head. "It was a surprise."

"There will be about six more people joining us today. You and Michael will start by picking a spot at the table and choosing a broomstick. We have small, medium, and large sizes of brooms in almost every color." Katie pointed out a far wall that housed several barrels full of thick sticks of varying colors and sizes.

"After you choose your broom, you'll take a look at our straws in the bins over there." She pointed to the right, where wooden racks held baskets filled with straws in various colors.

"Finally, you'll want to pick some twine and embellishments from the accessories area." She pointed to their right where a whole wall of fun accessories and rolls of twines, ribbons, and thin rolls of colorful metal wire were. "When you're done making your selection, you'll come over to the table, and I'll do a demo when the rest of our witches and warlocks get here."

A bell above the door sounded and a group of five older women walked into the shop. "Excuse me, Chloe."

Michael sidled up to her, having wandered off when Katie greeted her. "I put my jacket across two stools. You want to go pick out our broom stuff? Oh, and it's my treat, so get whatever size you want."

Chloe sighed happily. "This is perfect, Michael. My little goth heart is very full."

Michael chuckled, then raised his eyebrows suspiciously at the newly arrived women. "We better go rifle through the sticks before those ladies get to them. They look like they mean business."

Chloe laughed as they made their way from one station to the next. She was amused by how seriously Michael took his broom making. She knew he brought her here to cater to her and that it probably wasn't something he'd do by himself, but he was determined to have fun doing it. They both chose medium sized sticks with a bit of a curve at the top. Michael chose a walnut-colored stick and Chloe chose an almost black stained one.

Chloe stuck to the black theme and grabbed a large quantity of black straw, a small amount of purple straw, some black twisted twigs, some dried lavender, a few realistic looking purple leaves, some glittery black and purple striped ribbon, and black metal wire. Michael went with autumn colors–light and dark brown straw, yellow and orange leaves, and some brown twigs. He grabbed light colored twine and some orange ribbon.

Once everyone was settled around the table, Katie demonstrated how to arrange the straw and accents on the broom and showcased two different styles of finishing–a secure end open-bottom broom or a double-fixed broom with a longer, tighter upper broom tie and a mostly secured bottom tie. Michael chose the open style and Chloe, figuring it would fit better in her suitcase, chose the tighter style of broom.

They worked at the brooms for two hours, Michael asking for Chloe's opinion often and praising her ability to easily follow Katie's instructions and make a very put-together broom. Michael's twigs and leaves were giving him trouble, but Chloe's crafter's eye soon had them put right. She held his broom while he secured it, laughing at how he stuck his tongue out when he concentrated.

"Well, excuse me if my concentration face is not as adorable as yours," he said.

"I don't have a concentration face," Chloe answered back.

"You do. You purse your lips and frown," he countered.

"If you say so."

"I do say so because it's true. Hey, do you like Indian food?" Michael asked her.

"I don't know. I've never had it. But I like most food," Chloe answered.

He finished off tying his broom and looked up at her. "I think we are on our own for dinner tonight. I was going to take you to one of my favorite places to eat. My mom used to take Mindy and I there when dad was out. He doesn't like Indian food, and she always missed it so much."

"I like trying new things. I'm up for it."

Michael smiled. "Alright. We can walk that way when we're done here. It's about a twenty-minute walk, if you don't mind that."

Chloe wanted to say she'd walk a marathon with Michael if he asked her to. She wanted to tell him how special it was that he wanted her to eat at his mom's favorite restaurant, but she felt too awkward saying any of it.

She settled for a bright smile. "I like walking, remember?"

"I like walking, too. Especially with you." Thankfully, Michael was not shy about saying the things he wanted to say.

***

The host at the restaurant put them at a table near the window. A little oil lamp burned with a small, romantic flame upon a simple wooden table. The restaurant was mostly done in oranges and reds. Paintings of Indian stories and gods adorned the walls. The table was a four-person table with a booth and two chairs. Michael let her choose her seat, and she scooted into the booth next to the window.

Instead of taking a chair, Michael sat down next to her. "I like booth seats best, too."

"Well, I can share," Chloe said, thrilled to have his leg pressed up against hers.

Chloe had no idea what to order, so she let Michael order his favorite and asked that he order his mom's favorite, too. He chose Paneer Korma in her memory. He ordered with a bittersweet smile on his face. "Paneer Korma and Chicken Curry for our main dishes. Also, some naan and a vegetable samosa appetizer, please."

For drinks, they both ordered chai tea, which, when brought to them steaming, filled the air with a sweet and spicy aroma. It smelled a little like Michael's cologne, Chloe realized. Chloe closed her eyes and sipped her chai, marveling at the subtle spices, tempered by a splash of cream. She looked out the window at the darkening evening, the fire-colored leaves falling to the ground being rustled by a light breeze, and sighed happily.

Michael tentatively put his hand on her knee. She felt her face warm, but she smiled at him encouragingly. "This has been such a beautiful couple of days, Michael."

Michael squeezed her knee before removing his hand. The place where it had been felt so empty without the pressure of his long fingers.

He cupped his tea and sipped it before asking, "Have I done my job convincing you to stay, Ms. Mora?"

Chloe laughed. "You've been wonderful, but I won't say I've made up my mind yet."

The food was quick and when it was served, the scents set her mouth watering. The curry dish smelled a little of coconut and the paneer dish smelled sweet and a little like tomatoes and cream. The rice that came with it was unlike any Chloe had ever tasted. Tasting a spoonful, she was surprised by the nutty flavor and decided basmati rice was her new favorite. She took a tentative bite of the spicy chicken curry and mmmmed in the back of her throat. She immediately followed that by dipping some naan bread into the paneer korma.

"Oh my...that is the best thing I've ever tasted," she sighed over the bite.

"My mother would be very happy you like it. She always said it made her heart sing."

"I'm so happy you brought me here. It's so sweet of you to share something special like this, and it is the best food I've ever tasted. Please never tell my parents I said that."

Michael laughed and crossed his heart. "Promise."

They ate their fill of the sweet, spicy and creamy dishes, sharing a samosa, the mild flavor of which tempered the spicy heat building up in her mouth. They held hands and talked in between bites for an hour. Chloe was the first to throw in the towel and admit to being too full to eat another bite. Michael informed her they had a long walk back home to digest, which sounded like the perfect end to a perfect day.

They left the restaurant content and very full. The sky was darkening, and the air was crisp and breezy. The leaves fell with more purpose to the ground, creating little leaf tornados in the middle of the cobbled square where they stood. Michael grabbed her hand, his eyes smiling, and his broad shoulders relaxed. She twined her fingers through his, never relishing a touch so much as she had his.

They walked in a roundabout way to get back to the side street that would lead to another side street that would lead to his house so that Michael could show her the Bewitched statue.

Chloe had Michael lean into the statue with her and take a selfie of them. When she counted down, he leaned in and kissed her cheek. The resulting picture pleased Chloe beyond measure. In the picture, her face was pressed up against the face of Samantha. It looked like both she and the statue were posing for a very fun photo. Michael's perfectly timed kiss to her cheek was captured just as the shock of it hit Chloe's eyes. She immediately made it her profile picture.

She pocketed the phone and turned to Michael to find that his position remained unchanged. His body was turned towards her, his dark eyes serious. He leaned down to her and she leaned into him, pushing up on her tiptoes. His lips were warm and tasted of spices, coconut and chai tea. The kiss was quick and sweet. Having never kissed anyone apart from her parents and grandparents before, Chloe was shaking intensely, both nervous of messing it up and so excited by it that her knees were barely able to support her. Michael pulled away, but Chloe pulled him back down and kissed him longer the second time before parting, a dreamy smile on her lips. Her entire body was afire in a way it never had been before. She felt as warm as if she'd been running. She also felt a build up of pressure in her stomach, down.

For a moment, she mentally pictured where she'd shoved the condoms Bev supplied her with. That thought scared and exhilarated her.

Michael put one hand behind her head and moved a stray hair from her face with the other hand before leaning in a third time. Chloe panicked internally a bit. If he wanted more than just a regular kiss, she was out of her depth. Even so, she was excited to take that step. Unfortunately, fate was against her growth in this particular area. Michael's phone rang.

He sighed heavily. "Sorry, if that's my father, I have to answer, or he'll be very upset." Michael kissed her softly before taking his phone out, frowning.

He answered. "Hello, father."

Chloe was able to overhear Dr. Bath's stern, raised tone without having to try to eavesdrop. If she could have helped overhearing what he said, she would have chosen to. "Since you failed to travel back with your older brother today, I was left to call him repeatedly to reach him and insist he come back with me tomorrow morning. You have no idea how frustrating it is to have to work and take it upon myself to play nursemaid all day to your reckless sibling. When I was able to reach him, I heard a young lady in the background. Can you guess who he keeps company with these days?"

Michael turned away from Chloe, trying to protect her from his father's harsh words, but she could still hear him clearly. Michael answered, "No, I can't. I couldn't get ahold of him, either. I did try, father. You know he responds better when you reach out. He doesn't owe me answers."

"I'm sure you tried, but I doubt you tried very hard. Even if you don't get along with Ryan, his reputation affects us all, as does the company he keeps. He admitted to me that the voice of the young lady I heard was Lissa Thorne, that idiot Trenton Thorne's unmotivated hussy of a daughter."

Michael cringed over his father's adjectives and ground his teeth. Chloe immediately felt protective of the girl who she could not call a friend, but could not pretend to not care about. *Unmotivated? She was a student at freakin' MIT!* Lissa might have not been good friend material, but she was one of the most motivated people Chloe had ever met. Besides, she hated to hear Dr. Bath speak so vulgarly about anyone.

Dr. Bath continued, darkly, at the end of the line. "Can I surmise that your silence means that you already knew about this dalliance? You needn't deny it. Ryan told me he met Lissa at a party which Chloe attended with her, so I'll assume you were not ignorant of the connection and simply chose not to practice familial loyalty."

Michael sighed again. His shoulders grew tense, and his hand tightened around the phone. "Chloe did mention it, father. I guess I just thought he was probably not serious about Lissa. He's never serious about anyone."

Dr. Bath harrumphed. "Of course he's not serious about her. That's not the point. A girl like that can *make* someone very serious, if she's after our good name and money. Anyway, I told him to put a condom on it because if he impregnated that graceless twat from a failing household, I'd disinherit him on the spot."

Michael sucked in his breath. "Father, really..."

Dr. Bath cut him off. "Oh, grow up, Michael. Thankfully, he assured me he was only in for that very thing and would act accordingly. He also seemed to think you would have told me, since you were aware of the dalliance. I'm very disappointed by your discretion, son. Do you want that money grubbing whore to be the mother of your niece or nephew? Not that I'd let it get that far. Put your sister on, please."

Michael, his face red with embarrassment or anger, didn't miss a beat. "Mindy is in the bathroom. Maybe Lissa actually likes him, father. Did you ever think of that? What if she actually has feelings for him? Would it be so bad for him to be with someone who can stand him?"

Dr. Bath sighed heavily and answered, "If you're just going to be ridiculous, I need to get back to work. I only called to say I need you to come back to Boston tonight. I may have a surgery in the morning, and I cannot babysit your older brother. I demanded he meet me at the hospital in two hours. You will come and take care of this. Consider it a punishment for withholding information from me. He will stay in your dorm room with you tonight, and you will both make your way home in the morning. I suggest you act in better honesty and faith when it comes to family dealings from now on, or there will be consequences."

"I thought you wanted Mindy and I to entertain Chloe. I'm sure Ryan will come on the first train if you tell him to," Michael replied, his voice was all strained politeness.

"Mindy is able to keep Chloe company for the remainder of the night. When she is out of the *bathroom*, you can give her my directions to make sure our guest is happy for the night," his voice implied that he didn't believe for a moment Mindy was with them. "It will be too late for you to travel back tonight with your brother and keep curfew, so you'll just have to make your way home in the morning. I won't take any arguments about this. Do you understand?"

Michael mumbled that he understood and hung up before his father could say anything else that might embarrass him. He turned to Chloe. "I'm sorry about that. He shouldn't have called Lissa those things." He kicked a rock. "I was hoping to spend more time with you tonight."

Chloe's heart dropped. "I was hoping that, too. It *was* very unkind of him to say those things. Lissa isn't *all* bad. What if they really *do* like each other? How does being mean about her help him? I mean, if they did end up marrying or something," Chloe caught Michael's incredulous look, "which I know is unlikely, but if they *did*, he can't take words like that back."

Michael began walking, and Chloe followed him. After a moment, he said, "Nor would he want to. He thinks of it as Ryan betraying him. Lissa is no longer wealthy. In his mind, she's looking to improve her finances again, without looking to add any to Ryan's. Let's be honest, he's probably right in Lissa's case."

He paused to sigh heavily before continuing. "It's old-fashioned and strange, but my father is very strict about us not dating below our own social status. It's why he's so unkind about Kira. I mean, she's kind, thoughtful, entrepreneurial, and loves my sister like crazy, so what else could it be? I think Mindy's being a lesbian upset him, but it's always been clear that it's more upsetting that she chose to fall for someone who is not rich or socially important. Social standing is really important to him. Though, Lissa and Kira might be forgiven if they were famous or something. He still rattles on about how his descendants were barons and baronesses, however many hundreds of years ago."

"That's really horrible," Chloe murmured, feeling her own lack of social standing acutely. If that was the case, was Michael simply using her? It was possible that his father didn't know about her low class upbringing, since she'd been spending time with her aunt. She got the distinct impression that was exactly why Dr. Bath had been encouraging her.

"If you want horrors, Pickering Place has it in spades thanks to the good doctor," Michael mumbled, his carefree smile having been replaced with furrowed brows and a sullen expression of discontent.

Chloe couldn't help but shiver a little over Michael's tone and words. Dr. Bath grew increasingly terrible in her mind's eye. She wondered, again, about what Mindy said about not being present at her mother's death, at it being so unexpected. There were also the rumors the Thornes heard about Mrs. Bath not being faithful. Chloe could only imagine how unhappy being with someone like Dr. Bath would make a person. A growing, aching suspicion was overtaking her senses. She began to consider that her earlier imaginings about the late Mrs. Bath were not so far fetched. What if Dr. Bath was something much worse than oppressive and controlling?

"What kind of horrors are we talking here?" She tried to keep her voice light, but Michael arched an eye at her tone.

"Why don't you just imagine some horrors, then write me a good, gothic short story? I will probably be more interesting than the truth. Pickering Place is as good a title for a horror story as any." He tried to smile teasingly but failed.

"I think sometimes you tease when you're uncomfortable. I admit to not knowing much of the world, but I know what a happy home feels like. And I think I know what a very sad one feels like, now, too," Chloe answered.

Michael stopped, turned to her, and sighed. "You like vampire stories, right? Imagine living in one where the vampire didn't suck blood, but the actual life out of people. My father is like that. He sucked the life right out of my mother even before she died. My mom was all happiness and light when I was little, but she wilted more and more every year under his obsessive, possessive reign. Why not write that story? I can't say I'd enjoy it, having had to live it, but it would be properly gothic and terribly romantic."

Chloe bit her lip. "I'm sorry to hear that." Inside, her heart raced. She pictured Dr. Bath as a vampire of life. She pictured him looming over his wife, his hands outstretched, grasping in rage for her slender neck.

Michael started to walk again, his head hanging low. After a moment, he broke the heavy silence and said, "My parents never outright fought, but they weren't suited for each other. I think they married to please their parents. My mom's parents were interested in her doing better for herself, making her way in America. They were a wealthy family, but they wanted the American dream for my mom. My dad was already wealthy and was a doctor to boot. He can, as you probably can tell, be charming if it suits him. I think he must have once charmed her into thinking he was interested in more than his own self advancement. And maybe he even tricked himself into that. I don't really know. I only knew what they were like together after we came along."

"I'm sorry to hear that. I can't even imagine what that must have been like."

"I know. I'm a little envious of you."

"Me? Why? Are you jealous of the room I share with two of my siblings in a tiny trailer in Williamston? Being so poor that I make most of my clothing out of discount fabric and remake it so that it will fit my younger sisters when I grow out of it? Maybe living in a town of people where the median age is 60 makes you envious? Being one of only two brown girls in a place full of white people who purposefully whisper about immigrants taking their jobs while giving me nasty looks? Having people talk behind my back about how my dad ruined my mom's family's good name?" Chloe stopped herself, realizing she was raising her voice.

Michael frowned. "No, that is, I didn't know all of that. In cities like Boston, I guess people of color, like me and you, don't stand out as much. I actually didn't know that about where you lived. I guessed you were not as well off as your aunt, but I didn't know you were poor."

"Well, now you know," Chloe mumbled.

Michael nodded his head solemnly. "I was actually talking about your parents. You talk as though your parents are so in love. Maybe that's why I tease your romanticism. I don't quite understand it. I'm happy you had that, but my dad was never romantic and if my mother was, it was a poor match. I think the most romantic thing I can do is marry someone I know I can respect and love, so that my kids, like you, can dream their dreams, instead of hiding scars that their parents left behind."

"Do you think it will be possible to be with someone for romantic reasons if your father doesn't approve?" Chloe asked.

"I'm practical and understand that it's easier and better to have more money to live on than less, but it's not really my opinion that matters. My father has told my sister if she dates 'that destitute, good for nothing barista' he will cut her off. I'd hoped I could avoid all that by falling in love with someone who had money."

"And if you don't?"

"Well, then, I hope I can be as noble as I'd like to be, should that come up." He gave her a rueful smile, which did nothing to assuage her fears that this beautiful time together would end in nothing. "Anyway...we'd better get back. It's getting late, and I still have to go back to Boston, I guess. I'll text Mindy and ask her to come back to the house, so you're not by yourself."

~ Twenty-One ~

CHLOE TOTALLY KILLS HER CHANCES

The walk back was quiet, but not altogether unpleasant. Michael held her hand and squeezed it reassuringly. The dark, pervasive cloud that was Dr. Bath, however, could not be shaken after the call and only increased as evening darkened the shadows on the sidewalks.

Chloe was suddenly happy they would be inside Michael's house, as stark as it was. The decorations from people's porches seemed more ominous when walking past them than they had in a warm car, out of the wind that tugged at her hair and blew leaves and spiderwebs in her face.

When they got to Pickering Place, Michael excused himself to get a night bag together, and Chloe went into his mother's room to change into her pajama shirt. After dressing, Chloe sat on the bed, feeling defeated and frustrated. She didn't want to admit it even to herself, but she'd hoped to spend some time alone with Michael in the house, possibly in his room. She wanted to know what kissing him without measured restraint would be like. Turning on her side, she sighed into her pillow.

The door behind the screen rattled as the wind picked up outside. A chilly breeze crawled up her skin from under the cracks of the door. Her interest once again piqued, she could not help but wonder what was behind that door. Why had Michael's father insisted it be locked? Why couldn't his *children* even visit the room? Why was it cold to the touch?

Chloe pictured a specter of a woman standing behind the door, her cold, misty hands wrapped around the handle, begging to be released. She stood and crossed to the door, putting her own hand to the doorknob. It was so cold it stung a little to keep her hand on it. Chloe tried turning the knob, but it was locked, just as Mindy said. She bit her lip, thinking for a moment, weighing what she wanted to do in her racing mind.

Her romantic curiosity got the better of her logic. She ran to her purse, took out the card Tía gave her and ran it between the doorjamb and the door latch, like she sometimes had to do at home, when she forgot her key to the house and locked herself out. Old locks were not sophisticated. This one was no exception, and the card was thin enough to lift under the metal latch and release the lock. The door swung open.

Chloe took a tentative step forward, ducking under the arched doorway. It was very dark in the closet-like room. A sideways slanted window, a witch window, shone light from the moon on stacked boxes, tall paintings, and coffee cans filled with brushes. Chloe knelt to inspect a white framed picture that had fallen onto the floor, the glass on it cracked. The picture was of a beautiful woman in her thirties. She had long, black hair, a longish nose, and lively brown eyes. She looked so much like Mindy that Chloe instantly knew who she was. Another picture, propped up where this one had been, showed Dr. Bath and Mrs. Bath under a white flower trellis, holding hands in front of a priest. The picture was too dusty to make out the details. She went to wipe the glass off when she heard a knock at the door.

"Chloe, are you dressed?" Michael called.

"Yes," Chloe called back, without thinking. It was true, she was dressed, but if she meant to stall him it was the wrong answer.

Michael pushed open the door. Chloe sidled out of the space, closing the door quickly behind her, accidentally failing to latch the door in her haste. Michael stepped into the room, about to say something, when a breeze from the ill-insulated witch window pushed the door of the storage closet open. The door hit the silk screen, which crashed to the ground. Chloe, not able to hide the awkward guilt on her face, scrambled to close the door more firmly this time and bent to pick up the screen that clattered to the ground.

"Sorry. I'll get it," she mumbled, dashing about to fix her misstep.

"Were you in that closet?" Michael asked, his tone serious. "Didn't I remind you that my father says it's off limits?"

Chloe righted the screen, not meeting Michael's eye. She searched for words that would make her actions make sense, but she was not good at coming up with lies on her feet. Her agitation only made her more unable to speak dishonestly.

"Yes, you did, it's just that...Well, she couldn't say much about what happened to your mom and it seemed so strange of your dad to forbid you both to speak of it. And since neither of you were here when she passed and your dad shut everything away, and...well, you said that thing about your dad keeping his dirty secrets in there, and him being so unkind and vampiric...Well, I thought...well..."

She couldn't say it. It was too foolish, now that she'd expressed it. Even though her head spun with the sincerity with which she believed it, she could not tell Michael she thought his father was a murderer.

Michael crossed the room and put a finger under her chin, lifting it so that she was forced to look at him. His eyes were a mixture of hurt and incredulity. She immediately dropped her eyes again.

His voice broke a little when he spoke. "Let me see if I can understand what you're saying. You assumed that because Mindy was away and couldn't explain how my mother died, that her death was suspicious. You assumed that my father packing away her things and shoving all traces of her into this closet, locking it and forbidding us entrance was motivated by...what? Guilt? Not sorrow, but guilt? You assumed that he was hiding something more sinister than wedding pictures of a wife he misses and cannot bear to be reminded of? You think my father is a murderer? Is that it?" His voice was harsh now. His eyes were unbelieving.

Chloe stammered a bit, stepping away from him and looking, again, to the floor. She couldn't bear to look at those eyes. "I know it must seem impossible, but given his controlling demeanor, and Xaiden's friend John said your mother was healthy the week before...And, the fact that her death was so mysterious, that you weren't here, and your dad refused to talk about it, well I..."

"You came to the outrageous conclusion that my father killed her?" Michael took another step forward. "Chloe, look at me."

Chloe raised her guilty eyes to his. She expected to see more anger. He would have been justified in it if he were angry. But she didn't. She saw only hurt and that same unbearable incredulity, which, when centered on her, made her feel small and foolish.

His voice was strained when he spoke. "Mindy was not here when my mother died, but I was. I was the first to the room when she called out in agony for my father. I raced to this room. I flung open the door and I saw her clutch her head. I heard her last words. 'My head, Michael. Michael, get your father! Something's wrong.'"

A tear fell from Michael's control, then. His eyes were far into that terrible memory. Chloe's heart shattered to see it. She'd been such a fool.

"Xaiden's friend John was right." Michael threw out Xaiden's name as though it were something slimy and detestable; he threw it out as an accusation. It was clear he couldn't believe she still believed anything Xaiden had told her.

"My mother *was* fine the week before. She was fine the night before, only had a mild headache and went to bed early. That morning," Michael's eyes filled with more tears. More escaped his control and slid down his face, "that morning, after those words, she was *not* fine. She was *gone*. She fell forward like a rag doll. I ran to her, screaming. I tapped her cheeks, felt for a pulse, but I knew when I saw her eyes that she was gone."

He wiped the tears from his cheeks absently, staring at Chloe with that same awful incredulous, accusatory look.

What could she say to any of that? It was all so horrible.

"Oh, I see. I'm relieved to hear that I was so wrong." Chloe wished she was less awkward in difficult situations at this moment.

Saying she was relieved after what Michael just shared with her immediately sounded heartless and insipid. She scrambled to claw her way out of this impossible hole she'd dug. Tears threatened to fall as they gathered behind her throat. She fumbled for the right words to fix all of it. "That is, I'm so sorry, Michael. So, so sorry. I would never have presumed to think it possible if…"

Michael cut her off, for the first time looking almost angry. "You should never have presumed in the first place! I think I was wrong before, when I said your obsession with fantasy and romance was charming. I think there *is* such a thing as spending too much of your life in your own wild imagination." He turned on his heel, shutting the door behind him forcefully.

Our poor heroine was then rightfully ashamed. She spent a full hour, after Michael departed, crying heartily into the silk pillowcase on Michael's mother's bed. Exhausting herself so thoroughly that she didn't even hear Mindy get home, knock and open the door to check on her friend.

She didn't hear Mindy get ready for bed herself. She didn't charge her phone or call Tía or her mama or papa. She didn't remember to pick up the neglected card she'd used as a lock pick. She didn't hear when Dr. Bath's rideshare came pulling up to the house. She did hear him slam the door and yell for his daughter.

~ Twenty-Two ~

DR. DRAMA QUEEN RUINS EVERYTHING WHILE SALLY SAVES THE DAY

Chloe sat up in bed, Dr. Bath's feral yell for Mindy waking Chloe from restless dreams. She peered at the clock on the dresser, but the room was too dark to read the time by. She rose to find her phone in her jacket pocket from earlier. The time read 10:30 p.m.; the battery was low enough that the dim screen was hard to read. She shoved it back into the pocket, confused about why Dr. Bath had returned tonight when he said he wouldn't. She also worried that she knew exactly why, and her stomach clenched uncomfortably.

Chloe could hear Mindy rush out of her room and down the stairs. Dr. Bath's voice reached her in the room, here and there, but only in waves of harsh words. She caught "little adventuring bitch," "liar," and "out."

Those words were enough for her to know that she had overstayed her welcome. Michael must have traveled to Boston and told his father what she'd said. In a panic, Chloe began gathering her things and shoving them into her bag. She changed out of her pajamas and into warm black sweats and her purple hoodie, putting on the clothes she would wear in the morning when she left, so that she wouldn't be in the Bath's way for longer than necessary.

She had just finished packing the last of her things when Mindy knocked timidly on the door.

"Come in, Mindy," Chloe said, averting her eyes. *What had her father told Mindy? Would Mindy hate her now?*

Mindy came into the room and shut the door behind her. Her eyes were red, as if she'd been crying. She looked very uncomfortable and embarrassed to say what Chloe knew she would say–that Chloe would be leaving first thing in the morning.

"It's okay, Mindy. I know I'll have to leave in the morning. I expected as much when I heard your father come home so upset. I don't want to talk about it, but I assure you, it's my fault," Chloe said, motioning that Mindy could sit next to her on the bed.

Chloe's calm acceptance did nothing to assuage Mindy's feelings, however. She immediately broke down crying. When she'd composed herself enough to speak, she said, "I'm sorry, Chloe, but my father wants you to leave *tonight*." She sobbed brokenly over this injustice.

This alarmed Chloe. Travel in the dead of night? "Tonight? Is there a train so late?"

Mindy patted her nose with a tissue. "There is. There's one in thirty minutes leaving for Boston, and, I'm so sorry, but he wants you on it. He says you have to start walking now because he won't pay for an Uber to take you to the station. I can walk with you to the station, though. It's not safe for you to be out and about on your own at night. I don't care what he says. I'll go with you that far, at least."

Chloe felt that this reaction to her ridiculous assumptions was a little over the top, even for Dr. Bath. Nonetheless, she decided she deserved no better treatment. Her heart raced a little at the idea of making her way to the train by herself in the dark, but she resolved to be dignified.

"No, Mindy, you'll upset your dad further. Besides, I know why he wants me gone, and if he told you, you wouldn't be so kind.

Michael knows and he left very angry with me. He must have told your father. I don't blame him for being angry."

"I don't think so, Chloe. I don't know what passed between you and Michael, but I can't imagine he'd run to our father with it. Besides, there is nothing he could say that would justify kicking you out of his home when he promised to take care of you. Sending you, in the dark, to a city you barely know is despicable. Let me come with you."

Chloe shook her head. "No, thank you, but I'd better do it on my own. I'll call Tía from the station and have Bev pick me up. It'll be fine. I better get going, though, if I'm going to catch that train. I know it's a bit of a walk." Fear struck Chloe then. She didn't remember how to get to the station. What if she got lost and was wandering Salem for hours?

Mindy seemed to have this all figured out, though, and slipped her a folded piece of paper. "This has directions on it to the station. Oh, God, Chloe. I'm just so sorry. I should just go with you and not come back."

Chloe could see the fear in Mindy's eyes at this bleak prospect. She couldn't hurt both twins. As much as she wanted Mindy's company, she shook her head fiercely.

She took Mindy's hand. "No, Mindy. I won't have you do that. Michael and Ryan will be back in the morning. You might be happy you didn't make a fuss over me when they do. I'll text you when I'm at the station and when I get back to Bev's. I won't have you risking everything for me. I promise, this is for the best."

I deserve this. I deserve this treatment after thinking such horrific things about Dr. Bath. If she were truly honest with herself, however, she knew she'd never treat someone this abysmally for a like offense.

Without any more hesitation, Chloe stood, her shoulders set determinedly. Mindy helped her carry her bag down the stairs. Chloe was happy to see that Dr. Bath had not seen fit to see her off. She couldn't bear to look at him after what she'd accused him of.

She gave Mindy a hug for what she knew was the last time. Her only solace was that her sweet friend did not yet seem to know why she was being unceremoniously kicked out of the house in the dead of the night. It was a small comfort that would not be long lasting.

If the walk back to Pickering Place had been dark and gloomy earlier in the evening, the walk to the train station in the middle of the night was much more unsettling. Chloe's head swam with guilt, however, over how she treated the Bath family, and this preoccupied her so much that the clawing tree limbs, whistling winds and dark, dancing shadows in the night could not hold as much sway on her senses as they normally would. She was still frightened, but fear was not her strongest sensation at this point.

She unfolded the piece of paper Mindy gave her and almost cried when a fifty-dollar bill fell out of the paper and onto the streets. It was then that she realized she'd left the money card Tía gave her on the floor of Mrs. Bath's bedroom and would not have been able to pay for the train without this kindness from Mindy.

If she hadn't been ridiculous and nosey, she'd still have the card and money and would be sleeping soundly rather than fighting tears over Mindy's thoughtfulness. She didn't deserve this kindness, the detailed map in Mindy's careful hand, nor the sweet note at the bottom saying she was "So sorry and you are a truly wonderful friend." She picked the money up and pocketed it, grateful, once again, for Mindy's empathy and sense.

The walk to the train station took twenty minutes, and the train was already waiting when she got there. She quickly purchased a ticket in the machine, which, thankfully, accepted cash. She collected her change and ticket and boarded the dimly lit car, picking a mostly empty train car at random. Only one other woman occupied the space, and she was quietly snoring, her gray head lolling forward in sleep.

She unzipped her bag and fished her phone out of her patchwork jacket. Unfortunately, she flipped the phone open, only to find that it would not turn on. She'd forgotten to charge the stupid thing and it had died. She shoved the phone back in the jacket pocket and the jacket back into her suitcase, stowed the case above her seat and flopped down, dejected. She knew without looking that her charger was plugged into the wall of Mrs. Bath's room.

"Perfect!" Chloe said, bitterly.

Her chest tightened in anxiety, and a thickness in the back of her throat threatened tears. She must have made more noise than she intended, as it woke the poor old lady who'd been snoring a few seats down from her. She cradled her face in her hands and took deep breaths to keep from crying.

"Are you alright, dear?" a shaky voice asked from behind her. The old woman looked down at Chloe with a worried expression in her brown eyes.

"Yes. Sorry if I was being loud. I forgot my charger at my friend's house and my phone is dead. I meant to call my aunt to pick me up at the station, but now I can't. Unless, I'm sorry for asking, do you have a phone I could use?"

The old woman shook her head regretfully. "I'm sorry to say I don't have much of anything to my name. I had enough money to buy a ticket to stay warm on this train for a few hours, but I don't have a phone."

Chloe noticed, for the first time, the haggard appearance of the old woman. She was unkempt and a little dirty. "Are you hungry?" she asked the woman. "Is there food on this train?"

The woman stood. "There is. I think it will still be open. I'll show you." She gestured that Chloe should follow her.

The food car was just closing when Chloe and the old woman made it to the car. The tired-looking man stayed open for a few more minutes so Chloe could buy the woman something to eat and buy herself a coffee. She wanted to be alert if she was going to have to get to Bev's all by herself tonight. The woman thanked her for the food, and they walked back to their train car as the train lurched and made its way shakily down the tracks.

After eating, the old woman thanked her, again, all smiles, and fell back asleep. Chloe fell into a deep, morose reverie about how quickly life could shoot you down to earth when you'd just been walking on air.

The coffee kept her awake for the ride, but it didn't help her anxiety. She began to worry that she didn't quite remember Bev's address, and only vaguely remembered that it was somewhere along Charles Street, a few blocks down from the hospital.

She closed her eyes and pictured the black awning above the gray brick entrance to Bev's apartment. *Something Manor. Parkplace? Park? Park...Parkview. That was it. There was a pretty little walking park in between the apartments and shops on that street. Parkview was right.* She would just have to take the "T" to a station that stopped somewhere close to Mass General and retrace her steps from there.

She sipped her coffee, wincing at how bitter and burnt it tasted. Clearly, the brew had been on the warmer all afternoon. But she drank it, nonetheless, vainly trying to see past her reflection in the train window to the darkness beyond. When she grew bored with that, she closed her eyes and replayed the ridiculous confrontation she'd had with Michael.

Her face burned and her eyes stung, remembering how stupid she'd been. She tried to think of something more pleasant, like the fantastic kiss they'd shared in downtown, but her embarrassed traitor brain kept showing her the image of his face–confused and incredulous and angry.

When the train pulled into Boston thirty minutes later, Chloe nervously disembarked, feeling worse than she had when the ride started. The old woman followed her off the train and through the quiet terminal area. Chloe pulled her expensive bag behind her, the sound of the wheels clicking over the tiled floor of the station setting her on edge. It echoed off the empty columns and kiosks. The station had been full of people shoving and weaving and talking when she was last here. Now, it was a ghost town, unsettlingly empty and haunting.

The old woman wished Chloe well with a wave and a last thank you for her food before sitting down on a stoop just inside the train terminal. It was clear she planned to call the terminal her bed for the night until someone kicked her out. The thought made Chloe sad. No elderly person should have to sleep on the steps of a stinky subway station.

Chloe followed signs to the green/orange "T" line, and stopped in a near empty hallway to read the map of crisscrossing red, blue, orange and green metro lines displayed on the wall. She studied the map closely, trying to discern how to get to the red line, which seemed to be where the Charles Street/MGH stop was located.

Our heroine was not used to having to be aware of her surroundings, having been raised her whole life in a town where everyone knew everyone else's name, phone number, and business. Her latent trust in her fellow man kept her from becoming wary when a group of three rough looking young men who passed behind her, did a double take, stopped mid-conversation, and looked both ways down the hall where Chloe studied the map of the station.

One of the men cleared his throat and approached Chloe, a menacing smile in his eyes. "Hey, girly. You lost?"

Chloe, having just figured out her plan of action, nearly jumped at the man's voice, not having been aware of the men at all until this point. She turned to see him slinking towards her.

She eyed his friends smiling unpleasantly behind the wafer-thin brunette man. "I'm sorry. Did you say something?"

Chloe tried for politeness, hoping that, by being kind to the men, they would decide she was not a good target for unwanted attention. Unfortunately, the opposite is often true for young women, but Chloe had been too sheltered in her young life to know such things.

The man laughed cruelly, a hacking, wet laugh. Yeast and smoke sputtered forth from his hacking laugh, staining the air in a dive bar stench, and wafted her way. "Yeah, I said somethin', little lady. I asked if ya were lost. Me and my buddies here can see ya where yer goin.' It would be our pleasure." He dragged the word 'pleasure' out.

Chloe shivered involuntarily. She hugged her purse to her side, quickly realizing that kindness was not the correct approach to leering, lingering men in the middle of the night. She quietly undid the clasp on the pepper spray Tía made her take with her and went over Tía's instructions in her head.

Point the nozzle away from you and turn your head when you spray.

All three men began closing in on her. Chloe let go of her roller bag, stealthily turning the pepper spray nozzle away from her. She'd just raised the pink spray in front of her when a voice sounded down the hall she'd entered from.

"They went that way, officer. Looked *real* shifty!" Chloe heard a familiar voice say.

The three men turned away from Chloe upon hearing the word "officer." The wafer-thin man backed away from Chloe and motioned with his head for his friends to clear out. They ran down the hall as fast as they could, not waiting to meet the authorities. However, the only person to show herself was Chloe's old friend from the train. Her grin revealed a few missing teeth as she made her way toward Chloe.

"Those guys walked this way, looking like they were up to no good. I thought I'd better check on ya. You okay, dear?"

Chloe's hands shook as she clipped the pepper spray on her bag. Her throat was clogged with unshed tears from fear or grief or tiredness. She couldn't say which, but it hardly mattered. The tears began to stream down her face of their own accord, and she couldn't seem to stop the flow.

"Oh, dear. Come on, now. Where are you trying to go?" The old woman asked, coming up to Chloe and taking the handle of her bag. "I'll see you on your way."

Chloe nodded, wiping her nose on her sleeve. "Thank you. I just want to get to Charles Street station, if you can show me how?"

The woman took Chloe's hand with own thin hand, pulling Chloe's bag toward the green line with the other. "This way, dear. I'll wait with you at the green line. You'll take the green to Park and Park to the red line. Come on, this way. If you mean to get off at Charles Street, you'll be okay. It's a much nicer area."

Chloe wondered at the kindness of this frail, tottering, homeless woman. How did someone suffer through such things in life and still find kindness for anyone else in her heart? How did someone like Dr. Bath have everything he could ever want and still be so cold to those around him?

She couldn't answer these questions, so she wiped her eyes, took her heavy bag from the kind woman, and followed her to the green line.

The old woman's name turned out to be Sally. She was as good as her word, waiting with Chloe for the green line train to come, so she wouldn't be left alone with any lurking ruffians, should new ones show themselves or old ones return. Sally shivered in her thin, time-worn, long-sleeved t-shirt. The night was getting very cold. Chloe opened her bag while they waited for the train and fished out her handmade patchwork jacket.

Sally's jaw dropped when Chloe handed it to her. "Here, have this. You can keep it. I made it myself and I have another at home."

Sally pulled her arms through the quilted, colorful arms of the jacket and smiled her gap-toothed smile. "You made this?" She searched the quilted squares with her thin fingers, delicately patting them, a look of awe on her face.

Chloe nodded, zipping her bag. Sally buttoned the big yellow buttons on the front of the jacket, her eyes smiling. "You shouldn't give something so nice to me. You could sell something like this in a fancy store."

"That's okay. I'd rather you have it, as a thank you," Chloe replied.

The green line train pulled up not long after that and Sally shooed Chloe onto the train, reminding her to transfer to the red line once she got to Park Station. She waved at Chloe through the dirty train windows.

Chloe remembered something her grandma Jones once said–that guardian angels came in many forms. She wondered about that as the train pulled away from Sally, looking content in the patchwork jacket Chloe gifted her. The fluorescent lights of the subway shone against her gray hair, giving her an angelic glow.

Chloe switched trains and found Charles Street without further incident. She walked down the cold, quiet and peaceful city street, looking for familiar buildings. Lights from apartments fell down upon the sidewalk, giving the night a warm glow.

Charles Street felt just as safe and pleasant as MIT had. Some officers patrolling the area stopped to ensure she was okay. She took the opportunity to ask after Parkview Manor. They told her the complex was two blocks straight ahead and asked if she wanted them to take her there, but she shook her head. For some reason, she wanted to finish the last leg of her adventure on her own. It was her own foolishness that got her into this mess. She wanted it to be her own grit that got her out of it.

The city was beautiful at night, lit windows shining like a thousand candles through the gloom. The sounds of traffic were light, and the only ruckus noises were the sounds of laughter and music from a few bars and cocktail joints along the way. Joyful sounds. Chloe allowed herself to relax and see the city around her, not quite sleeping, not quite awake. She soon recognized the brick walks and colorful trees of the park in front of Bev's building. Her body flooded with relief.

When she finally came upon Parkview Manor, she felt a deep and satisfying sense of accomplishment. She pressed the buzzer labeled "Ikeda" and smiled in triumph when Bev's groggy voice rang on the other end.

~ Twenty-Three ~

THAT'S WHY THEY CALL IT GROWING PAINS

Chloe had a difficult time keeping Tía from trying to drive all the way to Salem on her bum foot. Tía was irate about Dr. Bath sending her barely-traveled niece home in the middle of the night without an escort or friend to guide her. She raged for several minutes in Spanish, throwing words around Chloe recognized as the same words she'd said when she reinjured her foot. She threw in a few choice English curse words, too, ensuring that Dr. Bath's name was twice cursed.

Bev got Tía to laugh when she threw in some Japanese curse words for good measure. Thrice cursed. Bev. shoved a steaming mint tea into Chloe's hands and ushered her to a long, black velvet couch.

"Spill it. Not the tea, mind you. I just bought the couch."

Bev and Tía sat on either side of Chloe, and she told them everything–how Dr. Bath made her feel, how he behaved toward his children, how sterile his house was, how oppressive it felt when he was in it, even the damning things the Twins said about his character.

Finally, tears falling down her cheeks, she finished off with the confrontation she'd had with Michael. She told them about invading the Bath's privacy by opening the closet and about the ridiculous conclusions she'd made.

"To top it all off, I left my charger and the money card you sent with me there, and accidentally gave my phone to a sweet homeless lady," Chloe sobbed, leaning on Tía's shoulder. She'd had to explain the phone situation in great detail, and the result clearly somewhat amused Bev, who covered a smile.

"It's a loadable card. I can put the remainder back in my account, so don't worry about that. As for your phone, we'll get you a new one, though your number will have to change. It's the least I can do, after trusting that prig with my niece," Tía comforted her.

"No, that's okay, Tía. I'll just call mom and dad tomorrow and ask them not to renew the phone plan. I don't deserve another one. I used your trust and my responsibility poorly." Chloe blew her nose.

Bev made a dismissive sound. "Oh, Chloe, you are being far too hard on yourself. Honestly, after you laid it all out like that, between what the Thorne's said, what you saw of his behavior and what the twins said, I can't blame you for thinking the worst of him."

Chloe made an incredulous face. "You would have called him a murderer to his son's face?" Her voice was thick with sarcasm.

Bev couldn't keep her laughter in, and it caught on. For a full five minutes, all three ladies laughed until they cried.

Finally, Bev took a deep breath and said, "No. I would not have said it out loud. You're much more honest than I'll ever be, dear."

"Did your papa ever tell you about great abuela Marietta?" Tía asked Chloe.

Chloe shook her head. Bev clapped and said, "Oh! I love the abuela Marietta story. Tell her, Miranda."

"Abuela Marietta was vilified, as a young woman, for marrying your great abuelo Juan Mora, when she was seven months pregnant," Tía explained. "Papa Luis told me she never once apologized for the baby she carried. She acted every day as if she deserved the love of a man who was not the father of her child. She unabashedly told those who asked that she met the Diné father of her child at a bar and that he was handsome, but not someone she wanted to spend her life with. And do you know what she told your great abuelo?"

Chloe shook her head. Tía continued, "She told abuelo Juan, he could marry her only if he treated baby Luis as his own. She said she was a catch at any stage of her life and her little boy was no different. She ignored the gossipers and whisperers. That little baby, abuelo Luis, raised his children with the same fight. She never said she regretted what she did that passionate night with a man she didn't want to stay with forever. We Moras don't make mistakes. We make opportunities for growth."

Chloe wiped her eyes. "I wish this opportunity for growth hadn't been so embarrassing, or the growth so painful."

"Growth *is* painful, mija. Do you think I wanted my app to be used by vapid influencers to trick people into buying weight loss products? To train young ones to be ashamed of who they are? *No.* I wanted my app to help people make informed human decisions about our leaders. The way I designed the algorithm, though, made it easy to use for purposes I'm not proud of. *That* was painful. I could allow it to embarrass me now. I could take to heart the comments of my peers who say they can't believe Miranda Mora actually made it to MIT on merit. I could let people who call me "Legally Brown" have power over me. I could listen when they say my descent is what got me into MIT, but I *know* who I am. I am Dr. Miranda Mora, and I am perfect in my imperfection. You are Chloe Mora. You are kind, smart, funny, and talented. You said something you're not proud of. Own it. Apologize only if you are sorry. Grow. That's all you can do."

Chloe smiled wonderingly at her independent, amazing Tía. "Thanks, Tía."

Bev covered a big yawn, and Chloe soon followed suit. Tonight had been exhausting–emotionally, physically and spiritually.

Tía kissed her niece's head. "It's late. Get some sleep, amor. We'll check in with your mama and papa in the morning. Let them know you don't have your phone."

Chloe, falling asleep where she sat, nodded her head. Bev showed Chloe to her office, which had a pull-down murphy bed. Tía retired to the full guest bedroom. Chloe was lulled to sleep by the faint and persistent city sounds playing outside the tall window.

***

Chloe spent the last two days in Boston with Bev and Tía. Chloe slept through much of her third to last day and spent the rest of it getting to know the wonderful Bev. They had a rainy romcom day with delivered take out and margaritas, watching *10 Things I Hate About You* and *Pride and Prejudice* while doing their nails. Tía got a lot of joy out of handing her "favorite virgin a virgin margarita."

The second to last day, they visited Chinatown before going to the Wang theater for a production of *Wicked*, which cheered Chloe considerably. She'd never in her life seen anything in a theater as big or grand as the Wang, and the show was life changing.

After having spent much of her life attending church plays or amateur theater in Williamston, Chloe never imagined the scale of a Broadway play. The music, costumes, sets and acting blew our young heroine away. Of all the things that could have convinced Chloe Mora to make Boston her home, this was probably the most convincing.

After all, new friends and relationships had brought her a mixture of joy and pain, and had ended only in tears. *Wicked* might have made her cry, but it didn't break her heart. It might have even healed it a little.

When her last day in Boston rolled around, Chloe was ready to return home. She knew she'd miss the city, but her strongest feeling, right now, was that of loss. Every time they passed MIT, her eyes would blur and threaten to spill over. She was ready to not be reminded of what she had and what she lost.

Tía and Bev dropped Chloe off at the airport a few hours before her flight. The three women shared in the perfect amount of parting grief before saying their goodbyes. Chloe was relieved to hear that Tía didn't order her the gate service this time around. She was ready to brave the reader boards, grumpy passengers, and boring wait by herself. And so she did, without any dire adventures or delays. She was not seated next to a handsome twenty something on the way home, any more than she had been on the way to Boston. But she was not grieved by it this time. Heartache was not as romantic as it seemed on the screen, and hers was too raw to want to pursue another at so early a date.

Instead, she was seated next to a sweet ten-year-old girl with two adorable jet black braids in her hair and a first time flier pin on her chest. Her name was Joon, and she was very nervous about takeoff.

"It's not so bad," Chloe assured her. "Hey, do you want to play I-Spy with me?"

Joon agreed to this arrangement, spying something white. This made the game extremely difficult in a plane made from mostly white materials. However, the goal was to distract Joon from her fear, and in this, Chloe was successful.

After the plane leveled out to cruising altitude, Joon admitted that "it wasn't so scary to fly."

"Most things aren't as scary as our imaginations make them," Chloe sagely informed Joon.

They spent the rest of their time dipping Lotus cookies in milk and watching in-flight movies. Their very attentive flight attendant gave them several packages of said cookies to ensure Joon's continued comfort and happiness. Joon chose *Encanto* for her movie pick, since she thought Chloe looked a lot like Isabela. Chloe decided that Joon was one of her favorite new friends. The new friends parted ways when Chloe got off the plane in Iowa, as Joon was flying on to Seattle. She drew a picture of Chloe dressed as Isabela on a napkin, so she would not forget her.

Chloe had a strange sensation, walking to baggage claim. She was nervous about seeing her parents. At first, she couldn't place why she felt this way, but she soon understood her own heart. She'd experience so much in the past week that she felt permanently altered. For a moment, she wondered if her parents would even recognize her in her new Boston clothes. She wondered if the grief of finding and losing something so significant would show on her face, if it made her look older.

Her parents, however, spotted her right away and swept her up as though no time had passed. Having spoken to Tía about the more difficult part of her trip, her parents understood their daughter had undergone a harrowing adventure, so they kept their questions light and smothered her in praise over how beautiful she looked in her new city fashions.

***

Once home, Chloe was immediately surrounded by noisy requests from her younger siblings for the promised souvenirs, which she happily fished out of her bag. The younger boys were not too old, at 13 and 14, for their Nimbus 2000 brooms. They immediately took their leave of their sister, running outside to play at quidditch. Sam, the oldest boy at 16, was helping at Grandpa Jones' farm, so she'd have to wait to give him his gift. Her younger sisters, however, donned their witch dress up outfits directly over their clothes and stayed to pepper Chloe with questions.

"What was Boston like?" asked Bella.

"Very busy and noisy and filled with buildings so high you can't see the tops of them," Chloe answered.

"What was Salem like?" asked Issa.

"It was beautiful. The trees were very colorful, and the houses looked just like what you see in the movies, painted in dark colors and gabled and everything. Everyone really gets into Halloween, there, too. There were a lot of people visiting to see the sites. All the houses are decorated with witches and ghosts and things like that," Chloe answered.

"Did you meet any people?" Bella asked, affixing her purple witch hat to her head with the clip it came with.

"Yes," Chloe answered, her voice choked. Her mind flooded with recent memories walking with the Twins, going to the LSC, having girl time at the Kendall with Lissa Thorne, looking out over the lagoon in Boston commons with Mindy's arm around her shoulder, sharing a kiss in front of the Bewitched statue with Michael, even being leered at by Xaiden Thorne over his hangover sunglasses. Then there was Michael's face when he realized how foolish the girl he'd been spending time with was...

"Are they your new best friends now?" Bella asked.

Chloe's throat tightened. "Well..." She took a breath. "I...I'm not sure."

"Why not?" Issa asked, her ten-year-old face a mask of confusion.

"Well, not everyone I met made good friends. And the ones that *were* good friends might be upset with me for saying something unkind," Chloe managed to say, her eyes threatening to fill with tears.

"You should say you're sorry, Chloe," Bella recommended, with all the wisdom and confidence her nine years gave her.

Chloe smiled at Bella. "You're right. I *am* sorry, so I should. I promise I'll do that."

"What were your friend's names?" Issa inquired.

"Well, we spent a lot of time with Bev, who is Tía's best friend. I really liked her. But the friends I spent most of my time with were Mindy and Michael. They are twins," Chloe answered. Her mother had wandered into the room and noticed the tightness in her daughter's voice.

"Boys and girls can't be twins," Bella insisted.

"Can too!" Issa yelled back.

"Nuhuh!"

"Run along, girls. You can talk to Chloe more about her trip later. She's tired now." Mama shooed the girls out of the living room.

"Are you okay, Chloe? Tía Miranda told me of the trouble you had a few nights ago. Do you want to talk about it?"

Chloe, her heart sore, and her eyes filling with tears, shook her head. Mama took her into her arms and held her, rocking her back and forth like she used to when she was her younger sister's age.

She cried into her mom's thin shoulder for several minutes before saying, "Oh, mama. I think I love him. But I was such an idiot. He won't ever want to see me again."

Her mom, not knowing the extent of her daughter's feelings until this moment, sighed heavily and held her eldest girl, wishing that her problems were as easy to fix as they had been when she was a grubby tomboy. But those days were over.

So she just held her daughter and let her cry. "Growing up is messy, sweetheart, but if this boy is half the man your father is, he will see the goodness of your heart and forgive you. If he's not, well, I'm sorry, but he's not worth any more tears."

Chloe knew there was wisdom in these words, but her broken heart hated to hear them.

~ Twenty-Four ~

PIRATE ISLAND IS FOR LOVERS

Chloe kept her word to her little sister about apologizing to Mindy and Michael. She messaged Mindy on Facebook the next day, confessing her ridiculous misunderstanding with Michael and asking forgiveness. No return message was forthcoming that day, however. The status remained unread, and Chloe despaired of mending ties with the twins. Michael did not use social media and she could not remember either of their phone numbers. She knew the address to Pickering Place, but she doubted the doctor would pass any letters she sent on. The situation felt hopeless.

Our heroine tried to fall back into the life she knew before her adventures changed her, but found that much easier said than done. She could not find solace in her over-used copies of *Twilight* or in watching her favorite movies. They reminded her too much of what Michael said about spending too much time in her own wild imagination.

She tried to visit Amy Bayers, but she was out with Tommy. She grew restless and grouchy in the trailer, in the room she shared with her two sisters. They insisted on asking her questions about her trip, each one of them a painful reminder of both beautiful and terrible moments.

She couldn't even find refuge outside their home, among their goats, chickens, and rabbits. The younger boys hassled her to play quidditch with them and complained loudly about her being boring now that she was eighteen.

She finally gave up and told her mama in confidence that she was headed to the crick, and to pretty please keep that information out of the ears of her siblings. Her mama chuckled, kissed her on the cheek and handed her a couple of warm biscuits wrapped in a blue checkered cloth napkin.

"Mums the word, love. Take these with you."

"Thanks, mama."

***

The late October day was fairly cold, so Chloe wore her new quilted jacket over a ribbed long john shirt. The fleece-lined black leggings and faux fur topped winter boots were just warm enough to keep the cold breeze out and kept her feet dry on the wet bank by the crick.

Recent rains had replenished the crick. It burbled noisily past the tree where she sat huddled in the Tetanus Fort she'd built with Sam and Tommy Tookers five years ago, smiling as she turned the hand painted sign that read "Nay, we be pillaging" to "Aye, we be in."

She, Tommy and Sam loved to play pirates best of all in the Tetanus Fort, which doubled as a pirate's ship, when times called for it.

She was almost too tall to sit in the boxy treehouse, now. The limbs of the large oak that housed the fort raked across the corrugated rooftop in the fall breeze. Her head almost brushed the top of the roof, sitting.

She rested her back against the damp wood pallet siding and protruding nail heads that made up the walls of the fort. She watched frogs and birds through the crooked cutout window on the far side of the fort. They flew and leaped through the tall grasses on the far side of the crick. The deep croaks of both ravens and frogs and the insistent buzz of cicadas filled her head with the racket of the country. So much different from the sounds of the city. The air smelled damp and thick, and there was a bite of oncoming frost in the air.

She closed her eyes and listened to the scratching of limbs, croaking, burbling, and buzzing of the world she'd always known and thought about how much she would miss these sounds if she left. Her mind drifted pleasantly through childhood memories the sounds evoked and would have done so for quite some time if the sounds had continued. But the animals and bugs were frightened into silence by the thump of a rock smacking the side of the fort.

Chloe sighed in frustration. "Not now, Julio, I'm being boring," she called to her little brother.

"I doubt that's true, Ms. Mora. You are many things, but boring is not one of them," a familiar voice called up to her.

Her heart skipped a beat. That voice belonged to Boston, to MIT, to Salem. That voice next to her Tetanus Fort, next to her crick in her Williamston, simply didn't fit.

She said nothing for a full minute before saying tentatively, "Michael?"

"I'd come up, but I don't think it will hold us both, and the name your mother gave it when she directed me this way leads me to believe I would need an updated vaccination to attempt it, anyway."

Chloe, her mind racing, rushed over to the crooked window of the fort and poked her head out, sure she was in the middle of one of her ridiculous, impossible daydreams. But, no, there he stood, next to the huge stump of a downed maple. The stump, she'd decided when she was thirteen, was called "Pirate Island," but she didn't think Michael needed to know that.

"Michael? Um...just a second. I'm coming down." Chloe carefully made her way out of the Tetanus Fort, down the two-by-four leftovers nailed into the oak that served as a ladder.

"What are you doing here?" His appearance was so surprising, she was having a hard time understanding why it should be happening.

"I'm sorry. I called your Tía, when you didn't answer my texts. Mindy was trying to contact you, too, before she got her phone, laptop, and pretty much everything else taken away last week. Father found out she'd spent time with Kira. If you had your phone, you'd know that I've been trying to call you for a few days, but your Tía said you lost it on the way back to Boston or that you gave it to a homeless woman?"

"Accidentally gave it, yes, along with my coat. Well, the coat was on purpose, actually," Chloe stammered, staring at the very real, very handsome Michael Bath, wearing a corduroy jacket, dark jeans and brown suede, newly muddied shoes that looked entirely too expensive to be worn near the wet banks of an overfull crick.

"You're going to ruin your shoes."

Michael laughed awkwardly. "The sacrifice is worth it, I assure you."

Chloe, still stunned and a little overwhelmed, just stood staring at him, several feet away. "You're in Williamston. Why?"

Michael, for the first time since she'd known him, looked self-conscious. "Well...to see you. And to say I'm sorry. I hoped it would be a welcome visit, but now that I think about it, maybe it's not? I mean, I wasn't nice to you the last time I saw you. You never answered my messages asking for forgiveness, and you never told me your address, so now I look like a stalker."

"To say you're sorry for what?" Chloe asked, still confused as to why Michael was the one apologizing. Her head swam and she found it difficult to believe any of this was happening.

"To apologize for my dad. Sending you out like that, in the middle of the night, on your own after he promised to look after you..."

Chloe raised her hands. "I deserved it. After what I said..."

"No!" Chloe jumped a little at the fervency in Michael's voice. "No one deserves to be treated the way he treated you, not even if he knew what you'd said. He didn't. I was a little dumbfounded by it and, yes, a little angry at first, but that's all over now."

He took a few steps toward Chloe, his face pleading. "You were wrong about what *kind* of heartless man he was, but your intuition about him was right. We all want to think well of our parents, but I just can't anymore. He may not have killed my mother, but he sucked all the joy out of her, making her death a sort of escape. When she wasn't there to pick on, he took the life out of our house, out of us. And he'll keep doing so as long as we let him. He doesn't do what he does out of love for us. None of it is for us. It's all about how *he* looks, *his* family name, *his* reputation. You've been excusing his behavior because you thought I told him what you said. I didn't. Do you want to know the real reason my father sent you out that night?"

Chloe, stunned, could only nod.

Michael took her hands, a bitter smile on his face. "After you and Xaiden had that falling out, Lissa did what she should have done in the first place before assuming you came from a rich family. She did some internet stalking on your social media profile and found out where you lived, that you lived in a trailer, that you had a large family and that you were...well..."

"Poor," Chloe finished for him. She wasn't afraid of the word. She wasn't ashamed of her trailer, of Williamston, of her loving family, of who she was.

Michael nodded, squeezing her hands and looking at his feet. "Yes. And she told Ryan, who spilled that information to my father in order to direct my dad's anger toward someone other than him."

"Your brother is an asshole," Chloe said.

Michael laughed and nodded, "Yeah."

"Your dad's an asshole," Chloe said.

Michael lifted his head and met her eyes. "He is. And I'm done answering to him."

"What do you mean?" Chloe asked.

"That night, my father put you in danger. Tía told me that you were cornered in the subway, that you could have been seriously hurt or worse that night. When I think of him putting you in that situation because he had misunderstood you to be wealthy, something you never claimed to be...his character was clear to me in a way it wasn't before.'

Michael's eyes shone with resolve. "When I left Pickering Place yesterday, I left it for good. I told my father exactly what I thought about him, about his stupid, nitpicky rules, about the way he made me feel like a pawn in a game I never chose to play, and I left. And I have no intention of ever going back."

Chloe put her hands to her mouth in shock. "He'll stop paying for your school!"

Michael nodded. "He already has. I was informed of that via text today. I am not afraid of it. I have a college account that he signed over to me when I first started at MIT as a reward for getting into such a great school. Legally, he cannot touch it now that I'm of age, and I have not used most of it, knowing that his temper was enough that I might need it someday. It will pay for two semesters of college. By the time it is done, I hope to be able to pay the rest with scholarships and loans. I'll have to do what other people do every day–make my own way. It feels...good. Freeing."

"If he cut you off, how could you afford to come here?! You can't spend money like that, Michael. Not anymore. You have to be careful, now..." Chloe started.

Michael held up a hand. "I may have bought the tickets here and the ticket back to Boston and rented the rental car with his emergency credit card he hides in the library..."

Chloe laughed, in shock, then shook her head. "Good for you! I can't believe he would do such a thing to his own son. I can't believe he'd cut you off over some words you said in anger." She sat down on the stump that was Pirate Island. It had been a very large tree at one time, and was big enough for Michael to sit next to her, which he did.

"He didn't cut me off because of that. It was because I told him I had every intention of begging you to forgive me and be with me. He cut me off because I chose you."

"Maybe if you tell him I said no, he'll change his mind..." Chloe said.

Michael's face dropped.

"Not because I don't want to! God, no! I *want* to. The last few days have been terrible. Thinking you thought badly of me was enough to make me completely desperate. I like you, Michael." She took his hand in hers. "I think I might even love you."

Michae's face brightened. His dark eyes danced. She had been worried about using the word love, been worried about scaring him away, but she saw no fear in his expression.

"And because of that, I can't see you suffer on my behalf."

Michael shook his head. "You think I'm suffering? Chloe, a great weight is gone from me. A cloud hung over me my entire life and it's been lifted. Not only do I now have the good fortune to hear that you don't think me an insufferable prat, I no longer have to ask his permission to be happy with the most amazingly beautiful girl I've ever known, inside and out."

Chloe beamed. "Yeah?"

"Yeah. Chloe, you make me so stupidly happy. I'm sorry if I didn't make that clear back home. I was afraid, but I'm not anymore. He can't make me afraid anymore."

Michael leaned in toward her under the canopy of leaves. The cicada and frog songs had returned in full force, almost drowning out the burbling of the crick. She leaned into him and felt that no romcom, no book, *nothing* had prepared her for the feeling of Michael's lips on hers without the possibility of interruption. They sat on that stump and made up for all the unwanted interruptions and expectations of others. After several minutes of increasingly deep kisses, Michael pulled away, as if shocked.

"What's that? What are those lights?!" He pointed at the weak, beautiful beacons of light sparkling here and there over the crick, flashing on and off over tall grasses.

"Lightning bugs. Have you never seen a lightning bug?" Chloe laughed, reached out her hand and caught one, holding her cupped hand up to his face.

"No. We don't have anything like that in Boston or even Salem."

Chloe nodded. "No. You don't. It's very different here. It has its own beauty and I've always loved it. But..."

Michael leaned forward earnestly. "But?"

"But I think I'm ready to have an adventure."

Michael's eyes were eager. "About that, Mindy hopes you'll consider BU. Her thesis advisor is on the admissions committee. She really misses you, and she needs a friend's support right now. She's still on father's string. Between the two of us, I think we could help her cut those ties."

Chloe frowned, feigning indecision. "I...I don't know, Michael."

His face dropped, and she could almost see his heart break. "Oh, you don't mean Boston, do you? It's fine if you didn't. I understand wanting to see what else is out there."

"Well, I don't know. I guess I *could* be convinced..." She moved closer to him, just inches from his mouth, and smiled.

"Ah." He smiled against her lips before redoubling his persuasive efforts.

~ Twenty-Five ~

IF YOU PLANT LOVE IN FALL, IT WILL BLOOM IN WINTER

Some would say that fall is the most romantic season on the East coast. Winter had the reputation of being the harshest, ugliest, most inhospitable season Boston had to offer. Chloe Mora would disagree.

The frigid temperature often forced Chloe and Michael to spend time snuggling in their dorm rooms at BU or MIT, visiting book and music stores on the weekend, walking hand in hand through the warm underground tunnels at MIT, or holding steamy cups of coffee at cafes in corner booths.

Mindy, Chloe's new roommate, was very accommodating about giving the young lovers' time alone. Her partner visited on the weekends, and Chloe always gave them the benefit of space and time together in return.

Dr. Bath still disapproved of Kira, but he did so from afar and without any say. Mindy had gone the way of her twin, whose presence at Pickering Place was the only thing that made the house a home to her. She had to pick up a part-time job and apply for loans, but she was making her own way in the world, and she was doing so with the same sense of freedom her twin now enjoyed.

Without Mindy and Michael to remind Dr. Bath of the light and love his wife brought to Pickering Place, his shadow darkened every corner of the house. He haunted the perfectly appointed place alone most of the days of the year except on holidays, where his meanest and most ungrateful child did his reluctant duty.

Ryan begrudgingly attended his father for necessary family holidays, feigning filial obligation in return for financial rewards. It was a relationship that neither seemed to find any source of comfort in, made all the more awkward by the many empty seats and spaces that used to be filled with more lively company.

It is not up to a narrator to tell readers what lesson should be gleaned from this book–whether it proposes to be in favor of disobedient children, breaking into creepy closets, exposing the skeletons of a life half-lived, or always carrying protection, just in case. The moral, as always, falls within the reader's discretion. It will be left to the discerning reader to decide who held the truest form of wealth, in…

The End.

ABOUT THE AUTHOR

H.M. Jones lives in the Pacific Northwest with her children, husband, dogs, bearded dragon and chickens. She is a teacher by day and author by night.

She is the author of more books than she thought she'd endeavor to write, including the award winning Monochrome Books–*Monochrome* and *Fade to Blue*. She is a National Indie Excellence Finalist (2016) for *Monochrome* and a Book Readers Appreciation Group honoree for both *Monochrome* and *Fade to Blue*.

H.M. Jones is the co-author of the urban-fantasy, time traveling and folklore mash-up series *The Immortal Brotherhood* Series, written in tandem with the fantastic Alesha Escobar.

She is a poet and a short story author, as well, with several poems and shorts in various anthologies. Her own short story anthology, *Witches of Barbery Hill*, has shorts set primarily in Washington State, where she is lucky enough to reside.

In her spare time, H.M. acts in local theater, thrives in fiber arts and consumes far too much Jane Austen literature and movies than is healthy.

Visit her website at **www.hmjoneswrites.com**.

Other Books By H.M. Jones

Monochrome Books:
Monochrome
Fade to Blue
Young Adult Books:
Al Ravien's Night
The Immortal Brotherhood Series:
The Immortals (1)
A Discovery of Faeries (2)
The Man Who Broke Time (3)

The Unexpected Queen (4)
Adella Darken: Wizend Undead Graphic Novellas
Poison and Fire (1)
Plots and Pitfalls (2)
Short Story Works:
Witches of Barbery Hill
Ariana Grey Chronicles
Tiptoe Through Time
Masters of Time
Magic Unveiled
Works in Progress
The Berenstain Effect (young adult)
The Potioneers (New Adult; in tandem with Hank Hayden)
Adella Darken Novella 3
Visit www.hmjoneswrites.com for updates about future projects!

FOOTNOTES TO INTRODUCTION

1. ^ If it is the latter, I submit for your consideration J.J. Field wiping mud off Felicity Jones' face after a horseback romp through the rain.
2. ^ Collins dictionary definition of novelette: a novel that is regarded as being slight, trivial, or sentimental.
3. ^ For reference, see Jane Austen's Mr. Collin's reading from Fordyce's *Sermons to Young Women*. This reference is just another nod to how Austen made fun of those who made fun of women who read novels. For who wants Mr. Collins' good opinion? No one.